Ties That Bind

L. P. Suzanne Atkinson

Cover Design—Adam Murray

Produced by:
lpsabooks
http://lpsabooks.wix.com/lpsabooks#

Distributed to the trade by The Ingram Book Company

Table of Contents

For David
(in appreciation for his patience and indulgence)

Thank you to Pauline, Wyneth, Heather, Pat A.
and my editor
Patricia Thomas

Other works by L. P. Suzanne Atkinson

~Creative Non-Fiction~
Emily's Will Be Done

Fate decides who walks into your life
You decide who you let stay, who you let walk away,
And who you refuse to let walk out.
Author Unknown

September——October, 2012

Chapter 1

The office door is ajar only enough to be open, yet not quite welcoming. She can hear two young women approach. As jute backing fights its way up through the flat wool weave, their reluctant steps tap on the Turkish hall runner. She's at her desk, focusing on the computer screen's cool white light, completely aware of the creatures standing at the door but not announcing themselves right away. They'll come in when they're ready—probably giggling about the initials. It's become a game over the years.

She's forty-nine and has been a professor in Cultural Anthropology at Callwood College for almost ten years, residing in the community surrounding this idyllic spot. Callwood Bay, on the eastern shore of Nova Scotia, is a town of about ten thousand. It's just far enough from Halifax that to travel into the city for a concert is inconvenient. You either arrive home very late or take on the additional expense of an overnight stay.

Dr. T. G. Norah Clarke's office is bathed in soft indirect light from an assembly of mismatched lamps placed with precision on the desk and on various side tables. A tiny clock radio shares a tune likely unfamiliar to others within hearing distance. Books line one wall from floor to ceiling. A large round coffee table sits on a tattered carpet surrounded by four old and clashing upholstered chairs. Tea things are assembled on the table and the kettle is filled and balanced on top of the bar fridge in the corner—ready to plug in when these two decide to make themselves known.

She is unaffected by the shabby conditions of her office, the furniture, the hallway, the building itself. Universities and colleges struggle everyday to survive. Purchasing a few recycled chairs from the local thrift shop and making do with the old carpet—smelling like dust no matter how much baking soda is used—is a small sacrifice for the privilege of such a vocation. Her parents were once in the retail trade with all its inherent threats and promises. It was a struggle to separate from that life. She has used the knowledge gathered from her time as a child in their antique shop, and as a young woman in the auction house, to propel herself into the comfort and pure joy of this institution.

The necessary soft tap happens and she responds with a raise of her arm and a motion for them to come in. As yet, she's not taken her eyes from the screen. "Have a seat, you two. I'll plug in the kettle and be right with you."

The girls, typical in that college campus kind of way, do as they're told and each chooses an armchair. They dress alike in their skinny jeans, layered shirts, short jackets, heels, long hair—one has hers tied back, the other, floating in froths of unruly curls around her face—and lots of chunky jewellery. One carries a paper notebook and the other an electronic tablet. It's consultation day for their term paper. The taller one, with all the loose hair, covers her mouth with her hand as a giggle dribbles out between her fingers. Norah smiles to herself, expecting her name is the reason for their conspiratorial looks. Few know what the T.G. stands for and most in her classes make sport of interpreting the infamous initials: Thank God, Too Good, Too Gross, The Great. It never stops. Maybe someday, she'll just take the bull by the horns and reveal her full name, but for now, she enjoys maintaining the bit of mystery.

She sees the girls exchange another look, this one more fatalistic, after catching sight of today's choice of tea—a red African rooibos concoction neither of them has probably ever tried before. Norah sees herself as a tea connoisseur and travels to a nearby town to satisfy her addiction for the rare and unusual at the tea merchant establishment there.

She lifts her taller-than-average frame out of the faux leather office chair and turns to face both young women with her introductory smile—the one that doesn't quite reach her eyes. The full smile, the one including the eyes, is reserved for those who show promise and work ethic. In this case, the facts are yet to be revealed. Hence, the routine consultation to discuss their outline and progress a full two weeks before the term paper is actually due. Some will have started—others not so much. In the span of a few minutes, Norah will decide whether or not to gift them with her smile of support and encouragement—the one she knows makes her eyes twinkle in the process. She leans across the end of the oversized desk and unplugs the kettle. The water is poured into the pot and the tea left to steep for a few minutes. One of Norah's few aggravations about her office is the lack of a sink. This means she can't heat the pot first before pouring the tea. That is a cross she must bear.

She sits. She looks at both her guests through glasses with large white Lucite frames reminiscent of the 1970s. Norah initiates by saying, "So, Ashley and Krista—correct?" They both nod although Norah expects they prefer Ash and Kris. "Tell me how you're doing. Give me a progress report and we'll have tea while we talk it over."

Krista, the one with the ponytail, flips open the protective cover of her tablet and taps the screen a couple of times. She spins the instrument around so Dr. Clarke can have a look at their outline. Her movements are brisk, no nonsense. Perhaps this consultation has promise. An outline. A good start. "May I?" She reaches for the tablet when Krista nods and Norah scans the entries in less than a minute. She holds it in her hand as she turns to Ashley. "Happy with the outline, Ashley?" She's suspicious Ashley might know little to nothing about the contents, but Ashley opens her notebook with authority and replies that they've worked on it together and have the research just about complete.

Norah pours tea. She knows her students most often do not like the tea. There are about three out of a hundred or more who actually seem to be tea drinkers, but it's important to her for the students to engage in a more human ritual at a more personal level than emails, texts, telephone messages, and simple exchanges. The tea creates activity. It's important. No one ever refuses the tea. "Tell me about your paper." She leans back in the dilapidated chair, holding her china cup in both hands, looking over its rim at the two women. Their project could have some potential, judging by the outline. Ashley is a Psychology major and this introductory course in Cultural Anthropology is just an elective, whereas Krista seems keen to major in Sociology and is showing considerable interest in Norah's field of expertise. She may want to do an undergraduate project with Norah. Time will tell.

The joint term paper is titled "Freud, the Collector". Norah is well aware of Sigmund Freud's penchant for Chinese, Egyptian, and Roman antiquities. She knows full well how his obsession propelled him around the world and how he often put his passion for collecting ahead of his work in psychoanalysis. At one time, he owned more than two thousand objects. Both take a sip of tea, with some reluctance, and Ashley nods her permission for Krista to begin.

"We chose Freud as our subject 'cause Ashley knows a lot about him," Krista begins. "He was a crazy collector and the point of the whole paper is to answer the question of why he collected what he did and how it affected him," she finishes, a bit breathless, looking satisfied.

At this point, Ashley chimes in. "He influenced the whole world of Psychology and we want to see if we can determine how his collecting obsession might have impacted that world. We also thought you'd like to read a paper that considers mad collecting, since that's what your PhD was all about."

Norah sits still, and looks from one to the other, waiting with patience to see if they have anything more to say. Her tea has started to cool and she takes a final drink before setting the cup on the table with care. She looks up and allows her eyes to twinkle at the two girls. Ashley leans back, crossing her legs. Krista's shoulders visibly relax as she adds, "We wanted the topic to relate to Psychology and Sociology. There are lots of references for us to use, Dr. Clarke. It won't be just stuff from the Internet."

Dr. Clarke smiles again and her gaze travels slowly from one to the other. "I look forward to reading your paper," she says as she stands, signalling the termination of the consultation. They haul themselves—hair, jewellery, handbags, and notebooks, both paper and electronic—upright and thank her with almost too much enthusiasm, for her time. As they shuffle to the door, still sorting belongings, Norah notices the full tea cups on the table. *Too bad. These two show promise.* She makes a mental note to do a little research of her own regarding Freud and his collecting habits. Her curiosity has been thoroughly piqued.

She checks her office diary. No other appointments this afternoon. She piles the tea things on a tray and pads down the hall to the kitchen behind the staff lounge to give them a wash. She wears a long skirt paired with a somewhat ratty blazer that should have gone to the Salvation Army a couple of years ago, but it's a damp and drizzly day, so when she dressed this morning for office hours and consultations, comfort was the name of the game. The remainder of her time will be spent on preparations for her two classes tomorrow. Some of her colleagues choose to recycle material and teach the same basic course year after year but Norah gets a great deal of satisfaction from shaking things up a bit. She likes to insert different topics into the same old course. This serves to challenge her and her students.

As she walks back to the office, the rattle of the tea things on a tray too small for the project, breaks the silence in the long hallway. She sees her phone as it blinks in the annoying fashion it does when someone or something is set to disturb her routine. The dog was sick this morning. Her first thought is that her husband is calling about her beloved Violet, a sweet little terrier mix with gastroesophageal reflux disease.

The tray meets the table with a resounding clatter and she reaches for the phone to check voice mail. Yes, it's Matthew, but Violet isn't the subject of the call. Matthew, Norah's boy toy as she so fondly refers to him, is a month more than ten years her junior and is a local contractor. The two of them are the subject of a great many rumours in Callwood Bay. Norah sometimes wishes their life could be even half as interesting as the talk about their life. In any event, Matthew is calling about the pocket doors intended to separate the living room and the dining room of their 1938 Craftsman bungalow. Part of the renovation involves restoring these doors—lost in the pockets of the walls for the last fifty years—to their former glory. Norah is sure money will have a significant role to play in this story. She returns to the coffee table, retrieves the tea things and stores them in their proper spots. Her office is much too small to support excess clutter of any sort. The sweet, yet woody smell of the rooibos tea still lingers in the musty air, and mixes comfortably with old books and dusty furniture.

Back at her desk, she settles in her chair and arranges the folds of the soft Tencel fabric skirt around her legs. The rain beats harder against the scrap of glass in the wall—the university is quick to point out the tiny aperture qualifies this as a windowed office. Norah clicks the speed dial to call Matthew.

"The doors are going to cost four hundred dollars to restore," he says in a breathless gasp when he picks up the phone. Good thing the caller ID function works on his end.

"Can they fix the cracks in the stained glass?" Norah silently hopes one person can do the whole restoration.

"No, but he has a guy and the price is included in his estimate. How's your day going?"

"Good, good. I'll be home by four. How's Violet?"

"She's fine. You worry too much. She just hurls for no reason. The vet said so. I think we should get the doors done, don't you?"

"Absolutely. Cheap at twice the price." She heaves a sigh. The house is costing a lot more to restore than she predicted but she loves it so much and her relationship with Matthew is courtesy of her house, so she's developed a soft spot for the old, decrepit thing. That aside, it's become akin to a demanding child: You keep pouring money out for school, vacations, and cars, but they never become independent. Her vision is for this to be their forever house so they will do what needs to be done. "See you at four." She hears him say, "Love ya," and her eyes smile as she hangs up the phone.

Norah settles into her chair and permits an escape back to the day she found the house and the day she found Matthew. She was a typical first-time home buyer. She fell in love with the house at first sight. So what if the roof needed replacement—and despite the lousy plumbing, the broken boards on the front porch, the absence of a garage or even a garden shed, and the cautious protests of her parents—those deficits made little or no difference. Although the price didn't seem unfair at the time, reality now says she paid too much, but the house spoke to her. She loved the oak woodwork and art deco fireplaces with their hand painted tiles. The quarter-sawn hardwood floors, the oversized windows, and the front porch—regardless of the broken boards—all reflected Craftsman architecture and her perceived sense of style. Norah always thought she should have been an adult in the 1950s instead of a child in the 1960s. The 1950s is her 'aesthetic'—no question.

Matthew, on the other hand, simply drooled openly over the prospects of a project like this one. She first met him when she interviewed contractors to fix the front porch and shingle the roof about a year after she moved in. He pulled into the yard with a cargo van that had seen better days. He sauntered up those risky front steps with a roll to his gait reminiscent of a boxer approaching the ring. Norah thought he looked like an overgrown kid and initially figured she was wasting her time with this one. He measured; he asked questions. He disengaged his extension ladder from the top of the van and climbed up on the roof to have a peek. He measured some more. He said he would call her back with a quote later in the evening and wondered out loud if she would be doing any restorations on the interior. Norah thought to herself, although completely tongue in cheek, how living with a contractor could be convenient indeed. He did not call with a quote. He came over with a bottle of wine.

"Buy a lady a drink?" He stood under the front light, straddling the broken porch boards Norah had taped up for safety reasons, holding a bottle of white wine as an offering. Violet barked up a storm.

She reached to unhook the latch on the screen door and he bent over to grab the pup. "If you're bringing wine to go along with the quote," she started after spying the folder paper in his shirt pocket, "then this can't be good." Although smiling when she said it, she really wasn't clear about Matthew's motives.

"Glasses?" He was grinning as he navigated the hallway toward the kitchen. Violet looked up at him with big eyes and stopped wiggling to get down. Norah ran for the cupboard and managed to find a couple of wine glasses that didn't look dusty. If she had known he was coming, she might have washed them ahead of time. She hauled open the silverware drawer with a bit too much force, which worked out well since the corkscrew seemed to propel itself with a clatter toward the front. She handed it to him, hoping she didn't look as dumb-struck as she felt.

After setting Violet gently back down on the floor and magically producing a dog biscuit from that same shirt pocket, he offered her a glass of wine preceded by a gentle nod of his head, motioning for her to sit. "I would love to work for you on this house, Norah. This place is gorgeous and could be restored, no problem."

"As long as I have lots of money." She had trouble keeping the irony out of her voice as she reached for her glass.

"I think my quote for the roof is pretty reasonable," he replied, lifting his eyebrows as he placed the folded paper on the table between them. She opened the quote. He picked up Violet and crooned softly to her while Norah scanned the figures. Her surprise was likely evident on her face because he said, "See? Not so bad." His grin made her feel a little flush. She wasn't usually at a loss for words.

"Okay, okay. I guess we have a deal. Violet will be thrilled to have her new friend hanging around." She laughed as she looked at her little dog rolling around in the lap of this big, gentle man.

Norah still feels he fell in love with her, as well as the house, over that bottle of wine. At first, he just did the work he contracted to do and then stayed for supper so they could discuss upcoming tasks, budgets, and so Norah could make decisions without being pulled away from teaching. After about three months, he started staying after supper and well into the night. Norah found herself growing fond of this thoughtful man who seemed unable to do enough for her. He did a beautiful job re-roofing the house. She came home from work one day and found him washing her truck. The recollection of him standing there in a white T-shirt and soapy hands still brings a smile to her lips. He tilled and weeded all the flowerbeds, too.

"Let's buy a few junipers to spruce up the curb appeal," he suggested one afternoon out of the blue. "We can fill in the spaces with flowers. What's your favourite flower?" Tulips had always been her favourite. She paid the contracted price for the roof but couldn't put a value on the pleasure she got from going to the nursery with him, picking out and later planting the bushes and bulbs they chose together. He was fun. They laughed, sometimes so hard they leaned into each other for support. She looked forward to arriving home after work and finding him there. She started to trust him back then and that made her uneasy. She assumed there would be a hitch.

She was jaded and she knew it. Perhaps he was just enamoured with her house. It happens. After all, she was looking forty in the eye at the time and he was a turning-thirty, independent contractor who could go out with whomever he wanted. Worried about the age difference, she finally came right out with it. "I'm ten years older than you. People talk about us, you know."

He peered at her over his reading glasses, as he sat on the couch holding the newspaper. His hair curled down over his forehead and he looked twenty, not thirty. "Does it bother you? And if it does, is it that I'm younger or that people talk?"

"Does it bother you?" Answering him with a question was all she could manage.

"I'm here because I think you're the best thing that's ever happened to me and I want to feel like this forever. So no," he said, while putting the paper down and reaching for her hand, "it doesn't bother me."

They continued on like this for almost two years, working on the house, going to concerts, having quiet dinners. They even took a trip to Cuba during March break. When he asked her to marry him, this independent woman finally, after years of choosing solitude, decided to risk marriage again, although she had once made a pact with herself to avoid that circumstance at all cost. He was so good to her. She knew he really wanted this and she was ready to try again.

Chapter 2

Cold rain trickles down the window. She jumps a little, startled by the presence of someone unexpectedly filling her doorway. Damien—one of her students. He smiles in a nervous way eighteen year old boys seem to do when talking to people in positions of authority. His hair curtains his eyes. He's wearing shorts that hang down below his knees and he carries a rucksack over his shoulder. "Okay if I talk to you?" he asks when Norah pulls herself together.

"Damien, when are you going to learn to make an appointment?" Norah responds, annoyed both by his presence and because he has appeared when it almost looks like she might have been napping. Her excuse would be that she was daydreaming about her hunky husband. How could that possibly be better?

"You don't look busy," comes the challenge, although his head is down and long, straight pieces of mousy hair block one eye. "I have a problem."

Norah nods and points to one of her ratty chairs by the table. He shuffles past her as the laces on his open sneakers drag behind him on the floor, the ends tapping out a sloppy slide rhythm on the bare wood. He collapses into the chair with a miserable exhalation of breath. Indeed, something may well be wrong with Damien. Norah wonders why anyone would be compelled to give a new baby such a name. Norah's memory is jogged when he looks with longing at the tea boxes He's one of the few tea drinkers among her students. "Shall I put the kettle on, or are you in a rush?" She leans toward him while remaining in her office chair, and gives him a questioning look over her glasses. "Are you okay?"

"Wow, Dr. Clarke. Two questions at once! This could be too much for me today. Tea would be great." He smiles, just a little, and heaves another sigh. Norah plugs the kettle back in and busies herself with her tea ritual while observing her student. He sits in the chair, legs stretched out in front, crossed at the ankles. He's made no attempt to take anything out of his knapsack or to start a conversation. From what little Norah knows, he's a good student but very much a loner and considered an oddball. She's never seen him chumming around with anyone or talking in class. He comes and goes, ghostlike. Other students simply ignore him.

With tea made, a simple chamomile this time—relaxing, calming, good for the soul—Norah breaks the silence. "What's on your mind?"

He seems nervous, and focuses on his tea. "The team term paper is due in two weeks and I have no partner. I think I should be able to do a paper without a partner." He speaks as if he's arguing with an unknown opponent. Norah has not said a word. "I have a good idea for a paper. I have the outline and some of the research done. There's no one for me to work with and it doesn't matter anyway because I prefer to work alone." He stops to take a breath, a sip of tea, and to finally look up at his professor, who is comfortable in the chair across from him.

"The class has an uneven number of students, Damien. I knew someone would have to work alone. If it happens to be you, that's fine with me. Your other option would be to work on a three-person team but I gather your preference is to be a one-man show." Norah keeps her voice calm and non-judgmental. Like being the last person picked on the playground to play Red Rover, being the only person in a class without a partner has the potential to become an exercise in ostracization. Risky for many.

He would know that, yet Damien is visibly relieved. His stress rolls away from him as the muscles in his face and neck relax. "I'm not much of a joiner," he contributes. "Only child, home schooled. This whole class thing is a big mystery to me." He shrugs his shoulders and smiles, this time with some confidence elbowing its way to the surface.

"Since you're here, do you want to go over your outline? Get it out of the way?"

Damien unfolds his lanky frame, takes a final drink from the china mug, and reaches for his sack on the floor. "Not today, Dr. Clarke. No need to bother you today. I'll make an appointment. Thanks." He's almost out the door before Norah has a chance to argue or comment. She wonders if he actually has an outline done, or was he just trying to make an argument for going it alone on the project?

"I have time, Damien. Tell me what you're up to."

He returns to the chair, still warm from before. With the sack teetering on his knees, he roots around for a scrap of paper and hands it to Dr. Clarke. *Is he slightly embarrassed?* He relinquishes the tattered and smudged document. She skims the outline and the list of references. It seems his family, particularly his grandmother and mother, are avid collectors of Trenton glass, a specific pressed glass made in Trenton, near New Glasgow, Nova Scotia in the late 1800s. There are only nineteen patterns and all have been identified via shards found during excavations at the three sites. His great grandfather worked at one of them. Damien isn't sure which one but he will find out. The paper will be about the family legacy of collecting and he plans to compare their collecting to King George V (1865–1936) and his penchant for stamp collecting. Today Queen Elizabeth II, who presides over the Royal Philatelic Collection, is a well-versed stamp enthusiast and her collection happens to be her biggest personal financial asset.

"It's a little rough looking," he says, pointing out what his professor silently observes as obvious. "I had no intention of showing you this today, but you insisted," he continues, grinning.

Norah leans across the coffee table and returns the outline to Damien. "So, your hypothesis is families can influence future generations to carry on their collecting passion. Correct?"

He nods. The grin disappears. "Younger generations can get caught up in the hunt. Like with osmosis, they can get interested and absorb that passion to collect," he adds, sounding oddly desperate.

"Although neatness is not supposed to count, Damien, remember I look for structure, proper English, and a professional presentation." Norah rises from her chair. She is being quite formal, not wanting her student to be too confident, but she knows full well this will be a great paper if he can pull it off. "I fully support your outline and look forward to seeing the finished product. Thanks for showing me, even though that piece of paper has obviously seen better days." She smiles a soft and supportive smile. He jams the paper back into his bag and hurries for the safety of the dim corridor.

After washing up the tea things yet again, Norah settles down for an hour to prepare for her classes the next day. She's good at her job, and the tasks at hand don't take long. Everything is organized in her mind long before she commits to paper, so it seems like the work is easy. She starts to revise her class outline.

Just as she's about to check email one last time and pack up to walk home, in wanders Peter Swift. Dr. Swift is a professor of Gerontology. He is a tiny, round man with a balding head and a growing midsection. He could be described as effeminate but Norah isn't sure he's gay. He never references his sexual status in any way. He lives alone. He attends functions alone. There are many rumours about him. He's a contradiction of sorts—very free with his opinions on decorating and personal style, while attending almost all university sports events and declaring himself the biggest fan on campus. He is who he is and he has created a feeling among colleagues and students that it would be inappropriate in the extreme to dig for details.

Peter was a huge help to Norah when she defended her doctoral thesis. She likes him a great deal and owes him—if the truth be known—but he would never expect her gratitude. He reminds her of someone from her past. She feels a personal connection but revealing this to Peter would be assuming too much. He is very political, especially as it relates to his field of expertise. Boomers are aging and the resulting issues will have to be wrestled to the ground. He doesn't believe the government is doing enough to prepare for the inevitable changes no doubt required in job creation, pensions, and everything related. Peter makes his feelings known to anyone who will listen. He feels governments of the day pay lip service to the problem and nothing more. Peter sits and looks at Norah. "No tea today," she says while stuffing a manila folder into her leather satchel—her office with a shoulder strap. "I'm on my way home to a sick dog and pocket doors that are desperate for a makeover."

"No problem." He crosses his legs and examines an invisible smudge on the knee of his khakis. "I hadn't seen you all day. I wanted to say hello. What's wrong with Violet?"

"She's still hurling almost every morning. The vet says it might be GERD. She eats and everything but in the morning she throws up this yellow, frothy stuff."

He mimics gagging. "Too much information! My God, Norah! Just say she's dead or alive. No diagnosis! No descriptions!" He flaps his hands for effect. "The poor little thing, though. I hope she's okay," he adds with a touch more sympathy and less narcissism in his tone.

Norah looks up and rolls her eyes. "You asked, Peter. Everything okay with you?"

"My class of first years are all idiots. Do they teach nothing in high school anymore? Don't answer. Anyway, run along. I'll catch up with you tomorrow and we can have tea between classes in the morning. Okay?"

Norah waves at his back as he drifts through the doorway. She reflects on her consultations today and how the word idiot had not crossed her mind when she thought about any of her students.

She glances out the window. The rain has slowed down, so the walk home won't be too bad. The fifteen minutes it takes can be brutal in nasty weather. Then she would call Matthew, but not today. On with the trench coat and sneakers, purse over the shoulder, office door locked and down the hall, off to the precious comfort of home.

Most often, she climbs over lumber, forgoes lighting in the room without wiring on that particular day, and peruses the disorganized contents of kitchen cupboards devoid of doors, but the solace of home remains, nonetheless. Despite the current chaos, Norah can visualize the finished space. She can see the kitchen with the refurbished doors and Craftsman hardware. She can imagine the tile countertops although right now her sink is being supported across the base with two-by-fours. People must think she lives in a dream world of the finished, while not facing the reality of the incomplete. It will get done.

It's wetter than she thought. Her rain resistant "trench" is no longer resisting and she has trouble appreciating the autumn smells of wet fallen leaves and dampened earth as she splashes her way down uneven sidewalks pooled with today's rain. Callwood Bay is an old town with old houses and streets lined with mature maples, birches, and oak. With the amount of rain falling today, they've lost their ability to shelter passersby. Water from their leaves soaks Norah's shoulders to the skin and runs down the outside of her leather satchel. As she turns up her street, a sense of pure contentment repels the discomfort of the weather. This street was created back in 1936 and over a four-year period, twelve Craftsman style houses were built using three different varieties of floor plans.

Norah loves the street. It's like walking back in time; like being on a movie set. Their house is the fifth one down on the left, almost at the end of the street that used to be a dead end but got connected to a newer subdivision about five years ago. Matthew's van is in the yard. She can see it from here. Her truck, a little Ford Ranger—another subject of discussion in this small town of sometimes even smaller minds—is tucked in behind the van, barely visible because of sagging wet branches. Although not dark by any means, the nondescript porch light is on. Someday, it will be replaced with something befitting the old veranda.

The pungent aroma of spaghetti sauce, one of her favourites, welcomes her as she climbs the stairs to the protection of the covered front porch. The inside door is open and Norah can gaze down the hallway, past the staircase and into the kitchen. Matthew, as tall as she is but no taller, stands at the stove stirring the sauce. He fancies himself a bit of a spaghetti expert and this suits Norah just fine. She cooks because eating is an essential evil. She gets no satisfaction from producing a meal, even a good one. If she could take a pill instead of eating, she probably would. One of the best things about living with Matthew is sharing a meal. They talk, mull over ideas, and listen to one another. He smiles across the table, teases her, and has eyes for nothing else. It somehow makes the act of eating more rewarding.

Violet slides to the door, nails scrambling for traction on the old hardwood. She's barking her hellos and Norah's anonymity evaporates as Matthew turns. She opens the screen door to let herself in. Hugs and kisses all around. Her wet trench and dripping satchel are whisked away to the mudroom in the back by Matthew. She bends over to pick up Violet. She's ten pounds of wiggling affection as Norah tries, without much success, to look at her dog's eyes and assess how she is, really.

"She's been fine all day," Matthew contributes as he returns from the back of the house. Norah steps around the two pocket doors, tilted on their sides and leaning against the wall supporting the stairs. They look like they could fall over any minute.

"Okay, okay," she replies, exasperated with the problem and not the players. "Are we going to take her to the vet again or what?" She sits down heavily on one of the vinyl and chrome chairs in the minuscule eating area of the kitchen. Matthew, without asking, places a large glass of dark beer in front of her. Violet has squirmed down and is busy shaking some unsuspecting stuffy within an inch of its life. "Thanks. This is nice."

"I took her to the vet," he finally admits. The grin on his face makes Norah's heart lurch at the sight, even after six years of marriage "They told me to get her some Pepcid. Do you believe it? Just give her a half a Pepcid every day and she'll be fine." He shakes his head and returns to the stove.

"She gets the first one a few minutes before she eats her supper. Problem solved." He turns to Norah and smiles from ear to ear. "I knew you were worried." He shrugged. "I had to do something."

She feels the relief flood through. What a guy! Exactly what had she done to deserve such a good man? Relationships aren't Norah's long suit and she battles the fear of failure daily; afraid that Matthew will eventually decide he can't tolerate her rigidity and inflexibility any longer and be on his way. She tries not to let her doubt show but knows, in her heart, it bubbles to the surface with minimal provocation. "So, my little one," she croons as she bends over and catches Violet's eye. "Daddy has taken care of you. I guess we know whose dog you really are." Violet gives the toy another shake and presents her lifeless prize to Norah. Tugging ensues as Norah asks about the pocket doors and Matthew plunges the pasta into the boiling water.

"I see they're out in the hall and no longer in the wall. Off to the restoration guy tomorrow?" she asks although the answer is not really important. It will get done when it gets done.

She knows Matthew is super excited about getting the doors fixed so they can resume their role of separating the living and dining rooms in the way the original design intended. "Yeah," he responds without turning around, focusing his attention on the task at hand. "He said to bring them to his shop about nine. It'll take a couple of weeks, but the timing's perfect. I have to finish the floors before reinstalling the doors, anyway. I thought the price was fair."

The table in the dining room is already set, cheese shredded, and bowls warmed. Crusty buns from the local bakeshop round out their feast. Norah assumes he thought about crusty buns on his way to or from the vet this afternoon. Remarkable.

As they chat about the day, the papers her students are writing, and next steps with the house, Norah's gaze falls on her collection of jadeite glass— stacked in a manner not safe for anything breakable—on the top shelf of the built-in bookcase in the living room. She started collecting this opaque green glassware as a child. Her parents owned an antique shop in Prestonburg, and the family lived in the basement apartment below the shop. Having something cheap and easily identifiable to collect, kept her occupied when she was out with her parents while they searched for stock. As a little girl, she just bought what she liked, but she accumulated some prized pieces over the years.

Mixed in with the jadeite are a number of rare and unusual porcelain cups and saucers, waiting to be placed in the china cupboard currently covered by a drop cloth. When she was little, sorting cups and saucers was her specialty.

Chapter 3

The phone's unexpected bleat invades her thoughts. Her mother instigates their evening conversation. On most nights Norah makes the call but Paige must be a little anxious about something tonight. She reaches over to the sideboard for the portable. "Hi, Mom." She sighs. "We're just finishing supper and I was going to call you. What's up?"

Her mother is breathless and unsettled on the phone. "Norah, I don't know if I can handle this. Beth has a whole crowd coming into the shop tonight—at night! I knocked on the door and asked what was going on and she said she was starting evening classes on quilting. There must be at least ten women there, some setting up their own sewing machines. I couldn't go to sleep if I wanted to!"

She stops for air and Norah shakes her head as she formulates a response. She can't be too hard on her mother. It's a huge change for her, to have given up the shop after Austin died in June, just five months ago. Selling the three story building to Beth, their upstairs tenant, who was just retiring from teaching, turned out to be the best possible solution. Despite this, her mother continues to look for issues. "You could join in." Norah knows full well her first suggestion will fall on deaf ears. "Or, just ignore the noise and watch TV," she continues.

Paige, of course, refutes any remedies, and continues to complain. "I want them gone," she whines to her daughter.

"I know," Norah responds, "but, Mom, you knew things were going to change upstairs and you still want to stay there, right? Spending all day in your apartment is a lot different than working above in the shop. Now you hear the foot traffic and the chimes whenever customers come and go." Norah smiles. "You used to like those sounds when I worked and you got to spend the morning downstairs making bread. It meant we were busy. Now, it's Beth's business and you consider those same sounds just noise. You knew this was going to happen and you told Beth it would be fine, even if she was open in the evenings. You can't go back on your word at this point. She was a great tenant and now she's a great landlord, Mom." She softens her voice as she speaks. Norah knows the call's more about comfort than about solutions.

"You know they won't be late." Norah continues to soothe her mother. "You could always dig some squares out of the freezer and take them up a snack," she adds, as she desperately tries to replace her mother's anxiety and annoyance with some positive scrap of something. She sighs. She's been doing this all her life.

"That's a good idea," her mother admits, much to Norah's relief. "I have those chocolate fudge ones from the Anglican bake sale. They're too sweet for me but those girls will love them."

"Mom. Have you ever wondered why Beth was at the auction when Dad died?" Norah hesitates to open this can of worms but the circumstances of her father's sudden death and her ongoing suspicions about his relationship with Beth continue to torment her. Sometimes, she can't seem to keep her mouth shut. It all started with finding a Bakelite bead in an unlikely location way back when she was in her last year of high school.

"I don't know what you mean, Norah. Beth was at the same auction as your father. It was just outside the city; some house auction where he thought he might find a couple of nice end tables and a few dishes. She went over to say "hi" and he looked like he was sleeping in his lawn chair. She tried to wake him up and realized he was unconscious. The ambulance came and took him into the city but he never woke up. I was really glad she was there. She even followed the ambulance into the city after she called me. I don't know what I would have done if it hadn't been for her. It took almost four hours before you and Matthew got here. She was with him until he died and then came home and helped me with everything until you arrived. I never thought about why she was there in the first place. I was just glad she was."

Norah chose her words carefully. "She doesn't like old things, Ma. You know that. What got her into going to auctions?"

"Well, I know your father helped her fix an old sewing machine she bought, and once he had to disassemble a loom so it would fit in her car. All that stuff she bought over a couple of years, she now uses as decoration in her craft shop upstairs. It worked out well for her."

Is my mother being purposely obtuse? Since she knows she isn't going to get anywhere, Norah decides to drop the subject. Austin's death was a shock to everyone, not just the family but everyone in town. He was well known, well liked, regarded as an honest businessman, and generous to his community. He was only seventy-four and considered in robust health.

On the day her father died, Matthew was working on a job site outside of town, building someone a new deck. It took awhile for Norah to reach him after her mother called. She thought she'd have to get in her truck and go get him, but he finally answered his phone. He came home almost immediately, but her mother was right. It was almost four hours before they got to Prestonburg. Paige had been surprisingly calm. Beth was not. After Beth helped Paige contact the funeral home so they could arrange to transport Austin's body back, she literally went to pieces. When Matthew and Norah roared in through the downstairs entrance to the apartment, Paige was busy making her tenant tea. Beth was sitting in the living room blubbering and hiccupping, repeating over and over that he had looked so peaceful, just sitting in his lawn chair in the sun at the auction. Norah focused on her mother, but she seemed quite stoic, all things considered. Matthew, with Violet under his arm, tried to comfort the inconsolable Beth.

Norah went with her mother to the funeral home to take care of details. They progressed through visiting hours and the actual ceremony in a blur of hand shaking and hymns. Not being particularly religious, the funeral took place in the chapel of Cumberland's Funeral Home and Crematorium just on the outskirts of Prestonburg. It was simple with an ecumenical service provided by a local minister. Beth never stopped sobbing, constantly blotting her eyes and digging for tissues in her oversized leather purse. Her face was puffy and red from crying. She wandered around, talking to people at visitation and at the reception, repeating her tale of finding Austin sitting in his chair on that Saturday afternoon. Norah remembers the auctioneer from that fateful day coming up to shake her hand during visiting hours. He introduced himself and expressed his condolences. Looking over at Beth, he leaned in toward Norah's ear and whispered, "She was sitting right beside him. I don't know why she's saying she came upon him. She was right there all the time."

All the old worries and fears about Beth and her father came flooding back that day. Norah continues to wonder if she'll ever know the truth.

****

"I'm going to go now and dig out those squares, Norah. Talk to you later." As her mother makes a quick goodbye, Norah is left looking at the receiver.

"Thanks for calling, Mom. Happy to help," she quips to the dial tone.

Matthew has already cleared the table. She can hear him rattling away in the kitchen, washing dishes by hand as the new dishwasher sits alone and beautiful in the basement. She'll go and dry them in a minute.

Her eyes wander back to the jadeite collection and she searches for the green glass Scottie dog with the ink blotter base, just to assure herself of its presence. The Scottie dog tea set is still safe and sound, too. She bought it in 1973 for twenty-five dollars. It's worth over eight hundred today—not that it matters. She thinks of her father and that day she got it. It was one of the best days she ever had in her life. She gets up and goes into the kitchen to dry the dishes with Matthew.

"Still troubled about your father and Beth? You know, you could just come right out and ask her." He looks at Norah from under the dark curls rolling across his forehead. His eyes have a bit of a sparkle and Norah knows he thinks that over twenty years is a long time to worry about whether or not her father had an affair with their upstairs tenant.

"Right! I've had such great success with that in the past." She grins at him and raises her eyebrows. "Seriously, I've tried to talk to her before, Matthew, but I never got anywhere. From what Mom says, she was going to auctions with Dad for a long time before he died. Maybe not going *with* him, but certainly meeting him there. I can see her now, packing lunches." The expression in Norah's voice is somewhere between ironic and sarcastic. "It shouldn't matter a bit." She shakes her head slightly and reaches up to place the bowls in the open cupboard.

"But it does matter—to you."

They finish up the chores in the kitchen. While Norah retreats to the living room to peruse the paperwork she carted home with her, her husband begins the ritual of making their after-dinner tea. As she plunks herself down on the brown velvet sofa, Norah looks around the living room, silently admiring, for the thousandth time, the stained glass windows on either side of the painted brick fireplace. They're balanced with appealing symmetry above the built-in bookcases. The couch and matching chair are auction finds from a couple of years ago. They're from the forties, but close enough to suit the old house to perfection. The coffee table belonged to Norah's grandmother and it doesn't matter if it's era specific for the house or not. The dining room table, along with the chairs and china cabinet are all retro from the forties as well. They found their way into the house when Matthew did a renovation for a couple who no longer wanted them.

He interrupts her revere with a steaming cup of Earl Grey. She puts her work aside, cuddles Violet in beside her, and smiles up at her husband.

1968—1981

Chapter 4

Norah is five years old and "working" with her mother in the antique shop on this sunny Saturday morning. Her father is attending a weekend auction, in the persistent act of pursuing and scrounging for good buys. The summer tourist season is fast approaching and although they've been searching and collecting over the winter, Norah often overhears her mother, Paige, worrying out loud. Paige is constantly concerned that they never have enough stock or won't have enough of whatever people want. She says trends come and go so fast, it's hard to keep up.

The little store is located on the side of a hill, backing toward the view and opening on to Tyler Street. Tyler is the top street of four that parallel the water in Prestonburg, a popular tourist community in the summer. Visitors park their cars down below, near the harbour, and walk through the quaint streets lined with historic storefronts. Clarkes Antiques and Collectibles is located in one of these buildings. The back entrance and daylight basement apartment face the water and this proves very convenient for the family. They can run downstairs from the store to their living quarters and access the car through the back door. There's even a patch of grass with a swing.

Since Norah started school this year, her mother often remarks on how much she misses her little helper during the week. Norah sits at the desk in the back of the shop, her legs swinging as she sorts a box lot of china cups and saucers, patiently matching tops and bottoms as she's been taught.

Norah is alert to her mother's moods as Paige looks around the shop at the shelves, the antique showcase counter, and the tables laden with glass and porcelain. Norah sees her concerns embedded in her expression like a continual frown.

"Well, I expect there won't be much business this summer," Paige says absentmindedly as she busies herself straightening the counter in preparation for the day. "I hope your father has enough sense to just buy the very best—if he has the chance and it's a good deal. It's hard enough to make a living selling other people's junk without having pieces that are chipped and cracked. The Americans are more concerned about the war than travelling this summer. I think it'll be slow." She turns her attention to the dinnerware set on a table in the middle of the floor and rearranges the dishes until she gives a nod of satisfaction.

Norah listens but knows enough to be still. Her mom constantly obsesses aloud about the bills, about the stock, about whether or not they can make ends meet, about how they will survive next winter's inevitable downturn. Things seem to work out each year, but her mother's lack of confidence and multiple anxieties wrap around the family like a threadbare blanket.

The brick building that houses their business and apartment is strikingly beautiful in its architectural detail. Everybody says so. Austin, her dad, bought it for a song before she was born. It was built about 1875 in the early Victorian style of rounded windows with curled mouldings and fretwork. Although her mother says the front windows are murder when it comes to the heating bills, neither one of her parents can bear to replace the old bubbled glass with something more efficient. They think it would ruin the front altogether, so they actually take pains to cover them with blanket-like curtains during the coldest months when they're closed to customers. This helps to prevent the almost constant winter wind from penetrating. The trim is painted a blue-grey hue that reminds Norah of the sea. The door to the shop has a huge century-old handle requiring two hands if five-year-old Norah is the one doing the opening. They have a tenant in the apartment upstairs. Her mother, of course, worries the tenant will leave, although there is no sign she will.

Beth Hanley moved to Prestonburg right out of Nova Scotia Teachers' College. The Clarke family is good to her, inviting her to dinner every now and then. Norah likes to visit with her and Beth invites the company of the curious and polite little girl. Right now, she's teaching Norah how to knit. She accepted a position at the high school just last fall, teaching English to students in Grades Ten to Twelve. Her first love is all things related to crafting and she's in the process of establishing a crafting guild in the little town. Norah loves being friends with an adult and appreciates Beth's generosity. Beth is both calm and funny in a fill-the-room kind of way. She's pretty and wears bright colours. Norah likes that, although her mother often says she's loud and overdone, whatever that means. They do crafts together, go for walks, play with her dog, and listen to music. Norah is excited that soon Beth will be teaching her how to sew and they will make doll clothes together.

Norah sorts cups and saucers, chatting to her Mom about school as she works. There are lots of teacups with feet in this box. She knows they're worth a great deal of money because many people collect them. They were made in Japan and she's just starting to understand the different markings on the bottom, recognizing Made in Occupied Japan as being the most collectible. She handles each piece with care, running her little fingers around the rims and bottom edges. Most often, "touch tells the tale." Her mother has said this a million times. She places a cup on the desk and removes the paper around what could be the matching saucer. But no, it's the saucer for the blue Aynsley cup she checked a minute ago. Good. This saucer is fine. Mom gets upset when Dad buys a box lot full of stuff with cracks and chips. "Good money down the drain," is the criticism and then he will look sad, smile, and say he'll be more careful next time. But Dad always gets excited at an auction and he wants to buy everything. He imagines all the collectors coming into the shop to see the rare and beautiful treasures for sale. Norah knows what he's like and finds it exciting. She goes with him whenever she can.

Norah likes outdoor auctions the best. She feels the excitement as she walks around while the breeze blows the tablecloths and the grass is still damp from morning dew. Her dad gave her something very special after the auction last week. It was a green glass Scottie dog with an ink blotter base so that it looks like the dog's sitting on the platform for a rocking horse. You roll the blotter over your writing so it won't smudge. It has wires on either end to hold the blotting paper. It's a little worn and Austin said he will try and find better paper. The glass is called jadeite and this is what she will look for when she goes to auctions from now on. It's nice to be able to search for something special. She hoped to go with him today but Paige wanted her to stay and help with sorting the things purchased last week—so here she sits, surrounded by teacups.

****

Bijou is the best dog a little girl of ten could have. She walks beside you without a leash and comes when she's called. She doesn't wander but likes to go upstairs and visit Beth when she hears her heavy footstep on the stairs after school. Most often, Norah and Bijou go together to visit the teacher.

Norah and Bijou deliver morning papers. They go up and down the quiet streets of Prestonburg, stopping at all the storefronts and apartments. They know everybody on Tyler and Seaview Streets. She delivers a paper to the variety store, the upholsterer, the two ladies' wear shops, a haberdashery, a jewellery store, another antique store—her dad calls it a junk store—and a furniture shop. There are also private homes, with front steps right on the sidewalk, just like the stores. Norah is convinced that in the olden days, all the buildings were built close together with their backs to the water and very close to the street in order to break the icy winter wind whipping off Prestonburg Harbour.

Despite the biting cold, Norah loves Prestonburg in the winter. It's like living in a picture postcard. If her mother didn't worry so much about business and heating bills, it would be perfect.

Norah bundles up to start her route. The papers are left on the covered step by the front door of the shop at about 5:00 AM. She carries them in around 7:30 AM, sorts methodically, and has one at each destination before going to school. If it snows overnight, many shopkeepers will be out shovelling or sweeping off the sidewalk in front of their establishments. Norah then has the opportunity for a quick visit with each one.

Mr. Kay owns Prestonburg Variety. He's quiet and Norah fights the urge to think he doesn't like children, or maybe dogs. He has neither—just a wife. They live upstairs above the store and Mrs. Kay seems to be sick most of the time. She only makes the effort to use the stairs when she goes to the doctor. Norah's family often wonders why Mr. Kay doesn't develop the walk-out basement like they have, so she would no longer have to deal with the stairs.

Norah's favourite place to pause for a visit is at Humphrey's Haberdashery— Men's Wear for Gentlemen. Norah doesn't know if Humphrey is his first name or his last. He responds to Mr. Humphrey even though he's made it very clear that a simple Humphrey will do just fine. He is a snappy dresser. He always has a laugh, a tip of his hat, and a pat for Bijou. Norah likes to hand Mr. Humphrey his paper. There are no bad days if they start out with this fellow.

Some of the businesses have no one around this early. The two ladies' wear stores—competitors, her dad says—are always locked up tight at 8:00 AM. They are owned by sisters who used to work in one store and then, when they bought out their competition about ten years ago, they had a big fight and each one took their own store. Their family differences make for some great clothing and accessory sales, according to Paige and Beth.

****

Norah and Austin walk down a street in Halifax peppered with antique and second hand stores. At eleven years old, she feels quite important to be in her father's company. Her dad's happy as he looks for special objects while scouring consignment shops. Norah knows that sometimes people put things in these shops and they don't know their true value. If Dad has a buyer for a particular item, he stands to make some money by combing these outlets. Norah finds all the streets confusing. There are lots of stores. They have been in and out of many and she's getting tired.

On their way down one street to get back to another with a particularly big shop, Norah spies a green child's tea set in a display window. She just sees it for a second as they go by. It's a long drive home, and her father's in a hurry but she's sure this tea set is jadeite and has Scottie dog decals on it. It looked like it was in its own box, too. They arrive at the big consignment shop and Dad is going crazy. He finds all kinds of interesting items from duck decoys to postcards. Norah waits and wanders through the aisles looking for jadeite. She finds a tiny flower pot for a dollar and takes it to her father. He smiles down at her, identifies it as agro agate, whatever that means, and adds it to the stash. After what seems like forever, he asks the clerk to add up everything while he runs out to the car, parked just up the street, to get his big "buying box." He keeps this in the car at all times, just in case he comes across a great hoard of stuff some place. Once they're packed up and settled for the trip home, Norah tells him about the tea set. "Norah, why didn't you say something? What store was it at? Do you remember?"

This is a lot of pressure. Norah remembers they walked by the store on the way back to the big place where they just finished. "Can we go backward and find it?"

Her father's shoulders heave as he lets a huge sigh escape. "We'll try." He sounds resigned. Norah hopes she's found something special so her mother won't be too annoyed if they're late.

They cruise the streets in reverse order and after about fifteen minutes, Norah almost jumps out the window of the moving car. "There it is; there it is," she shouts, relieved she's successfully spotted the shop.

Austin holds Norah's hand as they enter the store. "If this is too expensive, or if it has any damage, we aren't going to buy it. You understand, don't you?" The tea set is in the window, just as she said. It's jadeite, Laurel pattern Depression glass with Scottie dog decals. The box is with it—original and not in bad shape. He scans the price tag and gives her a look she interprets as "don't get your hopes up." Norah stands beside the box. She holds each piece with extreme care while she runs her fingers around the edges as she's been taught. Mint condition.

She turns her attention to her father. "It's perfect," she whispers. They go over to the clerk, who has been watching from behind the counter. "What's your best price?" pipes Norah in her clear, soprano voice.

The owner, an indulgent smile on his broad flat face, looks down at Norah, whose heart is flapping in her chest. "Half price, today, my dear. The set is yours for twenty-five. Wrap it up?"

Norah turns to her father. "I have the money at home from my papers, Dad. Can I borrow from you 'til we get home?" Her father removes the bills from his wallet. The pieces are wrapped one by one and they return. Norah holds the box on her knees for the entire trip home.

****

Making ends meet seems to be a struggle for almost everyone in 1975. Tourists are as scarce as the rare glass sought by the Clarkes. The Americans seem to all stay home this year. It's slow in the shop, even in the heat of summer. There are more sellers than buyers. Norah manages alone on Saturday mornings now that she's old enough. Her dad goes to sales and her mother uses the time to catch up on chores downstairs. It's most often quiet, so Norah can dust shelves, unpack a box not inventoried yet, rearrange the front window display—one of her favourite pastimes—or read a book while the radio plays easy listening in the background.

Today, she's scrunched into the window alcove, removing any and all things not matching her new blue and white theme. On the floor, just beyond stepping distance, lies an amassed collection of display pieces including her inspiration—an old textile called a crazy quilt because it has no pattern but is made of many different shaped fabric scraps. Norah's not sure of its origin but found it nestled in the bottom of a trunk, all laundered and priced—fair game for her new display. She's also gathered up a big transfer ware bowl, likely the base of a nineteenth century commode set, a number of cobalt blue bottles, an array of blue and white china pieces—some substantially older than others—and an apple ladder. Used for pickers to climb into apple trees, primitive ladders like this are wider at the bottom, narrowing to almost a point at the top, allowing them to settle into the tree without damaging the precious fruit or branches. Her father buys them whenever he can, regardless of their age. People like to put them in bathrooms for towel racks or even hang them on the wall. With the eye of a professional window dresser, Norah leans the apple ladder into the corner. She's methodical and careful not to damage the stock or be careless with an object. As she finishes, she steps outside to the sidewalk and reviews her completed work. One more stretch inside the window is needed to straighten a couple of price tags. It's always important for potential customers to be able to see the prices.

Inside, and pleased with her work, she starts to place unneeded pieces on shelves and tables, to fill in gaps and balance displays. The bells on the door tinkle an interruption as an older lady stumbles in carrying a large cardboard box. The bottom looks as if it will fall apart any minute. Norah rushes to the door, takes the box from the lady and sets it on the floor as carefully as she can manage. She's afraid she will lose her grip. The contents are obviously far too heavy for the box. Bijou wanders over to check out their latest visitor and to examine this foreign object. Puffing from her efforts, the elderly woman pushes a strand of grey hair off her forehead. She tucks it back under her felt fedora-style hat, smiles, and looks at Norah through rheumy eyes.

"You are very helpful, child. Is Austin around? I told your father some time back I might want to sell him a few things, so today's the day." All this is said in the form of a huge sigh.

Norah is more curious than anything else. She would love to open the box but knows from experience it's not her place. The woman satisfies some of Norah's curiosity. "I've brought him my father's inkwell collection, my mother's pickle castors, and my grandmother's custard glass breakfast set," she gushes with pride. "Austin said he would love to see them if I ever wanted to sell."

Norah says nothing but nods an enthusiastic response. She runs to the back of the shop. "Mom, Mom, there's someone here with some stuff. Can you come up?"

Miss Dixon looks both bewildered and flustered as Paige emerges into the shop from the back. Clad in a printed housedress and clean apron, she pats the bun at the nape of her neck to ensure it isn't misbehaving. She smiles and they exchange pleasantries. Finally, the older woman blurts out, "Austin said he would buy a few of my family's collectibles if I ever wanted to part with anything. I brought some things he seemed interested in when we talked. Is he here?" Her eyes dart around the shop.

Paige indulges the old lady with the smile Norah knows she reserves especially for the elderly and the sick. "Austin's at an auction this morning, Miss Dixon. We could have a look, if you like, or you can leave the box and Austin can go through your things when he gets back later this afternoon."

They all look down at the box Norah placed with such care on the floor. Norah dances from one foot to the other, like it's Christmas morning and no one will let her start to open presents. She hopes there are nice things and not a bunch of broken stuff, so her mother will be pleased.

Miss Dixon nods. "We can look," she relents. Norah pounces on the box and breaks apart the four flaps closing the top. She is assaulted with the smell of old newspapers as she unpacks and places each piece gently on the top of the sales counter. Miss Dixon has brought five pickle castors. Each one includes a silver holder but all the glass inserts are different. As Norah unwraps, Miss Dixon shows her which pieces go together. Next, Norah reveals the four items making up the pressed glass breakfast set. Without conscious awareness, Norah feels the edges of the pieces and checks for damages as she unpacks and sets each one on the counter. Once at the bottom, she retrieves three unusual inkwells. The first is a brass owl with a head that folds back to reveal the well. The second is a heavy square of glass with a round knob trimmed in gold. The final one is a dolphin mounted on a brass box and balancing a scallop shell that hides the inkwell. As a twelve-year-old, Norah's charmed, to say the very least. Everything is extraordinary and Norah thinks that they could probably go to ten auctions and not get pieces as nice as this.

Paige and Miss Dixon talk. Miss Dixon tells Norah's mother why things have been so tough the last couple of years. She wants to sell the old homestead but repairs are needed first and taxes are due this month. Her teachers' pension isn't enough to repair and run the place even though most everyone in town thinks she's loaded. Her cantankerous father put everything he had into the house before he died and there just isn't much money to spare.

Once she sells and moves, she won't have room for most of this stuff anyway. It might as well pay for the taxes. She says all this as if everything is worthless but then she adds as an afterthought, "I know people collect these kinds of things and Austin said they might be valuable."

Paige tilts her head, showing neither agreement nor argument in her expression. Norah knows her mother doesn't let the excitement of the find cloud her judgment for a good deal, like Dad often does. The Clarkes are not your typical business people when it comes to buying directly from someone liquidating their possessions. They determine the retail value of a piece and pay the person forty percent of that number. You don't want people to feel like they might be selling something of enormous value for next to nothing and it's important your neighbours can visit the store, look at the price tag on the item they sold you, and not feel ripped off. Norah is proud of the fact that this is why people come to Clarkes—because they are fair and honourable. "So, Miss Dixon, let me make a list and add everything up to see if we can offer you enough to pay your taxes. Norah, run and get my clipboard and a pen, please."

Norah scuttles off to the desk in the back and returns almost at once. She watches her mother. Paige is methodical. Each piece is listed. Some are more valuable than others. She goes behind the counter to retrieve a reference book, looks something up, and jots down a couple of notes. After a few minutes she returns to the centre of the shop.

Miss Dixon has been looking around but isn't moving far from her original position beside the now-empty cardboard box. Paige totals the column of figures and hands the list to the teacher. "This price is our standard forty percent of retail, Miss Dixon. These pieces are quite exceptional, although some will move more quickly than others. The inkwells are very collectible right now and there are always those who want cranberry glass, but we expect it will be a quiet summer so I can't offer more than our regular percentage." She's matter-of-fact and her tone indicates there will not be any negotiation.

Miss Dixon nods her head. Norah thinks she looks sad. "Your offer is fine, Paige. I appreciate it. I guess Austin would have come up with the same figure. The taxes will get paid, at least." Her tone is resigned. Norah thinks her father would have gotten all excited and paid way more. He always does, but she knows when to keep her mouth shut.

The cheque is written, the items are moved to the back where they can be cleaned and recorded as inventory. Norah becomes aware of hard times that day. She sees someone forced to sell family treasures. She learns things are not always how they seem as she listens to Miss Dixon explain her circumstances. She sees her mother as a disciplined but fair negotiator. Norah respects and admires her for this. As Paige returns downstairs to finish her bread, Norah hears her mutter about how they need groceries more than pickle castors but what are you going to do? You can't sell nice things if you don't buy nice things. Roberta Flack, singing "Killing Me Softly," filters through the now-still air as the sound of the radio returns to Saturday morning prominence. Bijou returns to snoozing, with one eye seemingly focused on the young girl working with quiet precision nearby.

Almost an hour after Miss Dixon departs, cheque in hand, the door chime tinkles. In flounces Beth Hanley, attempting without much success, to manage two glasses of lemonade while she pushes open the heavy front door. "Got time for a chin wag?" Running to assist, followed by the dog wagging with delight, Norah realizes she'll need a mop in a minute, if Beth's not more careful. The teacher has lived upstairs for a number of years. She's studying in the city this summer, upgrading all the time, it seems, but she travels back and forth and often appears at the door on Saturday morning when Norah works the shop. Norah thinks Beth is sophisticated and worldly, living on her own, managing her career. She's respected as well as liked at the high school.

Norah takes the lemonade from Beth and sets it on the counter she's just cleared. She scoots out to the sink at the back and returns with a damp cloth to wipe the drips from the floor and the damp from the glasses. Beth laughs as she settles her heavy frame onto the stool behind the counter. "I thought you'd be down here by yourself, needing some company and something cool to drink." It's a hot day and Beth is dressed for the weather. She's wearing red shorts and a tank top revealing more than appropriate amounts of her soft, fleshy curvature. Normally, Beth wears wispy and flowing blouses with extravagant scarves and palazzo pants or long skirts when out in public.

Although Clarkes Antiques is decidedly public, she seems to treat the place like an extension to her apartment, since access is just down her stairs, out to the sidewalk, and then into the shop by way of the front door. She doesn't appear to acknowledge the possibility of someone perhaps entering the store to look at antiques anytime she happens to be there. "It is so warm!" Beth exclaims as she takes a big gulp of her drink. "Want to go to the movies tonight? *The Love Bug* is playing. It's old but at least the theatre is air conditioned. Have you seen it? I haven't. They said on the radio it's quite cute." All this comes out between gulps of lemonade.

Norah leans against the counter and watches her. Although most would consider Beth to be a friend of her parents, Norah knows with certainty that, although Beth may be their tenant, she is really her friend. She likes Beth a lot because Beth treats her like a real person and not just as a kid. She also feels like she's in the inner sanctum of the teacher world. All the kids speculate about what teachers might do and how they might think when not in school, but no one else that she knows is actually friends with a teacher.

Norah treasures the relationship, would never say anything to hurt Beth's feelings, and loves to spend time with this outspoken, fun-loving woman so different from her mother. "I'll ask Mom. She'll be up in a minute." Norah wants to go but makes it a habit not to become too excited before receiving permission. This way, she can avoid potential disappointment. Her parents can be overprotective. Being an only child has its drawbacks. Norah takes another sip of the sweet lemonade, just as her mother's footsteps tap their way up the back stairs.

Paige comes around the corner from the downstairs flat for the second time on this muggy summer morning. Norah is alert to her look of surprise when she sees Beth piled up on the stool behind the counter, drinking lemonade, and leaving rings on the showcase glass. She smiles, but just with the lower half of her face, as she eyes Norah with a questioning look. Norah is completely aware of how her mother finds Beth a little pushy, a little too familiar, and loud in both personality and dress.

"I gather we aren't run off our feet with business, eh Norah?" She mutters this as she starts to organize the pieces just purchased an hour earlier from Miss Dixon. "I thought I would get this stuff listed before your father gets home. He'll probably have a couple of boxes of junk for me to shovel through." She turns away from their guest. "How are you, Beth? I thought you were taking a course this summer." Paige has yet to cast the merest glance directly at Beth.

Beth squirms ever so slightly on the stool that Norah imagines must just now be feeling far too small for her bum. Her mother has a way of revealing her judgment of people and situations without ever saying anything. "Saturday, Paige. And too hot for class, even if it wasn't a weekend. I just came in to bring your daughter a cold drink and invite her to the movies—a little Disney flick. Nothing too deep, but air-conditioned comfort nonetheless. Is it okay if she accompanies me to the early show?"

Norah sighs. The pressure's off. Paige would never say no to the teacher, herself. "My chores are done and I can tend shop the rest of the afternoon if you want to do something else," Norah contributes, trying to ensure her success.

After a moment or two, when all any of them hears is the slow drone of a single fly trapped in the display window, Paige consents. Norah knows that her mother is aware she could potentially be doing far worse things at the age of twelve than going to the movies with a teacher, albeit one her mother considers loud and outspoken.

Chapter 5

In 1980, at seventeen, Norah begins lifeguarding. Paige makes it crystal clear she's less than ecstatic about the idea because it'll mean more hours she'll have to spend tending the store, but her father says he's thrilled to see Norah getting out and doing something different. He tells her how he'll miss her company at sales or house buys, but she won't be lifeguarding all the time and she can still come with him whenever she's free. Norah has never been paid for working in the business so is anxious to make money and working at the pool will be great.

She was over the moon when she got the job at the outdoor pool for the summer. She's taken swimming lessons every year and is quite good. She took a course in lifeguarding and one in teaching beginner swimmers so she's willing and prepared to work as many hours as they'll give her; anything to make a few dollars and get out around other kids over the summer. Next year will be her final year of high school and she's anxious to be independent—to show her parents she can do other things. Beth has been encouraging her for three years. "Find out what you like; meet some new people," Beth says. "Set goals and go for it," she repeats. "If you like something, learn everything you can about it. Just go for it."

Norah followed her advice and now she's lifeguarding and teaching swimming. She met and has become friends with Joy Scott. The Scott family rented a cottage just outside Prestonburg and moved to the beach from Montreal for three full months. Mr. Scott is recuperating from some kind of illness and they wanted to get away from the city for a while. Norah liked Joy right from the start. Despite the fact that Joy's family is very religious, they accepted Norah without question and the girls have become close. Now that they are friends, they hope to go to the same university. Oftentimes, when Norah is working her Wednesday at the shop, Joy will pop by with her mother, who is a very good shopper. She loves beautiful glass and always finds something to pique her interest.

It's mid-week. This is the day Paige grocery shops and does laundry. It's the day Norah asked not to be scheduled at the pool. She worried her mother would find the disruption too much and she strives to keep the peace. Let her father be the disruptive one.

Norah settles in for the morning. Entering the shop from the back stairs, her nose is tickled by the familiar scent of dust and old things. Antique shops, regardless of how well you take care of them, always have a lingering odour of accumulated years. It's familiar and not unpleasant to her as she meanders on tanned, long legs over to the door, unlocks the deadbolt, and flips the sign from closed to open. She switches on the overhead globes. They don't produce the best light, but this isn't Eaton's, so the old yellowed shades do the job. Dusting and rearranging will be the order of the day. The front window was refreshed the week before. Norah turns on the radio and the melody of one of the year's biggest hits, "Fame," tumbles from the speakers. The sound in the background fills the room when there are customers in the store. It settles into the pockets of quiet when people are looking but not talking. Norah notices a dozen pieces of Cameo Depression-era glassware sitting on the back table. They're washed and priced, just not displayed yet. Left for her to do today. Her father says she has an eye for it.

She starts to create display space for the green glass when she hears a heavy tread fall on the back stairs. Her father is on his way up for a visit. He's not particularly motivated to deal with customers on Wednesday, unless, of course someone wants to sell something fabulous. He oftentimes shows up just to hang out with her. Mom never does this, just Dad. He appears around the corner, all tall and angular, a male reflection of Norah herself. He's carrying a cup of coffee and settles into the office chair, supposedly to "keep her company." This is a ritual they've fallen into over quite some time.

"How's it goin', kid?" He props his feet on a file box hauled from under the desk—old business records you can't throw away but never have anywhere to store.

"Dad, I just opened the place. Nothing is goin' yet," Norah responds, knowing she sounds a bit frustrated. Austin is dressed in his standard uniform of cotton shirt and khakis. He'll add an old cardigan if temperatures warrant.

Norah isn't sure she's seen him wear anything else except at weddings, funerals, or when he's in pyjamas. She smiles to herself thinking he would love it if she made him khaki pyjamas. Now there's a great Christmas present idea if ever there was one.

She admires her father because he never gets upset. He says his feathers don't ruffle easily. He lets Paige run the show. Details about business and life in general seem much more intense and important for her. He has a reputation for overspending; for getting distracted and losing track of time; for not taking things seriously enough. As Norah has understood the dynamic of her parents' relationship over the years, she's come to realize her father has much more control than any observer might think.

"Is there any place special you want to put the Cameo?" she asks.

"No, you be the judge. Maybe when you do the window again, you can do a green theme. Good idea?"

"What are you up to today, Dad? Paperwork?" Her mother hates to get behind in that department.

Austin smiles. "You are just like your mother, trying to steer me into doing a job. No. I am going to see an old lady about a dresser."

****

Summer melts into fall. Norah struggles. Her senior year of high school has arrived with far more pressure than she imagined possible. School is fine. It has never been about school. It's always about the life issues swirling around her—the antique shop, the money or potential lack thereof, her parents' relationship or lack thereof, and how Beth may or may not be involved. Any attempts to knit together the dramas playing out around her result in more tangles than stitches most days.

Norah applies to universities. Her path is not clear and, with advice from the school counsellor as well as her parents and Beth, she decides to take a general arts degree emphasizing sociology as she's interested in people and social development at all different levels. Norah has become a bit of a news hound over the last few years and is no doubt influenced by many stories: "The Iranian Hostage Taking of Americans in 1979" and the role played by Canada in securing their freedom; people like Mother Teresa and Terry Fox;

the decisions over the boycott of the Moscow Olympics; and by Canada's current Prime Minister, Pierre Trudeau.

She decides to focus on the things she knows and likes. Her courses will be heavy on theory but you have to start somewhere, she rationalizes. Both her parents want her to study nearby, at a small university a couple of hours away. Beth encourages her to stretch her wings while her parents seem to want to keep her close to home. Beth thinks she needs to explore the big bad world and go somewhere grand like Montreal. Joy might go to McGill in her home town but would like to get away to a smaller school, maybe nearer to Norah.

Norah has worked since she was a small girl, first by delivering newspapers, then minding the antique shop, and most recently coupling her ongoing responsibilities in the shop with lifeguarding and teaching at the local pool. She is always busy and always saving money. Her concern about the state of her university funding does not come from lack of savings. It comes from an ingrained sense of unease, learned over years of listening to her mother worry about the business.

If they have a good season, her mother's afraid to spend for fear next year will be poor. If the season is less than stellar, she worries about every dollar every day. Money, Norah knows, is a stress trigger, regardless of the circumstances. In point of fact, she's saved enough money for her first year, expects to land a scholarship from the high school, and will not have to get a student loan—at least for now. Her parents have never mentioned helping in any way and Norah hesitates to explore this option. She knows only too well how hard things can be for them, although at the moment the situation seems on an even keel.

Paige and Austin's relationship is another story and another stressor in Norah's life. She has asked a couple of times, to each parent in turn, if everything is okay and was met on each occasion with vague responses of "don't worry," "nothing serious," or "things will blow over," but Norah's radar continues to pick up signs and symptoms of conflict. Her parents are always on different wavelengths. This is nothing new, as her mother is rigid and set in her ways while her father is gregarious, flexible, and easy going. For every time Paige worries about money, Austin spends a bit more than he should. They relate this way. They balance one another. This has always been the norm—for them.

What has changed relates to Beth, and her parents' attitude toward Beth. Over the years, the young teacher has become part of the small family, invited to supper, babysitting Norah when she was a child, bringing down a gooey dessert to share with the family, and generally being the model tenant—albeit in a big-personality kind of way. She has never had any boyfriends and many times spends her Saturday nights at the movies with Norah.

Over time, little events and bits of evidence that indicate a possible relationship between Beth and Austin have accumulated in Norah's storage locker of a brain. Beth used to visit in the shop with whoever happened to be working. Over the past couple of years, she's stopped coming down when Paige is there. Norah isn't sure when this changed. Beth is out more on Saturdays, too. She seems to always be out when Austin is at sales or going to assess a house lot of antiques for purchase. Norah doesn't tag along as often, mainly because she does other things. It takes her father longer to visit people and do appraisals than it used to, and Norah isn't sure if this is because he's older and a little bit more eccentric about antiques or if something else is going on. Beth doesn't come downstairs to the apartment as often as she used to, either. Norah has to bug her mother to have her issue a dinner invitation and her parents never seem to look at one another while Beth is there.

Although not comfortable with having a conversation with her parents downstairs, Norah decides she'll be more direct and ask Beth what the trouble is. They have a date to go see Bette Midler in *The Rose*. Since Janis Joplin is a favourite of Beth's and therefore most certainly of Norah's, they're both excited about the movie finally running in the little local theatre.

Norah walks through the door of their apartment into the crisp evening air. She scoots around Prestonburg Variety and emerges on street level just in front of the door leading up the stairs to Beth's. It hasn't snowed yet this year but Norah feels winter's inevitable approach. She tilts her head for just a moment, admiring the salted velvet of the clear, late fall sky. She rings the ancient chime by twisting the small brass handle in the middle of the street-level door, pushes it open, and runs upstairs to what Beth refers to as the "real" door at the top of the stairs. Beth only locks the street-level door at the very end of the day.

Norah has traversed these stairs a thousand times. Beth has lived above the shop for all twelve years Norah has been in school. Every stair is familiar to her. Every tread, every knot in every piece of wood, and all the cracks showing in the original plaster walls—all are old friends assembled to greet her as she climbs her way to Beth's. Something catches her eye. It looks like a bead and Norah bends down to pick it up. *A Bakelite bead.* Customers collect Bakelite jewellery and her father buys as much of it as he can. It's becoming quite valuable and not everybody has figured that out yet. The secret to success in the antique business is to determine the trends ahead of everybody else. Austin has a nose for this and Norah understands the skill. *What the heck is a bead like this doing on Beth's stairs?* She shoves it in the pocket of her corduroys and continues up the stairs to the door at the top. Just as she raises her hand to knock, Beth appears with a flourish. "Heard the ring," she sings out. "Come on in. I just have to fluff the hair." The Captain and Tennille are on the radio serenading the empty living room with "Do It To Me One More Time" and Norah hears Beth chiming in on the chorus as her wide hips round the corner to the bathroom.

The apartment is simple and lived-in. The baseboards are oversized, original to the building. The ceilings are high. Everything is painted a soft biscuit colour and the wood trim is crisp in its whiteness. The room faces out to the street and is always bathed in the soft yellow glow of streetlights after darkness has fallen. Behind the living room is a tiny dining area spreading around the back to a tidy, although full-to-the-rafters, kitchen. Beth is an avid collector of all things yellow and it shows. She is not into antiques, but prefers new and yellow dishes, curtains, place mats, whatever is popular at any given time—picked up at Woolworths, most likely. There is a big bedroom and a roomy bath, both on the back overlooking the water. Although the apartment isn't large, Beth has made use of every available square foot of space. Norah likes it.

As she waits for Beth to finish getting ready, she casts her eyes around admiring all of Beth's possessions, thinking how someday she will have an apartment just like this. Not long now. First university and then she'll fly solo.

Her eyes fall on the sea shell full of Bakelite beads. She takes a closer look. The bead in her pocket is a match.

Last week, her father bought a collection of Bakelite at an auction. She remembers because she helped him clean everything. One of the necklaces had a very unusual clasp. It was a heart on one end with a key on the other. You put the key into the heart and turn it to fasten the necklace together.

Norah takes a step forward and looks down into the shell. Suddenly, she feels uncomfortable though she's been in Beth's apartment hundreds of times.

On any other occasion, she would just pick the thing up and look. The heart and key lie in the tangle of loose beads and necklace remains. It's the necklace she cleaned the other day.

Beth rounds the corner. Norah jumps just a little. "I found a bead on the stairs, Beth. I'm pretty sure it goes with your necklace." The statement is made with no expression. Her eyes are downcast.

Beth reaches for the bead sitting in the open palm of Norah's hand, and drops it in the shell bowl. "It fell and broke the other day when I was running up the stairs. I'm going to get the thing restrung as soon as I get around to it." She is sounding casual, but to Norah something about her words feels wrong.

"Did you get it from the shop, Beth? Dad bought one like this at an auction last week. I don't think Mom has priced any of it for display yet." Norah doesn't look up. She's standing and staring down at the beads. They're beautiful with brown and yellow swirls, shiny and perfect. Has she cornered her friend? She knows it's the same necklace.

"Your father gave it to me." Norah nods, still not looking up. "I guess he thought I deserved a present. I said I liked it. He gave it to me."

Norah's face lifts to look at her friend. She sees flushed cheeks. She smells musky anxiety. So, her father is giving Beth presents. Norah's only question to herself is whether or not her mother knows. She smiles at her friend, but it doesn't reach her eyes.

A couple of days later, Norah's in the shop with her father. She asks him what happened to the necklace with the unique heart clasp. He looks up with questioning eyes. "I can't remember. I think I gave it to Beth. She admired it. She's always so good to you; I let her have it for a gift."

"That's really nice, Dad. She loves jewellery." Norah's sad smile seems to contradict the words.

* * * *

Norah is accepted to Callwood College in Callwood Bay, some two hours away, and to McGill University in Montreal. After a serious and excited conversation with her friend Joy, who has been accepted to both schools as well, she decides on the former and sends in her application confirmation and deposit. It's a big cheque, amounting to half her tuition and twenty-five percent of her residence fees. She celebrates by taking her parents to a little waterfront cafe for lunch. They close the shop in honour of the occasion.

Her dad can't sit still. He squirms in the chair like a small child who wants to run and play in the toy room instead of remaining with the adults for lunch. Her mom gives him more than one glare but nothing seems to help the situation. Norah knows there's something going on. She figures they might have a high school graduation present for her but it's still just April and not time for presents. Mom is quite rigid about these things so maybe it's bad news, not good. Norah has spent six months waiting for someone to tell her that her parents are breaking up. The burden has been heavy and terribly unpleasant. *Are they going to say that now?*

Her dad turns to her mom after the third dirty look. "Can we tell her before lunch instead of waiting until after? I want to tell her." He actually whines a bit.

Paige heaves a sigh. "Okay, okay." Her voice is filled with a surprising measure of indulgence. "Go ahead."

Austin gushes at Norah. "You've worked in the shop since you were a little girl. You never asked for money and we never gave you any." He continues to shake and squirm in his chair. "But we put money away for you for every hour you spent there working and for every hour you helped out at an auction or went with me to buy a house lot. You've earned a great deal of money over the years, Norah." He's almost laughing.

The waiter appears and Dad waves him away. "Norah." He says her name again with more emphasis and intensity. He leans over so she can hear every word above the din of the restaurant. Her mother sits, arms folded, watching her husband and saying nothing. "There's enough money for you to pay your tuition and residence for the next four years. If interest rates keep going up, you'll no doubt have enough for graduate school as well!" He says the last with a flourish and slides a little blue bank book across the table. "This is for you."

Norah takes the book. Her questioning eyes look from one parent to the other. She wonders how they could have gone all this time without telling her, especially since she's expressed concern about the costs and her mother spends so much time obsessing about money. She smiles. There are tears in her eyes but her first response is for them. "Don't you need this money?"

Her mom, exhibiting both a calmness and reassurance Norah has not often seen, shakes her head. "Open the book, dear. The money is yours. You earned every penny." Her dad's grin is spread across his face to meet his ears. His nose is struggling to maintain position. He's barely controlling himself.

She carefully opens the book, her fingers caressing the linen-like cover. Every month shows a documented deposit representing the hours she contributed to the running of Clarkes Antiques and Collectibles. The balance in the account is more than six thousand dollars. Norah looks from one to the other. She rises from her chair, squeezing her way around the table so she's standing between her parents. With arms outstretched to envelope them, she lowers her head and kisses each one. Her mom is first as she fully appreciates the discipline her mother had to assert in order to keep up with the plan, and then her father just because he's so excited and so happy. "I love you both," she whispers. "This must have been tough for you to do. I will not disappoint you."

Her father turns and looks up at her with misty eyes. "You could never disappoint us, kid."

Paige pats her daughter's back. "Okay, now. You sit down and let's see if we can get our waiter's attention."

Chapter 6

Leaving behind the familiarity and comfort of the store front in Prestonburg and moving into a vine-covered dorm at Callwood College in Callwood Bay is not an easy transition for Norah. An only child suddenly plunged into the deep end of the pool with eighty young women under one roof can either go well—or not. Austin drives Norah to school. Her mother stays home under the predictable pretext someone is needed to keep the shop open, but Norah knows better. She suspects her mother doesn't want to exhibit any signs of weakness by maybe puddling up while waving goodbye to her only offspring as Norah stands alone on the front steps of her university residence.

They carry her things into the room she'll share for the next year with another female student whose identity will remain a mystery for a few hours yet. She wants her own space, or at least to share a room with Joy, but rooms were already assigned and single rooms are not immediately available to first years. She and Joy are both on a waiting list in the off chance single rooms will miraculously become available.

Her father helps place her new blue Eaton's trunk at the foot of the bed. He looks for a spot to plug in her tiny clock radio. The task list is small and now complete. The idea of being alone wedges itself between them no matter how positive Norah tries to feel. Her dad, looking forlorn, reaches out for a hug.

"You know, if you need anything, anything at all, just call. Call collect. I don't care what happens, you can call me. I'll come. I'll bring you home. I'll help." Tears puddle up in his eyes. He gulps for air. Norah is acutely sensitive to her father's emotions. She knows he is proud, scared, sad, and profoundly overwhelmed all at the same time.

She looks up from inside his embrace and smiles. "I'll be fine," she soothes. "Just don't forget to come and get me for Thanksgiving," she teases, as if her father would ever forget. Knowing him, he'll arrive a day early, pretending he thinks it's the right day. "Now off with you. Mom will be worried if you aren't back by supper."

He nods like an obedient child. She hooks her arm in his and they walk in silence along the hall to the main door. He turns to give her one more hug and starts to walk with reluctance down the steps and toward the car, his fists jammed hard into the pockets of his beige and bedraggled sweater jacket. She thinks he looks like he's forcing one foot in front of the other, so she shouts, "Hey, Dad." He turns his head. "Don't forget—this is what you wanted." She laughs and waves. He doesn't take his hand from his pocket but lifts it toward her in a mitten-like salute. She stands on the step until he turns the corner to the parking lot.

Listening to the sound of the Captain and Tennille floating down the hall, she trots back to the room. The song reminds her of Beth. Norah will miss her, no matter what the circumstances of Beth's relationship with her father. She's found her questions and suspicions lie between them like a pile of rocks requiring navigation each and every time they meet.

* * * *

Norah's roommate proves to be a challenge on many levels. She stays up all night and sleeps all day. She shows no interest in attending classes and Norah reaches a point where she spends every moment either at the library or in Joy's room, hoping against hope that Cookie, for this is her roommate's name, will drop out. Cookie is a wiry young woman whose wardrobe consists of jeans and T-shirts; who bathes only on occasion; swears like a sailor; and often remains out all night. This last quality is a bonus for Norah, who's able to sleep on those occasions.

Just before Thanksgiving, Norah is notified by the Residence Coordinator, that a single room is coming available in a different building. It will be more money and most of the rooms there are occupied by third- and fourth-year students. There's also a rule about no noise after 11:00 PM but if she can cope with this, the room is hers. *Cope?* How about survive and thrive! Best of all, Joy has been offered a single room there, too.

When her father arrives to take her home for the long weekend, she's packed and ready to move to the new dorm. He meets Cookie and understands. He helps Norah move her things and then they laugh all the way to Prestonburg.

****

Friday noon until Tuesday noon is not much time to do all the things Norah wants to do. Of course, spending time with her parents and Bijou are the top priority. Seeing Beth is a must. A visit with high school friends, also home for a couple days, is important, too.

Bijou is not herself. Her excitement at seeing Norah is tempered in a sad and distant way. She lies on the couch, looking down at the floor, casting her eyes up toward any voice speaking to her, but she moves as little as possible. The vet simply stated the obvious—Bijou is old—more than twelve, and suffering from congestive heart failure. She gets short of breath as her lungs fill up with fluid. Norah spends her weekend sitting with Bijou, understanding the inevitable. An appointment is scheduled for Tuesday morning, to have Bijou put to sleep. Norah insists she'll be the one to take her dog. She won't return to school and have her parents take Bijou when she's gone. She refuses to take the coward's way out.

Tuesday dawns crisp and clear. It's the kind of fall day where the sun is warm but the wind off the water has a hint of icy winter. Harbour wind has a way of gobbling up each block on the calendar, leading the community toward yet another coastal season of snow and freezing rain. Norah is in the front seat with Bijou curled up on her lap, when Austin comes out to start the car. She rubs the dog, one long stroke followed by another.

Bijou's eyes are closed and she's safe and secure in the arms of her person. Father and daughter are silent. Austin's eyes are brimming as he starts the engine. It's a ten-minute drive to the vet's office and they arrive in what seems like seconds. Norah expects they'll both go in, but one look at her dad's face tells her she's on her own. Tears roll down his pale cheeks and he folds his arms over the steering wheel, drops his head to rest on them, and weeps like a child.

Norah touches his heaving shoulders. "It's okay, Dad. You don't need to come in. I'll take her." She climbs out of the car, Bijou and a dog blanket in her arms. Dry-eyed and stoic, she forces herself up the steps and into the office that smells like antiseptic mixed with damp German shepherd, no matter when you turn up.

The assistant is prepared, so ushers her without waiting, into an exam room. The stainless steel table twinkles under the fluorescent lights. Norah spreads the blanket and places her dog gently on top. Bijou obviously knows where she is. She's not afraid. She likes the vet and her tail produces the shadow of a wag just as Dr. Curtis opens the door. He's a kind and gentle man, just like all vets should be. He's a mountain, likely weighing more than three hundred pounds, but he handles animals as if every patient were a kitten.

They don't have to talk much. He tells Norah what's going to happen next and offers to take Bijou into the other room so she doesn't have to witness anything. Norah is aghast. She will not leave her dog. No one can make her. Dr. Curtis asks about Austin and, as much as she would prefer to have him by her side, she simply states that he's waiting in the car.

A tourniquet is wrapped around Bijou's little front leg, just above her paw. She resists a little and Norah leans down. She coos sweet nothings into Bijou's ear and rubs the silky head, calming her. Dr. Curtis starts injecting the liquid into the vein. Norah continues to pat her dog and whisper. Norah holds Bijou in her gaze until the light is gone from her dog's big brown eyes.

Norah is struck by how relaxed Bijou seems now. She hasn't looked this way in a very long time. After stretching the little dog out on the blanket, she removes her collar and wraps her up. Bijou will be cremated and they'll bury her ashes in the corner of their yard. She puts out her hand to thank Dr. Curtis. "I will go get Dad to come in to pay you." Her voice is strained and formal.

"No need for that today, Norah." The big man smiles down at her. "I'll see Austin gets a bill when he comes in to pick up Bijou's ashes. Don't worry now." She nods her thanks and navigates her way toward the door, not looking up at the people and their pets in the waiting room, acutely aware of the leash and still-warm collar dangling from her fist.

In the car, her dad is all apologies and ready to go in and pay the bill. Norah repeats what Dr. Curtis said to her, touches his hand to let him know she's okay—which seems to satisfy the questioning look in his eyes—and asks if they can just go home. She has a few more things to organize before the trip back to campus. She's thankful she had no classes scheduled for today. Her father would have been a basket case if forced to do this alone, or poor Bijou would have been sick for weeks longer until someone scraped up the courage to take her in.

Back home, she makes a beeline through the house and gathers up dog food, dishes, toys, and her old sweater that Bijou used to sleep on when up on the couch. Everything goes out to the galvanized garbage can by the back fence. In a tiny corner of her mind, Norah doesn't understand why her mother didn't do this much. Paige comes down from the shop when her husband goes up to take over. She watches her daughter in silence, not interfering.

They have lunch together in the store and then Austin drives Norah back to college. It's a drive like no other she and her father have ever made, exchanging less than ten words. Each remains lost in their thoughts. Norah is angry with her parents and proud of herself for stepping up. Her heart is broken but she knows she did the best for her dog. She didn't want them to take on the responsibility without her, but she feels they weren't even up to the task of helping her. She's anxious to get back to school and throw herself into a paper about anthropology that's due in a couple of weeks.

It's Friday, three days after her return from Prestonburg. Norah is sitting in a first-year biology class. The professor is lecturing about arthropods and she realizes tears are pouring down her face. Dr. Arnold is talking about spiders and scorpions while she cries like a baby. She mops herself up and makes her way to the park immediately after class. She acknowledges no one. The tears don't stop for a long time. The grass is damp and the ground cold as she sits with her head on her knees, letting the grief pour out of her. The wind blows just enough to cause a chill. He was talking about caterpillars and metamorphosis, for God's sake, not Bijou or dogs at all.

Her loss of control is a surprise.

****

Living in a residence with older students suits Norah just fine. Some of the girls are very mature and some not so much. She thinks her relationship with Beth, growing up in Prestonburg, is serving her very well as she carves a niche for herself in Hammond's Hall. Her room is Number 101 and located near the beginning of the first-floor hallway. Having her friend, Joy, in the same building is perfect and she meets a lot of her other neighbours by simply leaving her door open.

This all starts one Sunday afternoon when Joy stops in for tea after returning from church. She thinks a visit is in order before going up one floor to her room to study. Norah's door is ajar. She and Joy are talking. Just as the hot water meets the tea bags, pushing out the pungent aroma of cranberry, a freckled and spectacled face appears. "That tea smells fabulous! Hi, I'm Amy from down the hall—105."

"Cranberry tea. There's lots. Come on in." Norah's always happy to share tea. Amy looks over at Joy, who hasn't said anything to this point. "This is Joy. She's a freshman, too. Upstairs in 203."

Joy, always shy at the best of times, uncurls her legs off the end of the single bed and stands up to shake Amy's hand. Norah thinks her friend is being a bit formal, but continues to prattle on. "Have a seat. Are you in third or fourth year?"

Amy pulls out the desk chair and flops down, her long red hair hanging across the desk surface and brushing the papers Norah has scattered methodically on the work surface. "Barely holding on to third year. I'm starting to think science is not what it's cracked up to be. I was a whiz in high school, but just the middle of the pack, here. The physics is killing me!"

"This is just what you need—a tea break." Norah and Joy both look at Amy with a measure of sympathy and understanding. "Everything's harder in university than it was in high school."

"Yeah," she replies. "I'm working on a paper but I needed to get away from it for a while. I heard you two chatting and smelled the tea. Thanks."

Amy is the first of her neighbours to stop by unannounced, but certainly not the last. Girls coming back from class or the library poke their heads in to say "hi". As time passes and they get to know Norah better, they stop to share an experience or wax on about a certain professor. They often pause on the way out, to ask Norah to join them on a trip to the student centre or the library. Norah quickly gains a reputation as being reliable, able to keep a confidence, and as a hard worker. She is liked and respected by students throughout the building. They soon learn the kettle always has water and tea will be ready when there is occasion to celebrate a new boyfriend, a passing grade, or a successful shopping spree. Tea's also shared over tears for loves lost and marks not fit to write home about.

****

Nothing about the approach of Christmas feels right. Everyone runs around residence, wrapping parcels, giggling in corners, or trying on goofy reindeer sweaters while wearing antler contraptions on their heads. Norah lacks the spirit. All she thinks of is going home to a house without Bijou. She wonders about Beth. She still doesn't know if she'll bring up the relationship she's convinced

Beth is having with her father. Perhaps she'll try and find a way to fly high over the situation in order to make observations from afar. She vacillates from worrying and wanting to interfere back to feeling it's none of her business.

The dorm is chaotic on the first floor. The party noises of the season tumble into Norah's room and she closes her door. What an odd time to want to be alone. With her dad arriving tomorrow, right after lunch, Norah hauls her suitcase from under her bed and lays out the clothes she'll take home for the two-week break. Everything irritates her.

She wants her dog. She wants things to be the same as they used to be with Beth. She wants to be able to look at her father the way she used to. She wants to know if her mother knows. The house won't be the same and no one she loves seems, to her, to be the same, either.

****

Beth clatters down the stairs, through the outside door and into the shop almost the minute Austin grunts and drops Norah's suitcase in the middle of the well-waxed floor. The dark blue fabric bag looks odd surrounded by parlour tables and antique glass twinkling under the old ceiling globes. She's barely had time to hug her mother when she finds herself wrapped in the dough-like upper arms of the increasingly voluptuous Beth.

Norah decided a long time ago, if she were ever destined to gain weight, she would follow her friend's example and consider herself voluptuous instead of fat. Beth sways back and forth with Norah wedged into her cleavage. "I have so missed you," the teacher croons, smiling at Austin and ignoring Paige's look of outright hostility.

Paige's laugh sounds forced. "Now, Beth. Let the poor child go. She just got in the door." Beth drops her arms and grins around the little circle. "I am just over the moon you're finally home, girly. I had no idea how much I was going to miss you. Now you're in university, we can be big-girl friends." She claps her hands for effect. "I didn't see much of you at Thanksgiving." The second the words leave her pink-lipsticked lips and enter the dusty air in the little shop, they fall with a thud on the worn hardwood.

"Thanksgiving was a bad weekend." Norah smiles at Beth but she can't prevent her eyes from telling the tale. The little basket is long gone and the absence of welcoming wags and barks at the door can never be replaced, no matter how contagious Beth's excitement. "Are you going to close up, Mom? Let's go downstairs. Beth, will you come for tea?"

Beth tells them she's off upstairs to finish some wrapping. Perhaps Norah would like to come up for a visit later on? She slips out the front door, leaving behind the echo of the little bell and the rhythmic thump of her steps as she retreats up the stairs to her apartment.

Paige closes the shop. Austin carries the suitcase down to the apartment and stashes it in Norah's room. Norah follows her father and goes into the kitchen to put on the tea. The little bit of Christmas spirit she was starting to feel as they drove into her hometown and turned on to Tyler Street has evaporated as the reality of loss rears up to meet her. It had to happen sooner or later, but oh this is going to be hard. She looks up and sees her dad leaning on the old cream door casing, arms crossed in his sweater jacket with the baggy pockets, as he watches her. She wonders if he misses Bijou as much as she does.

Norah doesn't go up to visit Beth that night as invited.

The next day is Christmas Eve. She helps her mother prepare lobster chowder—a family tradition—and takes time to call on Beth early that afternoon. Plans are for Beth to spend the evening with the Clarkes and then go to her cousin's house for Christmas Day. Beth opens the door before Norah has a chance to knock. "I heard the door chime," she says. "I thought you weren't going to get up for a visit."

"Can we talk?" Norah replies. Beth has never refused a talk in all the years she's known her.

"Depends on what you want to talk about." Beth turns toward the kitchen, looking for glasses and cider, removing herself from Norah's line of vision. She returns in a couple of minutes. Norah is still standing, admiring the little tree with the soft lights and angel ornaments. Beth is a lover of all things angel. "What's on your mind?"

"Dad." Norah thinks she sees cold fear rippling through Beth, who hesitates, just for a second, and then sets the glasses down on the coffee table.

"No, Norah. We are not going to talk about your dad, or your mom, for that matter. I want to hear all about your classes and how your first semester grades turned out. I want to know about any papers you wrote and projects you researched. I want to hear all about you. Without doubt, I do not want to talk about your father."

Norah does not miss the emphasis. At no time during the visit does Beth ever refer to Austin by name. Perhaps using his name would make it all more personal. They have their cider, chat a bit about school, and Norah returns to her parents' apartment. It appears things will never be like they were.

October, 2012—January, 2013

Chapter 7

Norah opens her eyes. The light in the bedroom is muted, the shadows without edges. It's early, just after six. Matthew rumbles with contentment beside her, both arms stretched above his head, feet sprawled across to her side. Violet is still curled up on her little pillow on the floor by Norah's night table. It's so quiet she can hear the soft whir of the air exchanger and absolutely nothing else. She loves waking early when she doesn't have to get up right away. The master bedroom is the one room in the house where the renovations are finished. The original quarter-sawn oak hardwood floor is buffed to a soft shine. The dark wood casings around the doors and windows are restored. The baseboards and crown mouldings were replaced where necessary. The room is painted a mat tan called doeskin and the colour is warm and soothing. There's an old fireplace in this room—considered an architectural detail in a Craftsman house—and they spent the money to fix and convert it to propane. The antique stained glass windows on either side of it match the glass above the double window on the other side of the room.

Matthew made the headboard for the bed. It's an original door, discovered in the basement after she moved in. Turned on its side and trimmed with mouldings in keeping with the rest of the room, it's by far Norah's favourite element. The space is stunning.

She turns to study her sleeping husband once more. Sometimes she finds it hard to believe he's real. Such a nice man. So good to her. Her mother's voice creeps into her thinking space, and suggests yet again, that maybe she's just not worthy of such a good man; that everything will eventually fall apart. Perhaps she doesn't deserve him.

Norah's always preferred making love in the morning more than at any other time. She likes the soft warm smells, the already rumpled sheets, the cool air drifting through the open window, the morning energy. She thinks about waking him. She runs her finger down the inside of his outstretched arm. He smiles and turns toward her.

Later, in the shower, Norah looks ahead to her day. She has two classes and promised to have tea with Peter Swift during the time between. She expects a productive morning followed by open office hours in the afternoon. Students will stop by for a chat without an appointment, if they don't mind waiting or sharing time with someone else. It has the potential to be very interesting, with five or six in the office at once, exchanging ideas and competing for attention.

She dresses in her usual teaching apparel. She always wears comfortable clothes but when she'll be in front of a class she focuses on being a bit more put together. She chooses grey silk pants with a matching long-sleeved fitted pullover. She slips a soft white cashmere tunic over top. It floats past her narrow hips and ends about mid-thigh. She picks up drop earrings with multi-coloured crystals and slides her feet into red sandals, mirroring the red in the jewellery. She almost skips down the stairs to greet Matthew and Violet who appear to be enjoying Matthew's corn flakes.

"She ate her own food, hasn't hurled, and now wants my breakfast." He crunches his cereal with a smile. "I think we might be out of the woods. I guess I don't have to say good morning. Already did that." He winks from under dark curls dusting his brow.

Norah grins and tries to control a pink flush. This always happens. His sexual innuendos never fail to embarrass her, even after six years. Norah struggles with the concept of herself as a sexual being, fully aware she's repressed in many ways. She works very hard at overcoming her hang-ups. It's a never-ending struggle.

She helps herself to cereal and coffee, as she moves through the construction zone of a kitchen with an awkward ease. She's used to the disarray. "I think I'll walk," she remarks as she bends down to give Violet a cuddle before sitting at the chrome table. "It's going to be a beautiful day. If the weather changes or if I have to bring a bunch of stuff home, I'll call for a lift. Are you around?" Norah never assumes Matthew is at her beck and call.

"I'm working here all week. No new job contract for ten days or so," he replies between sips of coffee and mouthfuls of cereal. "Want to deal with the floors while the doors are out being finished. Maybe by the end of the week, you'll even have ceramic tile counters in your kitchen." He grins again, revealing cereal bits between his teeth. Norah has learned to show outside enthusiasm without allowing herself to get too excited inside. One never knows what might come up to get in the way, especially if a call comes to build a deck or install a kitchen for someone else. "The shoemaker's children always go barefoot." Isn't that the saying?

"I still like the tile we chose six months ago, so it's all good," she can't help but say as she leans over and kisses his cheek, then makes a move to finish in the bathroom before leaving for the college. So, she did it again. She chastises herself for managing to point out how long the tile has been sitting around, despite trying to be supportive and enthusiastic. This is an inherited quality from her mother and she's attempted, without success on many occasions, to curb it. Matthew, of course, being the good guy he is, takes very little to heart, remarking the tile is no doubt out of stock now so he had better not make any mistakes. He punctuates his response with another grin.

The fifteen-minute walk to work is uneventful. Norah notices the kids waiting for the bus and her mind drifts back to her last couple of years in high school. She recalls working all the time but admits, with reluctance—if only to herself—she must have had a bit of fun. What crowds out the recollection of fun is that they never had vacations like other families. The antique shop was their singular focus in the summer. Someone always had to work the shop, regardless of whether it was a good year for tourists or not. While her friends were going to the cottage, on car trips, or even on the train or in a plane to visit friends and relatives, Norah would be stuck at the antique store. Norah jolts herself back to reality as she just misses stumbling up the scarred, granite steps of the Sarah McCall Sociology Building, built in 1954 and unchanged over a half century later.

Her first class is Introduction to Cultural Anthropology and is located in a basement classroom. There she'll meet with thirty students much like Damien, Ashley, and Krista. It's a seventy-five minute class starting at 8:30 AM. She'll then have forty-five minutes for tea with Peter before her graduate students meet upstairs in the lounge for a two-hour seminar propelling her through lunch. She absently digs in her bag for a granola bar to hold her through until 12:30 PM. Office hours start at 2:00 PM. Busy day.

After depositing her bag in her office, Norah makes her way down the cement back stairs to the basement. Chairs scraping on the naked floors and voices echoing up the hall indicate her class will no doubt be full. University classes are often like exercise classes. Everyone starts out well in the fall or just after Christmas, but the faint of heart will fall by the wayside early on. This bunch appears to be quite enthusiastic. It might just stay this size for the duration. Norah, silk trousers rustling, enters the room as Dr. T. G. Norah Clarke. The subject of discussion today centres around European Wunderkammern or "cabinets of curiosities." She provided the class with various references to early European collecting in the modern age of the seventeenth century, when travelling became readily accessible to those with means. Their assignment today is to share ideas based on the information gleaned from the references.

Peter isn't there waiting when she gets back to her office, which is odd because he tends to be prompt. She, on the other hand, is running a bit late since the class turned out to be quite chatty. Norah expects a group of them to show up in the afternoon as well. She puts her portfolio on the desk, grabs the kettle, curses for the umpteenth time that she does not have a sink, and makes her way down the dim corridor to the lounge kitchen. She looks up and sees Peter locking his office and coming her way. "Sorry I'm late," he sputters. "Is your office open? I'll just go in and wait for you." He eyes the kettle. He appears rattled. Norah nods and keeps going, as she wonders what's on the poor guy's mind. Things can't be so terrible in his classes already. It's only October after all.

She fills the kettle and starts back up the hall. Before Peter sees her, she sees him slumped in one of her shabby armchairs, looking troubled—defeated somehow. "Okay, okay, don't lose the faith. I'm back and the kettle will be boiled in no time. Who died?" The second the words are out of her mouth, she regrets them. Perhaps someone *has* died. Peter's life is such a mystery, how could she know?

He looks up, appearing a bit uncomfortable when she breezes in the room. He holds his hand up to indicate nothing dire is occurring right this minute. "I'm fine, Norah, just depressed and a wee bit jealous. Your students love you. They come and visit. They attend your classes!" He says this last bit with a lot of emphasis and a bit of a whine in his voice. Norah curbs her annoyance.

She will not defend herself. It's not complicated. Her enthusiasm for her subject rubs off on her students. She has high expectations of them and they seem to appreciate that. She remembers her conversation with Peter last night and his reference to idiots. She doesn't teach idiots. She sets out the cups, settles on a blackberry and current tea with a wonderful aroma, and chooses her response with care.

"Peter, this has nothing to do with me but I'm happy to help if I can. What's the problem, really?" She pours a cup of tea and places it on the table in front of him—a gift designed to help improve his mood. He picks it up and holds it with a lack of appreciation she finds a little bit offensive.

"How do you compel your students to take an interest in the subject matter, Norah? This semester is just like the two last year. The students seem to hate the gerontology courses. They don't relate. There's only so much you can do to spice up theories of aging. They seem to be more interested in my sexual orientation, for God's sake! I'm out of ideas." He takes a sip of tea, closes his eyes, and leans his head back against the chair.

Norah is still reeling from his statement about his students and sexual orientation. She's glad he's closed his eyes for a minute in case her face betrays her surprise. In all the years they've worked together, this is the first time he's ever mentioned the subject.

"Peter, I can only tell you this. Students have to find a way to relate to the subject matter. They all know someone who's over fifty. Maybe they need to talk to aging adults to get perspective. Maybe they need to use some of the interviewing techniques they're learning in their methodology course to interview some old people. I don't know, Peter. It just has to be real; that's all I can tell you." She sighs. People have to make their own decisions. It's a helluva lot easier to stand at the front of a room and spout theory than it is to work with young people and explore the reality of that theory. Peter might have to roll up his perfect Brooks Brothers shirt sleeves.

His eyes pop open and he raises his head, takes a gulp of the cooling tea and smiles from ear to ear. "You are a star, my dear. I think I'm going to shake it up a bit. I can feel an assignment coming on." He leaves his half-finished cup of wonderful tea sitting on the table and dashes, without grace or ceremony, out the door and back to his office. Norah is a bit miffed. He wasted a tea bag and the answer to his issue was quite obvious, after all.

****

All Matthew said on the phone was supper would be takeout because the kitchen is otherwise engaged. Her already active imagination is in overdrive on the walk home as she analyzes all the options of what could be happening.

She is rendered speechless. He's managed to rehang all the cabinet doors and drawer fronts, put on all the hardware, build a plywood top, and lay all the tiles before she returned home. She and Matthew decided some months ago they'd use a sea-mist green, four-inch square tile for both the top and the backsplash. With the invention of waterproof adhesives and grouts, they are able to employ traditional tile to reflect the era of the house without compromising ease of care. They match the vinyl on her art deco chrome kitchen set to perfection. The original cabinets are oak, sanded and re-stained by Matthew in a golden honey shade. The doors and drawers have an outside frame with an inside flat panel. The original hardware was brass with knobs for the doors and d-pulls for the drawers. A week at the auto body shop has resulted in a revival of these irreplaceable collectibles to a perfect antique finish, not too shiny but not overdone, either. The grout between the tiles, tomorrow's chore, will be a biscuit almond, complementing the oak.

So, right now, they have no kitchen sink, but she knows that after tomorrow, once the grout has dried, it will be full speed ahead to a magical, restored Craftsman kitchen. Norah's in heaven. She smiles and laughs as the love of her life dances from one foot to the other. He holds a squirming Violet, while Norah takes it all in. The result, although still incomplete, is picture book stunning. The retro-style appliances, purchased specifically to reflect the theme of the kitchen, are like works of art in beautiful snow white with their rounded corners and curvy handles. As she crosses the kitchen and hugs them both, she closes her eyes and breathes in the scent of her family mixed with wood stain and ceramic glue. She imagines the old house sighing with the pleasure of being loved, cared for, and returned to its original glory. Surrounded by yesterday, she rocks, contented and safe in Matthew's arms.

****

Norah supervises four graduate students in pursuit of master's degrees. Each one must write and defend a thesis and part of her role is to mentor them toward the ultimate goal of completing their dissertations. She meets with the group once a week. She reads their outlines, examines reference lists, and edits chapters. The necessary balance appears to be to assist without undue influence. They're an interesting bunch. For some she has grave concerns while others appear to be well on their way forward.

Charlie has been with her the longest. He's completed all the required course material for his graduate degree but has registered for another year in order to finish his thesis while working part time in the campus bar. Charlie's parents emigrated from India before he was born. They are traditionalists and much of his research has been about trying to square the circle of his Indian heritage and Canadian identity with theory. He's interviewed a great many subjects but rather than seeing patterns he seems to be digging an ever deeper pit of confusion for himself. He sits in one of Norah's old chairs, disconnected from the group as he stares out the window at the tinted grey light reflecting a shadowy November afternoon. Charlie is tall, dark, and handsome—just like many male protagonists in romance novels. His olive skin and thick black hair bequeath him movie star qualities. The girls tend to swoon a bit when he's around. He appears not to notice and there's no visible link to a girlfriend, even the casual variety. He is, thankfully, one of her tea drinkers and savours the local blueberry variety Norah has set before him.

Penny is an odd young woman. She sits on the floor and leans against the bookshelves, physically apart from the group by the tiniest of margins. It appears she has virtual friends as her iPad is always open to Facebook, but real, in-the-flesh friends seem scarce. There's a chair for her but she prefers the floor and Norah no longer offers. The girl can sit wherever she likes. Her soft-sided briefcase bulges with papers. She is obsessive about her work but disorganized to the point of despair. Norah always attempts to ask for any documentation just prior to the seminar so Penny can do her interminable rifling through her papers prior to their start time.

Norah is convinced Penny hears voices and has visual hallucinations. It's more than just talking to herself. That happens regularly, but Norah thinks her student sees things as well. She's tried broaching the subject when they're alone, but Penny always finds a way to give a noncommittal response that merely serves to create more suspicion on Norah's part. She's an attractive young woman in her very early twenties. She wears clothes that hang off her, obviously garments many sizes too big. She always covers herself with a trench coat and her natural curly red hair is most often left to its own devices, sticking out in all directions, refusing to stay poked behind her ears. Penny is continually dragging it back. She says she doesn't like elastics when offered one by another student.

Maisie is a devoted student. She's "mature." This is the university's description of someone who is out in the world making a living before they decide to advance their education. Maisie owns a second hand store in a town nearby. Norah relates to Maisie because they're of similar age and because Norah spent so much time in the retail business as a child. Maisie has a long way to go, but is taking first steps in trying to mix the culture of collecting and the theme of recycling and reusing in the modern day world of "going green." Norah helps as much as she can. The challenge for Maisie has more to do with her lack of a writing skill set. She and Norah spend a fair amount of valuable time discussing things like sentence structure and paragraph building. She suggested Maisie return to the undergraduate classroom for a course in creative writing, just to build up her abilities.

Maisie is plump and plain. She has settled into middle age with comfort. She pays little or no attention to her appearance, in a different way than the younger students. They seem to present rumpled and mismatched as a style. Maisie is simply rumpled and mismatched. She drops herself into the biggest armchair and, with a breathless disregard for any ongoing conversation, asks if there's any way she might be able to have some real tea.

Joe Waskiewicz is Norah's fourth and final graduate student. He doesn't look old enough for graduate work and is impossible to read. He's not appeared for an individual session with her as yet, only attending seminars. He asks for no input. Strangely, once in the seminar session, it's hard to control him enough to allow the opinions of others to creep into the conversation. If talking could be transformed into the written word, Joe would have a thesis of massive proportions. Norah has been given to understand, via her ever-gossiping colleagues, that Joe is living with two women—not girls, but women—and no one has any understanding what, if any, relationships exist among the three. He's a perfect gentleman and exudes a kind of old world charm, often seen assisting someone with their packages, sweeping off a building step or opening doors at just the right time. He's a curiosity just like Peter Swift. Norah practices her father's philosophy of live and let live. Joe slurps blueberry tea, as he organizes his satchel of texts and papers.

Today, each student presents their description of their thesis research to the group. They talk about various approaches to research, but through their own work. Will they be using a qualitative approach, a quantitative approach, or a blending of the two? There are no rights or wrongs here. Norah listens and provides feedback. She encourages her students to be open to questions and critiques from both herself and their seminar colleagues.

At the conclusion of their two-hour session, Norah reminds them to think about attending the Department Christmas party in early December. She's chairperson of the planning committee and wants them to feel welcome at the annual gathering being held in the Sociology Lounge on a Friday afternoon. Charlie provides a confirmation on the spot. He will be there for sure. Maisie will have to think about it as her store cannot run itself and this function is pretty close to Christmas. Joe and Penny make a surreptitious exit without committing.

As she cleans up the tea things and tidies her office, wiping up tea rings and removing slightly used napkins, she thinks about her own Christmas. They'll be going to Prestonburg this year—not her favourite option, but the plans were made with Paige before Norah could be sure the kitchen in the Craftsman would be finished. Now she must face her first Christmas without her father.

****

Norah gazes about her office on the day of the Christmas party. She's careful with decorations—only a few white lights trail like vines through her massive bookcase. A twig wreath, capable of celebrating any number of different occasions, hangs precariously from a plastic thumbtack on her door. Norah is mindful of the shifting cultural tide in which her work ebbs and flows. Being too over the top about Christmas tends to come across as tacky and thoughtless these days. She's tried to ensure the party is a vehicle for inclusive seasonal celebration. Others who might disagree with her approach can plan the gig next year.

She chose her clothes with care this morning. Norah sees this first get together of the year as a platform to show who she really is, not to put on an act or airs of any kind. It will start about 3:00 PM. Matthew will arrive a little later. She takes this social opportunity to give students a peek at her as a person—not just as a professor.

Teachers are human, too. She learned this lesson from Beth. Norah's wearing cranberry silk palazzo pants, tight at the waist and wide in the legs. She loves the deep pockets. She's paired them with a cream angora sweater that fits her to perfection. It's in that fifties style of tight waist and somewhat puffy sleeves. The only other embellishment, besides her cranberry-coloured, framed glasses, is a multi-strand necklace of hand-painted glass. It's uncanny how it resembles Christmas ornaments, the old-fashioned ones with the different colours and caved in sides to reflect the light. She proceeds down the hall to the lounge to complete preparations.

Earlier in the morning, she and Peter set up the tables for the punch and snacks. The iPod and speakers are ready to plug in and Peter has assembled lots of festive tunes for the remainder of the afternoon. The wine is chilled. She arranges plates before pulling the food from the attached kitchenette. Peter rushes in through the door. He tears toward the corner and fidgets with his iPod until Brenda Lee bursts forth with "Rockin' Around the Christmas Tree." He's wearing a bright green sweater with Santa on the front and an unruly crowd of elves on the back. He's behaving like someone who has already made a few trips to the bar. Norah looks up and smiles with caution. "Everything okay, my friend?" She has to project her question over the music.

Peter turns toward her. "Could not be better. Tomorrow I'm off to New York City for the whole holiday." He puts the emphasis on "whole" by swinging his arms up and around in a circle about three times. "My mother is going to my sister's and I don't have a care in the world."

"Visiting with friends?" Norah is cautious. She would love to ask, "who are you going to see?", but knows better than to be too pointed. Peter is Peter. He smiles. He winks. He turns to the door just as a group of students and two professors wade into the music-filled lounge.

Maisie and Joe are among the attendees. Maisie is all dolled up, her retro look working well as an advertisement for her business. Although still chaotic in her appearance, with messy hair and shabby shoes, she's managed to build a Christmas-themed outfit of various shades of red— skirt, sweater, and shawl. They don't match but they don't clash. The whole thing is topped off with a vintage sequin necklace and earrings of exceptional gaudiness.

Joe is alone except for walking in with Maisie. His mystery women are nowhere in sight. Wearing grubby jeans and a navy cotton pullover, he's made no effort to dress for the occasion, although he always looks fresh and scrubbed, like he just jumped out of the shower. His sandy, straight hair has little room for styling, cut close as it is to his head. He has on boots. Norah watches the two come in and she smiles. At least they turned up, which is more than she can say for many others. Norah makes her way toward the door to greet the newcomers.

The gathering is well underway when Norah, her back to the door as she discusses vacation plans with a small group of first year students, feels Matthew's presence and turns around just as his imposing frame and dark curls fill the entry. The room doesn't go totally quiet, but something changes as he saunters over to her with that rolling gait she's come to love, puts an arm around her waist with protective ease, and kisses her cheek. "It looks like things are going well," he whispers in her ear. Deciding to come in his professor gear as he calls it, he is decked out in a pair of dark khakis, a plaid shirt, and a corduroy sports jacket with the compulsory leather elbow patches, creating the look. No tie. He could be ten years younger than his actual age and Norah wonders to herself with a certain measure of chagrin, if she now looks twenty years older. *Great!*

They mingle. They refill glasses. Matthew pitches in by pouring wine and handing out punch. Soon, people start to drift out. It's Friday night, after all. Two days of classes next week and Christmas vacation starts. Many, like Peter, are finished already.

Things wind down. Joe approaches Norah just before making his departure. "I'll stop in to see you after vacation." He raises one eyebrow and smiles, reaching out to shake Matthew's hand. "It was a pleasure to meet you. Don't worry, Dr. Clarke." He grins, looking back at Norah as if conspiring to do something inappropriate. "I'll make an appointment. Merry Christmas to you both." He turns toward the door, asking Maisie if she would like him to walk her to her car. They both leave, and in Shakespearian fashion, he makes a tiny bow and sweeps his arm forward to the door so the rouged-and-sequined Maisie can breeze through the exit ahead of him.

At the end of the evening, Peter stays behind to help them clean up. He's subdued. Matthew cocks his head at Norah and casts a sideways look toward him in the kitchenette.

"Hey, Peter. Did you have a good time?" Norah attempts to start a conversation.

Peter pokes his head out from the doorway. "Do you know? One of those idiot students thought they had the right to ask me if I have a boyfriend in New York! Just because we're at a party doesn't give someone the right to pry into my personal life! You two can hug and kiss and no one says a word." He has a second thought. "They stare and talk about you behind your back, but they don't say something right to your face! I think I'm going home now. You two can finish up, eh? See you in the New Year." A couple of flounces later and the back of his green sweater disappears into the dim corridor.

Norah, having developed the ability to ignore Peter's oftentimes off-the-cuff remarks over the years, directs a tired smile toward her husband. "He'll be fine. I hope he has fun in New York. We're just about done and then we can go home."

Chapter 8

Prestonburg never changes but seems to have changed so much. Matthew, Norah and Violet roll into town in Norah's little truck. The streets always seem narrower than they did when she was a child, the buildings less imposing— their lavishly ornamented beauty fading.

Norah stares out the passenger window, remembering the Prestonburg she loved as a little girl but seeing the reality that comes with a downturn in the economy. The sidewalks need repair. Buildings cry tears of peeling paint. Windows are iced in the cold, almost obscuring "For Sale" and "For Lease" signs that hide empty spaces. Dust and cobwebs are all that hang on display.

Dusk will soon begin to elbow its way past the fragile winter light of this December twenty-third. Norah cuddles up to her dog and sighs along with the sad little town, as she silently reflects on the old Prestonburg, the one built on tourism. Until 2001, Americans and Europeans flocked to the seaside community to buy property at half the cost they would have paid at home. They summered in the town, sailed in the Harbour, attended the amateur theatre, and supported the flea markets, the shops, and the market gardens. In the fall, they boarded up their summer retreats for the winter and arrived again like the robins in the spring. They would socialize with the quaint locals and buy everything in sight because the permanent residents just seemed to want to give their stuff away.

Well, time's progression has not been kind. From September 11, 2001, through Hurricane Katrina, a falling US dollar, the sudden need for passports, and continual rising costs, the tourists have almost stopped visiting. Since they aren't coming, the local government decides just last year to forfeit the ferry to the US and eliminate any upgrades to the scenic tourist routes. It's a vicious circle—trying to save the minimal tax dollars contributed by a shrinking population—resulting in the ultimate neglect of everything important. The little town now holds on by frail fingernails. Still, residents haven't stopped trying to breathe life into the poor old dear. This is Father Christmas decoration time and everyone who can, decorates their front stoop with a rendition of Father Christmas himself.

As Matthew and Norah approach the building once housing Clarkes Antiques and Collectibles—now Beth's Creations—they're met with an eight-foot-tall version of Santa, braced with precarious precision on the front step, permitting only the barest passage into the craft shop.

Norah laughs, shakes her head, and motions Matthew to drive to the lower street and park in the back. No more going through the store and down the back stairs. The inside door down to Paige's apartment is locked. All the rest is Beth's territory now.

Violet squirms. She's just now figured out where she is and starts to whine and snivel in her anxiety to get inside to see Paige. For all her rigidity and lack of emotion, Paige obviously loves Violet and the little dog knows it.

After the truck snuggles into the parking spot beside Beth's Malibu, Norah opens the door and puts Violet down on the grass. The little dog bolts in through the back door without a glance to see if her people are following. If Violet is in possession of anything, it is a firm sense of self.

If the saying is true, "the older you get the more you're like yourself," then Paige is definitely the proof. She has become increasingly frail in the eight months since her husband's sudden death. It has taken a lot out of her. Norah notices her mother's hair as Paige bends to reach for Violet. It's grey streaked with soft brown now, like a reversal of fortunes. She continues to wear a bun cinched at the nape of her neck. After all these years, its slightly askew position is now the trendy look on the models at Paris Fashion Week. At seventy-four, she's a more anxious and nervous version of her forty-something self. She has never had issues with weight but often rails on about the work it takes to maintain her girlish figure. She wears pants now, most often velour ensembles with zippered jackets, in sizes too big and in jewel colours like purple and cranberry. She watches lots of HGTV and can't give a rational reason why. Norah thinks she's developed a taste for observing paint dry but Matthew argues her mother just wants to look at the hunky carpenters.

Norah surveys her surroundings. The absence of her father wraps her in foggy sadness. She thought she was prepared until she walked in the door.

When she was a child, her father always managed to over-decorate the apartment for Christmas. Today, there is a pathetic little ceramic tree sitting on an end table. A myriad of cards pepper the top of the sideboard.

Matthew places their suitcases in her childhood bedroom while she organizes Violet's water bowl and basket. Her mother and Violet are busy with a new tug toy that has appeared like magic from behind the couch.

Her old room is stripped of all things Norah. This happened years ago. It's now the official guest room with the obligatory double bed, Eastlake dresser, and Gibbard end table with a small, hand-painted satin-glass light, and an ornate wicker chair—once used by a photographer in the late nineteenth century.

On the wall are four antique Currier and Ives prints: American Homestead Autumn, Summer, Fall, and Winter. Paige just couldn't part with them when she packed up stock for auction after the shop closed. A complete set is difficult to find. Her dad loved these pictures. Her mother had each one framed to match and here they hang.

Norah stands in the doorway waiting for Matthew to look up as he finishes with the bags. He kisses her forehead, squeezes her hand, and they return to the kitchen without a word, to make tea.

"Beth expects you to turn up sometime before the end of the day, Norah." Her mother is matter of fact and continues looking at Violet and away from her guests. There is stew bubbling in the slow cooker. The apartment is cozy, although somehow empty at the same time. The little tree casts a combination of a sad and festive glow.

"I'll run up tonight, Mom. We'll take Violet for a little walk while supper finishes. Is there anything I can pick up while we're out?"

"Not a thing, dear." She finally looks up and smiles as she accepts a cup of peppermint tea. "You must have loaded your truck with everything you had at home as it is." Her mother isn't far from wrong. Norah managed to bring buns and bread from their local bakery, along with a Stollen loaf for Christmas morning. They'll make lobster chowder for Christmas Eve. Norah and Matthew brought all the ingredients and fixings with them.

"Did you invite Beth for supper tomorrow?" Norah would not assume anything.

"Yes. She still goes to her cousin's for the big day although her cousin has been sick so I said we would be happy to have her here."

"Good. I'll go see her after dinner and firm things up." Finishing her tea, she glances over at Matthew, who's been reading his book "Are we ready to take a walk, now?" Violet jumps from Paige's lap and runs for the door. After being cooped up in the truck for two hours, she's enthusiastic.

Tyler Street is a mere shadow of its former self. Changes, over the years, have turned the once-vibrant seaside community neighbourhood into a collection of storefronts, some active and others empty. Their building is now the one example still housing people; still providing a home to someone. Most of the old upstairs and downstairs apartments are vacant or have become storage spaces clogged with broken bits from past lives. It's depressing.

Mr. Humphrey, of Humphrey's Haberdashery, is long dead. The store was rented by the family to someone making stained glass but in the end, the building sits like an old lady no one will take to the beauty parlour or a doctor. The family must be just letting it go.

The two sisters who owned competing dress shops, of course, are also long gone. The stores are now a big hardware store, joined together. Norah expects the sisters' spirits are very put out.

Mr. and Mrs. Kay just died in the last year, within weeks of one another. She heard they were in two different nursing homes and when the government, acting like it was doing them a big favour, offered to put them together to share a room in one facility, Mr. Kay gave them a flat "no." Since his wife had been sick and housebound most of their married life, he was probably happy not to be forced to deal with her in his last years.

Norah tells this story to Matthew as they trot down Tyler and cross Seaview Street. He laughs out loud and you can hear the echo bouncing off the line of storefronts serving to break the wind from the Harbour. It's starting to get dark.

Closer to the dock, things are a little brighter. A couple of the bigger restaurants stay open all year round and The Captain's Inn looks very festive in the gloom of evening. Its white twinkle lights reflect in the dark waters across the cobblestoned street. Tomorrow is Christmas Eve and Norah plans to bring her mother to the Inn for tea while Matthew and Violet keep each other company. It'll be something different, a new tradition just for Norah and Paige.

After supper—a divine blend of beef stew and crusty buns with mincemeat tarts for dessert—Norah and Violet circle the outside of the building. She rings the bell and climbs the stairs to Beth's apartment. The stairs don't feel so long and steep anymore. Beth waits at the top, resplendent in a multi-coloured polyester extravaganza wrapping around her abundance and drifting like feathers to the floor. Norah is reminded of Eclectus Parrots. Beth's freshly tinted blond hair froths around her still-beautiful, although aging face. She is sixty-six. This retired teacher and long-time friend has taken grooming and fashion to another level over the years. Her manicured nails are designer. Her clothes include long, colourful sweaters and skirts that drift on the floor boards. It appears to Norah she is, with limited success, doing whatever it takes to detract from her ballooning BMI.

The apartment looks smaller. Beth and her stuff appear to take up even more room in an ever-shrinking space. Violet races past Beth with a tail wag of recognition and trots straight for the dog toys tucked into a corner behind some rug-hooking paraphernalia. "I guess she's happy to see me." Beth laughs as she wraps Norah in a bear hug. She rocks her back and forth as she croons something loving and indiscernible, the way she always has since Norah was small. "I have missed you. When's your house going to be finished? I'm dying to come and see it. Have you had a peek at the shop since I've gotten it all set up? Your mother thinks I did a pretty good job and that's saying something. You know your mother."

She releases Norah as they both manoeuvre their way into the living room where the decor now includes plastic stacking boxes piled to the ceiling with additional stock for the store below.

"Poor Mom. She's doing her best to cope." Norah sighs and watches Beth assemble the tea things already stacked on the water-marked coffee table. "I gather you're enjoying your first winter not teaching?" The question is asked with a smile and Beth grins in return. It's more than obvious how much retirement suits her. Norah continues. "The kitchen is all done, now. It's gorgeous and I could have had Christmas in Callwood Bay but it seemed important to Mom for us all to get this first Christmas over with here. Next year we'll do it and you can come and bring Mom." She adds as an afterthought, "Of course, if you make other plans next year, Matthew will just come over and get her. No problem."

Beth pours tea. They talk about Norah's work and they talk about the craft shop. Norah will meet Beth for an official tour the next morning. Although silence doesn't totally fill the room, there is still awkwardness. It's always there, since Norah's graduation year from high school. This time it's different, somehow. Austin is gone.

"Let's talk about Dad, Beth." Norah's abruptness has a startling effect and Beth almost spills her tea as she looks across at Norah. "I miss him a lot," Norah volunteers, as a way to get a conversation about her father started.

"I miss him, too. He was very good to me." Beth makes a great issue of mopping up tea that hadn't really spilled at all.

"Beth, I want to talk about your relationship with Dad. No judgments. I need to know, Beth." She tries to suppress a tiny whine that seeps out with the words. "It doesn't matter anymore. I just need to know."

After what seems like forever, this woman who has been such a presence in Norah's life, heaves a huge sigh, leans back in her overstuffed lounger, and looks Norah straight in the face. "Your father was good to me. You know what he was like. He was kind. I thought the world of him. You remember the Bakelite beads? I admired the necklace and he gave it to me. That night when you found the bead on the stairs—I almost said I'd stolen the necklace. I thought if you knew he gave it to me, you'd suspect something was going on between us, and that's exactly what happened. You wanted to know. Now you know." Beth has gone from teary eyes reflecting the twinkling lights of her Christmas tree to chubby droplets running down her perfectly made up face. Without waiting for a reply from Norah, she struggles to her feet and makes her way to the kitchen for a tissue.

Norah gets up from the couch and follows Beth. Uncomfortable to be pushing Beth further, and with genuine sympathy for her old friend, she wraps her arms around her. She just isn't sure she believes Beth's rendition.

The next day, Beth gives Norah and Matthew a tour of the craft shop and studio. She's closed for the holiday week, but will reopen for classes in the New Year. The wall shelves behind the glass display case are filled with a rainbow of yarn skeins. The display case holds samples of rug hooking, quilting, sewing, crocheting, and knitting. Beth teaches classes in all these crafts. There are tables all around the floor, each with notions and tools. One wall has file cabinets full of patterns. The display window is a sight to behold, decorated for Christmas with a myriad of gift suggestions, all handmade and ready to go. As they admire the window, Beth looks at Matthew and grins. "I learned a lot from this girl. She was decorating this window when she was ten years old. No one has an eye like Norah. Do you remember the green glass display, Norah? It created a lot of foot traffic that summer."

Norah just nods and smiles at her husband as Beth prattles on about new threads and serger manufacturers.

Early in the afternoon, Paige and Norah, bundled up against the biting wind, trundle down the hill to the Inn for Christmas Eve tea. They have reservations; this traditional English tea with all the trimmings has become quite the event in Prestonburg over the last few years. Norah hopes they'll still have room for chowder tonight. The Inn's dining room is tarted up with red cloths on the tables. Each boasts a compliment of crystal vases and candle sticks, along with silver butter pats and napkin rings. There are centre pieces of pine and fir woven through with clear, green, and silver miniature balls. The place is awash with twinkling lights and soft carols float through the warm evergreen-scented air. Paige's grip tightens on Norah's arm as they stand at the entry, waiting to be seated. Her sparkling eyes reflect the season as she gazes around the room. Norah is relieved her mother seems pleased with their decision to attend.

"These old buildings are as drafty as a barn," Paige had told Norah prior to making the reservations, so they're seated at a table not too close to the windows. Their timing of tea must be early enough not to ruin supper—also a good idea. They are served Earl Grey tea, and scones with Devonshire cream and raspberry jam. All the dishes are Royal Albert china: Old Country Roses and Lavender Rose patterns with a smattering of Silver Birch and Petite Pointe thrown in. They are given the option to put milk in their teacup prior to affixing the strainer but both women prefer the "aristocratic" version and add milk later. They laughed about this prior to going to the Inn. Paige did her research about traditional high tea and if the cups look too fragile, the milk would need to be added first. After what turns out to be the perfect diversion, Norah and her mother navigate the hill to Tyler Street arm in arm as a light flurry of snow starts to fall.

They go through the motions with their family meal of lobster chowder and brown bread, one of her father's favourites. Once again, Beth is dressed like an exotic bird when she appears with music for the evening. She has *A Motown Christmas* from 1973, Kenny Rogers from 1983, and Michael Buble from 2011. Paige just rolls her eyes at Norah. Matthew shares stories of growing up on a dairy farm just outside Callwood Bay. His fondest memories are of when both his grandparents were alive and three generations celebrated Christmas together. His parents live half the year in Arizona now and his brother runs the farm.

Norah's family, as it is, sits around the dining room table, reminiscing about other Christmases. She knows they are doing the best they can to fill the empty space created by her father's absence.

****

It's early January, cold and overcast. Norah is at her computer, enveloped in a cashmere throw and sipping rooibos tea. She scans her emails while waiting for Joe Waskiewicz to appear for his first thesis appointment. The office is drafty so the curtains that frame the leaking window are pulled. Lamps are lit and Norah has done all she can to create cozy in this decrepit place. She hears footsteps coming down the hall and within seconds, Joe stands just beyond the doorframe. He sports a down-filled, knee-length parka in bright orange, covered in pockets, and trimmed in what looks like raccoon. His narrow face is flushed from the cold and one hand holds a briefcase while the other arm cradles a bundle resembling a bouquet of flowers.

"Hi, Joe. Come on in. Make yourself at home. Flowers for me?" She speaks with just enough irony and a hint of teasing.

"This is not a bribe," he states in a matter-of-fact voice as he crosses the threshold, places the flowers on her desk, and drops his briefcase by the nearest chair. "They are symbolic of my thesis and I could not resist them." He starts to unpeel the layers of hat, mitts, scarf and the enormous coat to reveal his standard apparel of jeans and a cotton pullover. "Are you sharing?" He looks at the teapot with longing and Norah smiles.

His grin is mischievous as he reaches for a cup off the shelf. Norah exposes the contents of the parcel wrapped in multiple layers of tissue, cellophane, and paper. *Tulips*. He managed to find tulips in Callwood Bay in January. She adores tulips. She has a history with tulips. As the crunch of the cellophane drowns out any potential conversation, the white and yellow petals reveal themselves to a room that didn't appear to need flowers until these existed in the space. A definite spring-like spirit bounces off the bouquet and into the dusky room. "They are my favourite." Her voice is soft. Memories collide.

She tries to keep the years from slipping away so she can focus on Joe and the task at hand.

He sits directly across from her and seems relaxed and confident as he tells her about his plan. His brown eyes sparkle as he talks, and he runs the hand that isn't holding the tea mug, through his hair periodically. That gesture has the effect of punctuating his sentences. Norah likes Joe a lot. She especially likes his enthusiasm for his topic.

His thesis will be about Tulipmania which occurred in the early 1600s, peaking and crashing in 1637. People traded in tulip bulbs and the market became rich to the point where traders could net what would be equivalent to forty thousand dollars today, in a single month of bulb trading. Joe is fascinated by the flower business for some reason. It has nothing to do with his background. He hails from northern Alberta—the grandson of Polish immigrants. His father still farms their original homestead, first secured in 1948.

The topic is compelling. Norah is pleased he has finally shared his outline and asked a few questions. After about twenty minutes of academic discussion, Joe takes the conversation into more personal territory. "I suppose you, like others, wonder about the stories of me living with two women." He's blunt but looks at his almost-empty tea mug and not at Norah.

"I believe in live and let live," Norah replies. "People always want to know what they don't know or what is none of their business."

"They are a couple." He smiles, but not in a joking way. "I'm their cover so people will think one of them is involved with me. Even in this day and age, they still seem to think they won't be accepted on their own. I guess they had a bad experience before they came here. In actual fact, I'm the handy man who gets free rent. Kinda' sad and weird, eh?"

"Not at all," she states, thinking of Peter and how precious his privacy is to him. "Seems like a mutually beneficial arrangement. Some people are just afraid to show the world who they really are—afraid of being judged. We all want to think society is improving, but people still judge and make assumptions. Why was it necessary to tell me?"

"I trust you and I wanted to tell someone. I want someone to know me for real. The one thing wrong with this set up is, in order to keep their secret, no one gets to know me. Now you do."

"My full name is Tallulah Gertrude Norah Clarke." Her eyes dance as she leans over toward Joe. This gesture serves to eliminate most of the space between them. "Now we have reasons to trust each other. And, thanks for the tulips."

Joe gets up and starts to pile on the outerwear. He appears happy with his meeting and his decision to trust her. If he needs a place where he can be himself, Norah will gladly provide that spot.

Following Joe's departure, Norah pours herself the last lukewarm cup from the teapot. She returns from the lounge kitchen with her water-filled ceramic vase, gathers up the tulips and places them, as the prized possessions they are, inside. Now the memories can be permitted to rush forward, just for a little while.

1983——2003

Chapter 9

Norah first meets Sam in the late fall of 1983. Well entrenched in her third year of undergraduate work, she spends increasing amounts of time in the library, researching, writing, and preparing. Sometimes she digs through the stacks and startles other researching strangers pinned between walls of reference texts and periodicals. More often, she hovers over a dilapidated desk inside a glassed-in study room. From this vantage point, she's prevented from directly experiencing the sounds and smells of knowledge being sought just beyond the see-though walls. Remaining open to the visuals of rushing, searching, and aimless wandering, she's learned to ignore what is going on beyond the glass. She focuses her attention on what presents itself on the workspace in front of her. These rooms, located on the exterior walls of the library, provide shared isolation for up to six serious academics.

He says nothing. He merely nods with a look of vague recognition each time he enters the space. He often sits and gazes out the darkened exterior windows at the reflections of his surroundings. He always leaves before she's ready to abandon her work for yet another night. He is Sam Sampson, a man of slight build and immaculate grooming. He wears Oxford cloth shirts with button-down collars and khakis with a crease down the front that could slice a tomato. The pants always have cuffs and he walks just a bit up on his toes. Norah suspects this is because he's not more than five feet eight inches tall. His face is broad and just out of proportion with the rest of him—which is not broad at all. His hairline is receding and this makes him look older than what she expects his actual age to be. His hands are square and the fingers short and stubby. She always notices hands. She thinks this is from the many years she examined fragile objects and watched others do the same. He never seems to study or research much. He just sits at the desk, faces the outside, and stares out the window. Sometimes he shuffles through a few papers hauled out of a beautiful, beaten leather satchel.

Eventually, Norah breaks her silence and introduces herself. No one else is in the study room, so the only person she might disturb is Sam. "Perhaps I should introduce myself since it appears we're going to be regular study mates." She smiles with unexpected nervousness and puts out her hand across the limited space.

"You're Norah Clarke." He responds by extending his hand and smiling back. "I'm—"

"F. G. Sampson, also called Sam," she inserts before he finishes. "I guess we've both done our research." The very second this statement propels itself from her mouth, she regrets it. People don't have to research others. They can just learn casually. It now sounds like she made a concerted effort to determine his identity.

Which she did. Hence the blush.

They shake hands, and in a condescending manner she finds oddly off-putting, he adds, "I'm Forrest Godfrey Sampson, named for my long suffering grandfathers. You can call me God."

"Well, we have something in common." Norah attempts to cover a little prickle of discomfort as she reveals herself to him. "I am T. G. Norah Clarke, named for my grandmothers whom I don't believe suffered very much at all, Tallulah and Gertrude."

Sam laughs out loud, a large, full-faced laugh that leaves his mouth sounding much bigger than the body from which it came. "With those names, I'm sure they suffered." Suddenly, she isn't so sure this is going at all well. She feels that little prickle of discomfort again. They exchange some pleasantries about the college and what they're studying. He's using this year to upgrade his arts degree in an attempt to qualify for a Bachelor of Education next year. She tells him her focus is Sociology.

He leaves ahead of her, as usual. The next evening, it seems he's not coming to the library, at least not to the study room. Norah works late. It's near the end of November and papers are due. There are three other people in the glass box. Just as she's packing her things, getting ready to go back to residence, the door opens and Sam pops his head in. He thrusts his hand through the opening and presents her with a dozen white and yellow tulips, in front of witnesses. "Walk a lady home?"

Their relationship begins in earnest. They have many common interests. They like the same music and read a lot of the same books. They go out for dinner. Sam is very romantic and creative. He finds ways to have intimate dinners in his room with candles and tulips and unusual food combinations prepared with imagination in the toaster oven. Norah is smitten. He's wooing her and she's falling in love.

Sam is a drinker—much heavier than anyone Norah has ever known before. She tries to keep up but can't. Getting sick and having headaches is not her idea of fun so she tempers her role when it comes to alcohol, but Sam can really tie one on.

By the time Christmas vacation rolls around, they're considered a couple on campus. Norah has gone out with other guys before, but always with groups and never with any measure of seriousness. She's a virgin, which has become troubling over time. Most of her contemporaries sleep with their boyfriends. They take risks. Norah is not a risk taker and she knows it. She makes an appointment at the clinic on campus. She'll go about obtaining birth control, as she anticipates their relationship will proceed down a path to intimacy. Norah treats the act of losing her virginity as a project requiring management. She remains clinical and speaks of her circumstances to no one, not even Joy, whom she knows will most decidedly disapprove.

Sam makes a few noises about her staying over but never pushes the point. He has a double room in the men's residence and it wouldn't be an issue for her to stay as she knows there would be no roommate to consider. He revealed at one point that he had a roommate when he first arrived on campus, a third year named Jim Brooks who Norah met quite by accident once. He appeared at Sam's door when Norah was there. They were introduced with some haste by Sam and then Jim turned on his heel and left without another word. Norah wants to take the plunge and stay overnight as she's certain Sam is the one, but pragmatic to a fault, she will take care of herself first.

In the end, the two of them make a plan. They will have sex for the first time after sixty days of Norah being on birth control. They count down the days. It's a time of intense intimacy. No one knows what they're talking about when Sam winks at her and says, "Twenty-two." They giggle together. When the big night finally arrives, Norah turns up at the room of her first love, swarms of butterflies beating their way through every part of her. She fights reluctance, making an unexpected appearance in her made-up mind. Sam has been drinking more than usual. Norah spies a bottle of scotch just behind a stack of books on his desk. She concludes this will not be the night she expected.

They don't make love that night. They have sex. It's awkward and unpleasant. Norah holds him in her arms and whispers that everything is okay. They'll get better at it over time. She lowers her expectations and determines the value of their friendship and having him in her life is far more important than great sex, whatever that might be.

Just as dawn breaks, she gathers up her things and returns to her dorm, arriving just before alarms start to ring. She's in the big, hollow-sounding shower letting the soothing hot water erase any evidence of the night before when her neighbours begin their morning routines.

****

Back in Prestonburg for the summer, working in the shop, and helping out the local auctioneer, the last person Norah expects to see is Jim Brooks walking through the big front door. She's in the back corner of the shop, unpacking the standard fare of cups and saucers, china candy dishes, and Depression glass pieces when the familiar tinkle of the bell propels her attention toward the entrance.

There stands Sam's ex-roommate Jim, filling the space in that tall and imposing way he has of doing everything. Jim is, without doubt, a beautiful young man supporting an athletic build sculpted from regular visits to the gym. His olive complexion and deep blue eyes create a startling contrast in a chiselled, magazine-model sort of way. Due to the circumstances, Norah and Jim became good friends over the last number of months at school. They often sat together in the student centre waiting for Sam or played cards long into the night while Sam watched, preferring to drink. The three of them would dine together and then Jim would make a subtle exit when he thought his time with them was over. She's surprised to see him show up on her doorstep in Prestonburg unannounced.

"Hi," he states simply as he closes the old door with quiet precision behind him. "I hoped you'd be working today."

"Jim. What in the world are you doing in Prestonburg? I thought you were working in Callwood Bay all summer with Sam. He told me you two were doing research for a professor in the Education department. Is something the matter? Is Sam okay? Is he with you?"

Norah suddenly realizes she has not heard from her boyfriend in about a week. This is unusual as he tends to call every few days, if only to talk for a minute or two. Sam is staying with his grandparents in Callwood Bay for the summer. His parents spend most of their time in Florida, now. He doesn't seem too anxious to visit with them for some reason he doesn't share. Family details are hard to glean from Sam. Norah is sure something happened between Sam and his parents before he moved to his grandparents' but she can't get him to talk about it.

Jim ignores her questions. "I'm staying at The Captain's Inn; the one down the hill? I thought you might like to have supper with me."

Norah notes how he sounds nervous. "Why don't you stay here and have supper with us? I'll introduce you to my folks. You'll like my dad. He's a character." She knows by his expression this is not an option.

"Not this time. Come down to the inn about 6:30 PM. I'll meet you in the bar. We can have a drink and then go to dinner." His voice is determined and he looks at the floor.

"Sure. I'll be down in a couple of hours." She moves a few steps closer and rests her hand with light affection on his arm. "I'm delighted to see you, Jim." The bell sounds once more as he eases open the door and retraces his steps down the street.

When Norah arrives at The Captain's Inn just before the appointed time, she glances through the window and sees Jim sitting in an alcove at a small table for two, nursing a beer and gazing into space. She's anxious and a bit put out he would show up out of the blue, act like something is wrong, and then make her wait to find out what it is. She's convinced he's come to tell her Sam has found someone else. She steels herself as she enters through the archway into the bar.

He stands when he sees her, motions to the seat across from him, and catches the eye of the waiter who magically shows up with a glass of white wine.

She can tell almost immediately, upon close scrutiny, that he's gotten a considerable head start in the drinks department. His eyes, those beautiful blue eyes, seem cloudy and hooded. His voice is soft and rolling, facial muscles relaxed, and posture too loose for the situation. Norah knows the signs. She's alert to Sam all the time. She's never seen Jim drink too much. The two of them have gotten into the habit of watching Sam tie one on while they each nurse one drink for the evening.

"Jim, it appears you've started without me." Norah's tone is blunt. "What's the occasion?"

"Be patient." He smiles at her and she feels as if he can look through her or into her somehow. "We'll have dinner and we'll talk." She hopes dinner slows down his steady progression toward complete inebriation.

Dinner turns out to be better than expected. They talk about generalities. Jim starts to sober up a bit and Norah relaxes, beginning to enjoy his company again. She's always liked Jim although he's sometimes morose. She wishes he would get himself a girlfriend rather than continuing to hang around with her and Sam.

After dinner, Jim convinces Norah to come up to his room for a nightcap and then he'll walk her home. She has reservations, but it's Jim, after all, so no harm. Once inside his room, he closes the door and seats her in the red-and-white striped wing-back chair in the corner. With methodical precision, he pours her a glass of wine from a prepared tray on the desk and sits in the leather office chair facing her. His eyes are hooded again but there's nothing resembling relaxation in his face. "Norah," he begins after taking a deep breath, "I came here to tell you I think the world of you. I want to go out with you. I want you to break up with Sam and if you continue to see him, I am not returning to Callwood College in the fall." He leans back in the chair and closes his eyes after completing his apparently much-rehearsed speech. "There. Mission accomplished. This has been driving me crazy for months."

Norah is transfixed in her seat, her glass of wine frozen part way to her lips. What could possibly possess Jim to think he could betray Sam's trust this way? She sighs. "Jim, you're my friend. You're Sam's friend. I'm in love with Sam. You know this. He knows it, too. Where's all this coming from?" Norah tries to be fair and honest. She doesn't really believe Jim's feelings for her are anything more than a crush built on familiarity and friendship.

"Sam is fine. He doesn't know I'm here and I don't want you to tell him, Norah." He throws the words across the space between them. "I made up my mind I wanted to talk to you before school starts again. There are things you need to know. He's bad for you, Norah. He'll make you unhappy. He's not who you think he is. Have you ever wondered why we aren't roommates anymore? Has the thought ever crossed your mind he might be using you?"

"Using me how, Jim?" She tries to remain calm, keeping her voice flat and even.

"He made a pass at me, Norah. I like the guy, but I couldn't share a room with him—not after that. He just wants a girlfriend as a cover. He figures he'll never get a job teaching otherwise." Jim's voice is angry. He hurls his words at her.

Norah gets up and turns toward the door. She refuses to get into a discussion about this with Jim. "Thanks for dinner. I'm going home now. No need to get up; it's just a short walk. I hope we can still be friends and you change your mind about returning to school."

Chapter 10

Norah's senior year at Callwood College is filled with preparations for graduation, plans for the future, Sam, and all the necessary work to get to the finish line. Sam lives in an apartment off campus now, as he completes his Bachelor of Education degree. Norah is focused on her Bachelor of Arts, majoring in Sociology, and writing a thesis based on the overall concept of the collecting nature of human beings and what this says about society in general. She works hard. She spends time with Sam. Since he's moved to his own place, she sees his drinking increase, his studying decrease, and their relationship slide into a pattern. She might visit the apartment over the weekend. They might cook dinner together but more often than not he'll want to order something in and add it to an ever-ballooning charge card.

Norah craves intimacy with the man she has come to love, but most of the time he drinks too much and she spends the night back at Hammond's while he snoozes on the battered couch absconded from his grandparents' basement.

It's high time she takes him home to meet her parents so they decide to travel to Prestonburg for Thanksgiving—although Sam is more than a little reluctant. They'll go in his 1967 Mustang. It's a powder-blue hardtop, two-door version of the Ford classic, certainly not restored. It looks the worse for wear.

Sam will stay at The Captain's Inn, courtesy of Norah's parents. The Clarke apartment has only two bedrooms and sleeping on the couch is out of the question. Arrangements are made.

Norah eyes the car with a nervousness she's developed through experience. She loads her suitcase into the trunk and hops in the front seat Her eyes scan for liquor store bags or any telltale signs of Sam's own personal weekend plans. The drive to Prestonburg is uneventful. Sam is sullen. After almost an hour, able to stand it no longer, Norah blurts out, "You didn't have to come, you know."

"I suppose your parents don't drink. Hope they don't mind if I pick up a bottle of scotch for me and wine for dinner."

The problem is revealed. Norah has become ever vigilant about alcohol consumption. She can tell if he's overdoing it. She can tell if his mood is going to change. She can tell when it's time to leave by herself, or in the case of gatherings away from his apartment, when it's time to take him home. It's become an occupation of sorts and she continues to hone her skills. "There'll be wine for dinner." Her response is flat. "No need for scotch, okay." There is no question in her tone. There will be no scotch and no getting sloshed at her parents'. He watches the road and anxiety starts to nibble away at her, as is often the case these days.

They arrive in Prestonburg early Saturday afternoon and drop things off at the Inn for Sam. He's clearly not impressed with the old place. He notices plaster cracks and points out deficiencies in the decor. Norah, with some annoyance, reminds him he's not paying the bill and the Inn is the best spot in town. They finally make it to her parents' apartment and park on the street as the back only has room for two cars. The antique shop is open and seems to be busy. Sam is obliged to park at a distance of almost a block. He carries her suitcase back toward the building and they circle the side to enter at the back. It's no small feat to maneuver down the incline and Norah experiences an overwhelming urge to apologize for what she suddenly feels is the inconvenience of her much loved childhood home.

Norah sees her mother, standing at the door, obviously ready to meet the young man who has stolen her daughter's heart. She is cool from the beginning. Norah can sense her mother's uneasiness straight away. Once inside, Norah grabs Sam's hand and guides him up the stairs to meet her father. They round the corner just as the bell sounds and his last customer leaves. Norah is a bit gushy with the introductions. It's very important to her, for Austin to like this man. They shake hands.

Sam wanders around the store. He fingers a bisque statue here, a jardiniere there. He makes a point of noting his grandmother has many of the same sorts of things but they're bigger, older, or more valuable. At one point, he picks up a sterling silver candy dish, observes the price tag hanging from the foot, and guffaws aloud. He remarks that he can't understand how the Clarkes manage to make a living with these prices—not clarifying whether he thinks the price is too low or too high. Norah makes a mental note to tell Sam the last thing any antique dealer wants to hear is what your grandmother has in her cupboards. It's a standing joke. Everyone thinks their kitchen cupboards are filled to overflowing with valuables. Norah watches her father's reaction. He appears underwhelmed.

"Beth is coming for supper," Austin shares to the room at large. "She's going to a friend's for Thanksgiving tomorrow, so will dine with us tonight." He finishes with a flourish, having successfully emptied his mouth of words into the silence of the little shop.

"I think I'll just go out the front and down to the Inn so I can get settled before supper. What time do you want me back?" Sam is direct. Norah can tell by his tone, there's no point in arguing or suggesting they run upstairs to meet Beth.

"Supper will be at 6:00 PM," Austin pipes up.

Sam lets the old door bang closed as he dashes out, turning toward the Mustang and ultimately to the Inn on the street below. Norah thinks her father looks pleased he's gone.

The appointed time comes and goes. By 6:15 PM, Norah is jumping out of her skin. Beth has been there since 5:30 PM, dressed to the nines and ready to grill the boyfriend. Norah senses her father's nervousness, and her mother is just plain cross. Annoyed and embarrassed, Norah dons her coat and tromps down the hill. She knows, in her heart of hearts, what she'll find. Sure enough, there he is in the hotel bar, ice swirling in a glass of amber she suspects is charged to the room for which the Clarkes are paying.

She stands in the doorway. There aren't many people around. Eventually, he turns enough to notice. He motions for her to join him and as she moves forward, he begins a flowery introduction to the room at large. Sam is just entering the danger zone. She has to get him home before he becomes the kind of man she would not invite for the weekend to meet her parents.

They will walk up the hill, even though he insists with more volume than necessary, he should be able to drive. "Sam, honest to God, if you cause any kind of disturbance tonight, it'll be over between us." She grabs his arm in a vice grip and off they go. The crisp, cool breeze off the water assists Norah in her struggle to reign in his attitude as they make the climb. By the time they reach the door, Sam is apologetic and contrite.

He meets Beth. She's not her bubbly self. At the table, Norah has a keen awareness of Beth's reticence. Her father tries to be sociable. Her mother pays undue attention to the correctness of serving chicken curry and then apple pie. Sam drinks wine and helps himself to glass after glass. It doesn't take long for him to become tipsy yet again. Dinner ends with abruptness when Sam leans over to Norah and stage whispers, "Man, is she fat!"

Beth gets up and makes an excuse to go back upstairs to her apartment. Norah is at a complete and utter loss for words. She looks with pleading eyes at Beth who gives her a watery smile as she takes her leave. Austin suggests perhaps he'll assist Sam back down to the Inn while Norah helps her mother clean up. There's not a lot of protest from anyone except Sam, who seems to feel as if he can manage under his own steam. Nevertheless, the two men leave together.

The silence roars in Norah's ears as she clears the table and tries to start a conversation, to apologize, to try and make excuses. Her mother's only comment is to tell Norah she needs to go talk to Beth. Norah trudges up the stairs after she rings the old front bell.

Beth waits at the apartment door. She's changed into a velour sweat suit and her generous mounds of flesh are concealed in a manner creating a navy Michelin Man look. Mascara shadows her cheeks—evidence she's been crying. "Beth, I am so sorry. He started drinking at the Inn. I thought he was sobered up and I didn't keep track of the wine. He can be an ass, but when he's not drinking, he's a great person." It all came out in a rush.

"God, girl. Get a grip!" Beth rips into Norah, exhaling her anger with words. "The guy's not just an ass. He's gay! Surely to God you've figured that out by now! How long have you been dating? A year? More than a year? He acts like an ass when he's around his girlfriend." She leans over so her face almost touches Norah's, and draws this out for particular emphasis. "Because he is frigging gay!"

She will not let Beth see her real feelings. She will not let her know this has been nibbling at the edges of her consciousness ever since Jim came to see her in the summer and never turned up for school in the fall. She asked herself, then, if Sam had a thing for Jim or maybe it was the other way around. She wants to know the truth but doesn't have the courage to open the subject. "If Sam is gay, he has an interesting way of showing it. We have a perfectly normal relationship, Beth."

"Be honest with yourself, at least." Her reply is wrapped in more than a small measure of annoyance. "The man is as gay as the flowers and deep in your heart, you know it. I can't believe you think so little of yourself, you started going out with him in the first place." Norah isn't sure she's ever seen Beth so angry.

Norah apologizes again and returns downstairs. Her father's home and looks grim. "I left him in the bar. He wouldn't go up to his room." His face turns to Norah and he shakes his head. "He won't be coming back tomorrow. I told him to go home to Callwood Bay and I would drive you there on Monday."

Norah is shocked. She's never known her father to intervene in such a resolute and final capacity. She starts to sputter an argument, but the look on his face makes it crystal clear. The evening is over and decisions have been made. She thinks better of going down to the Inn. Sam has had way too much to drink and, despite her efforts to appear on top of things, she knows she wouldn't be able to talk to him anyway.

****

Back in Callwood Bay, Norah finds a message in her mailbox. It is a request for her presence at a dinner the following evening at Sam's apartment. She knows he'll be contrite. The thought of refusing never crosses her mind.

Norah knocks at his apartment door at the appointed time. He answers with a flourish. She eyes him with increased intensity and is surprised to realize he hasn't been drinking. He's prepared a wonderful stuffed pork tenderloin dinner with roasted potatoes, steamed vegetables, and a raspberry dessert he eventually admits came from his grandmother's freezer when she wasn't looking. There are exquisite fuchsia-coloured, ruffled tulips on the table. They have wine, but Sam has very little. Norah feels he's trying to impress upon her the gentleman he's capable of being, and how much he cares about her and wants to be forgiven. She laps it up, and cannot believe her eyes when he returns to the table with coffee and a small blue box. He places it, with care, down beside her cup. She looks at him, speechless—a circumstance to which she is not particularly familiar.

"What's this, Sam?"

"Open it and see."

She removes the lid of the Birks box, revealing the silver ring case inside. Lifting the cover, she struggles to compose herself when she sees the beautiful vintage-style diamond engagement ring.

"So—shall we make it official and get married?" He reaches into her hand to take the case from her. "Let's put it on."

Norah drops her left hand to her lap, extending her right out to touch his arm. "We need to talk, Sam. Thanksgiving was a mess."

"I know. I know. It'll never happen again. I promise. I was nervous, meeting everyone. I should never have spent time by myself at the Inn before supper. I got scared they wouldn't like me."

"Beth says you're gay, Sam. Are you? Why do you want to marry someone if you're gay? Did you have a thing for Jim? Am I your cover?" The questions fall out of her mouth and drop like marbles on the vinyl kitchen floor.

"Beth is a cow." He gets up and goes to the cupboard where he reaches for the scotch. "What does she know? The fact of the matter is that I'm attracted to both men and women. I want to spend the rest of my life with you. The people I've been with in the past have no bearing on our relationship. I don't care who you've dated, do I?"

Norah feels familiar prickles of anxiety as she watches his reaction to Beth—how he immediately grabbed a drink—and hears his rationalization for wanting to get married. She thinks about her conversation with Jim last summer. In a soft but determined voice, she asks if he could please put the scotch away and sit down and talk with her.

To her surprise, he dumps the drink down the sink and returns to the table. He holds her hand. He kisses her ear. He runs his fingers down the line of her jaw. "I love you, Norah. What I've done in the past doesn't matter. I want to be with you. I want to have a life with you. If it means not drinking, I won't drink." He retrieves the ring and slides it on Norah's finger, running his lips across her palm in the process.

She looks at the top of his head, as if she's sitting up in the ceiling, peering down at strangers. This is really happening. She's going to marry Sam, the love of her life. He wants to be with her. He'll do whatever it takes to make the relationship work. Look at what he's done to make up for Thanksgiving? Everything will be fine. She leans her head into his hair and whispers how much she loves him.

They set a date for early August. Sam applies for teaching positions in Montreal. He wants to teach English in a private boarding school. He stands a pretty good chance. His French is flawless. It looks like Norah will be living in Montreal, although she's not just sure what she'll be doing. She'd like to attend graduate school and do her master's at McGill University, but Sam seems to think they'll need extra money so she plans to get a job. Not speaking the language will be her challenge. Her parents seem resigned to the fact their only child will marry someone they both struggle to like. Beth is just plain pissed. She even suggests, at one point, that Norah's making a fool of herself. In the end, she volunteers to make Norah's wedding dress and help with the preparations, successfully avoiding alienation from the whole process.

****

Sam doesn't return to Prestonburg until the Easter before their midsummer wedding. Beth is going to host a small reception to celebrate the engagement and work with Norah to complete the dress. The wedding will be small. Joy will be Norah's attendant, and Sam has asked a Language Department professor, a man Norah has never met, to be his best man. They will marry in the small university chapel at Callwood College with the local chaplain officiating. Norah is more comfortable with an ecumenical service if it must be something other than the town office, which would suit her sensibilities much more. Sam, and especially her maid of honour, Joy, would never endorse a town-hall wedding.

Beth's party is set for Easter Saturday evening and Sam is coming to town just for the occasion. He'll stay overnight at the Inn, as he did on Thanksgiving, and return to Prestonburg the next day. Norah worries about the drinking. She's always worrying about the drinking. There have been issues, complicated by his so-called promise to quit when he proposed. Sam continues to drink when he's upset about something. He drinks to celebrate. He also drinks when it appears he has nothing better to do. Johnny Walker and Norah are getting to be quite good friends now. When she sees Johnny on the counter, she has a clear vision of how the evening will progress.

At the appointed time, Sam arrives at Norah's and they go up the long flight of stairs to Beth's apartment. He has not decided to start partying early, and relief is written all over Norah's face as Beth responds to the ring and stands waiting at the top of the stairs. Paige and Austin are right behind them. The party has brought together an array of people who have known Norah all her life. The guest list includes school teachers, a group of faithful and admiring Clarkes Antiques and Collectibles' customers, and a smattering of high school friends also in town for the long weekend. Beth has gone all out, as only Beth can. She has wrapped herself in pink chiffon and seems to float around the room as she attends to her guests. The place is cramped, as it has always been, but there's lots of room for cocktail wieners, mini meatballs in the slow cooker, little pastries stuffed with spinach and cheese, crackers, a veggie plate, and a tray the size of her kitchen table covered with every kind of sweet imaginable.

Of course, there's punch. As Norah drifts into the kitchen to see if anything needs to be moved out to the front room, she catches Sam as he tips a pint bottle of rum into the prepared refill container of punch in the refrigerator. She gasps. He grins and raises one eyebrow, just like he always does when they conspire together about something delightful. She retreats back to the guests. With a little luck, no one will notice. The bottle isn't very big, and there's lots of punch.

The next morning, Norah runs back upstairs to help Beth clean up. The party was great. Sam got a little tipsy, but did nothing to offend anyone. She's relieved, but Beth, it turns out, is not a happy lady. "I know what your so-called fiancé did last night, Norah. Did you know?"

Norah feels defensive and on the spot but she's honest nonetheless. "I saw him in the kitchen," she responds with a slight smile on her face. She doesn't want to act like this was a terrible thing. "Sam will be Sam," she adds, hoping to make them sound like an old, married couple. "He managed to maintain a semblance of dignity, Beth. He didn't call anybody names." She rolls her eyes for effect.

Beth cannot be pacified. "Listen, missy, there were people at my party who do not drink, for various reasons—health, AA—and your man," she says the phrase with what sounds like an intentional slur, "put liquor in my punch. You're lucky I caught it right away or we would have had a mess on our hands." Her voice rises and even her hair shakes a little when she adds, "He is a drunk, Norah. He's wrong for you. He's gay and he's a drunk. I cannot, for the life of me, figure out why you feel you have to marry him."

"I love him, Beth. His previous relationships have nothing to do with his relationship with me." She can feel herself parroting Sam's words of defense. "He loves me. If he were a man who had a history of all kinds of girlfriends and said he was going to get married and settle down, everyone would believe him—or at least give him the benefit of the doubt. Well, this is the same thing. Our relationship is about us and not the past. And he isn't drinking as much. He said he wouldn't and I believe him." She adds this last part more to convince herself than Beth.

As Norah leaves, Beth thanks her for the help and just as Norah is about to close the door, she says, "So, I was right. He *is* gay."

Chapter 11

Norah arrives in Montreal at the Place Bonaventure train station early on the morning of Thursday, July 4, 1985. Joy, always ready and willing to help, is patiently waiting.

Joy, at home with her parents for the summer, does missionary work for her church in the city centre. They are a well-to-do family and live just off Sherbrooke Street West, near Grand Boulevard, deep in the heart of Anglophone West End Montreal. It's a middle class neighbourhood of huge duplexes on tree-lined streets. Norah is to be their guest for the next few days as she attempts to secure an apartment and interview for a job. Joy and Norah have remained friends ever since Joy spent that summer in Prestonburg back when they were seventeen. Despite their obvious differences, they've continued their friendship all through their time at Callwood College.

Joy is a Christian, but not the kind of Christian who goes to the local Protestant church each Sunday and complains about how the board spends the weekly collection. She's the kind of Christian known in various circles as "born again." She has accepted Jesus Christ as her Saviour and is trying to live a suitable life. In the beginning, Norah suspected Joy befriended her to convert her. As their friendship matured, Norah joked she was the "token heathen" in Joy's life.

Joy is the model student. She always looks fresh and scrubbed, goes to class well prepared, is never late under any circumstances, and is reluctantly respected by her peers. She almost never wears jeans and she always ties her long brown hair back at the nape of her neck. She bucks the trend of girls her age and doesn't wear any make-up. Her dark eyes and balanced features don't seem to miss the additional attention.

As Norah walks across the huge marble expanse of the train station lobby underneath the Queen Elizabeth Hotel, Joy beams from ear to ear. She's dressed as she always is, in a cotton skirt and a matching blouse with a button-down collar. Her hair is tied back and her horn-rimmed glasses seem too big for her face. She looks like she's wearing her father's spectacles. Norah makes a mental note to volunteer her company to look for glasses the next time Joy gets her eyes checked.

They'll search for apartments together. After doing research based on budget, size, and location, Joy has narrowed the viewing down to a few. Until Norah actually secures a job, it's hard to plan being close to work. They've already determined Sam will have to commute, as the school where he'll be teaching is in Pointe-aux-Trembles, about thirty minutes by bus from downtown. Norah is anxious to find something, and grateful for the preliminary work Joy has managed to do.

Between the two of them, they manhandle Norah's suitcase to the bus stop and catch the next one to travel down Sherbrooke Street. All this is so foreign to Norah. She has never lived in a big city; has never experienced public transit, for that matter. Her high school French lets her down at every turn and Joy translates as they go. Most signage is in French only. Norah feels her brain twist inside out in her attempts to remember the phrases and words she learned as a child.

Arriving at the Scott house is a blessing. Norah's been on the train all night and feels in desperate need of rejuvenation. Joy's parents are at work and she shows Norah to the guest room with adjoining bath on the third floor. When Norah returns downstairs following a luxurious hot shower, her friend is busy with the chamomile tea. A list of potential flats is laid out on the oak table in the spartan dining room. They'll spend the afternoon looking at apartments. Norah will try to pick one and then call Sam, who's at work in Callwood Bay. He didn't want to make the trip. Norah found this odd. He'd been interviewed and hired for the teaching position at Ecole Notre Dame, all via the telephone. She thought he'd be excited to get a look at the school and the area, but he seemed nonplussed about the whole thing. His one qualification for a place was he should have no more than a half-hour commute.

They visit five apartments during the afternoon, no small task in a city the size of Montreal, but Joy was thorough when she screened them to meet the basic criteria. She kept her search within walking distance of the area around De Maisonneuve and University where the major auction houses are located. Norah has a budget and a minimal number of things on her want list. She is flexible about size, amenities, and elevators or lack thereof. In the end, the best fit is a sunny walk-out located on the main floor of a four-story converted mansion—one of six in a row at the end of a small street just off Sherbrooke. There's no parking but the Mustang will be sold once they move. The apartment has just one bedroom, but the rooms are large. The kitchen is dark, old-fashioned, and in the middle of the suite. The living room and bedroom have huge windows and there's a quiet and private garden—a little oasis in the centre of the city. They allow small pets, a piece of information Norah keeps to herself for the present.

Sam's response on the phone is benign. By late Friday afternoon, the apartment is secured. It will be painted and made available to them on August fifteenth.

Norah's nervous about getting a job in a huge French-speaking city, but has scheduled a meeting with one of the partners, Bertrand Le Blanc, at the auction house known as Le Blanc and White. Due to her time constraints and the fact no auction is scheduled for the weekend, her interview is first thing Saturday morning.

She arrives at the building, a converted 1930s art deco theatre, wedged unceremoniously between two imposing glass structures right in the heart of the city on Rue Sainte Catherine. The building's brick facade is imposing with a huge arched window and intricate detailing. The theatre marquis and canopy have been retained. The letters for Le Blanc and White twinkle in the early morning sunshine. Underneath, information about an upcoming estate auction, the following Wednesday night, is displayed. She's been told to ring the bell, as the building is not open for viewing until after lunch. The hollow sound echoes in the cool dark lobby and brings Monsieur Le Blanc to the door.

He presents as a no nonsense man, this Bertrand Le Blanc. He speaks impeccable English and switches with seamless ease to French when a worker approaches him to ask for information regarding what Norah believes to be the storage of a dresser of some sort. M. Le Blanc's hairline is receding and it appears he's employing teasing and hair spray to try and coax the few remaining strands to cover an emerging dome. Their attempts are yielding little more than sprigs of coverage. He's forthright and particular. Does Norah know about glass and china as his colleague from Nova Scotia suggested? Is she good at displays as has been inferred? Can she stay long enough to look at a few things and give him an idea of her expertise? Things go well. She feels she has managed to impress him with her knowledge of Canadian pressed glass and her ability to initiate research into anything she doesn't know off the top of her head. She wonders about his partner, White. There's no sign of him or her. Since she won't be having direct contact with the public, her poor French won't be an issue. When will she arrive in Montreal to live? Can she start work right after Labour Day?

Norah is ecstatic. She'll be working for Le Blanc and White, Auctioneers and Appraisers in downtown Montreal. Her father will be so impressed. She'll be appraising glass and china prior to auction, researching rare items, and creating displays for auction previews and catalogue photography. The pay is not great, but will cover her half of their projected expenses, with a few dollars to spare.

****

In Prestonburg for her last summer, Norah once again takes up the reins at Clarkes Antiques and Collectibles while she plans her wedding and the subsequent move to Montreal. Sam spends the summer back in Callwood Bay, working for Dr. Guy Coderre, a professor of French in the Languages Department. Sam is doing translations for him, both into English and into French. It appears Dr. Coderre has better things to do than translations of his own research. Guy will be Sam's best man and the explanation to Norah is vague, with references to friendship and mutual respect.

When together, the two men converse in French and Sam appears delighted with this. They go out for drinks after work and often have dinner. For some reason she doesn't understand, Norah feels suspicion rumbling away at the edges of her thinking. Being in Prestonburg for the summer puts her at a disadvantage. She would like to get to know this person, Guy, but has no chance. Sam doesn't make plans to visit during July, so they just talk on the phone a couple of times a week.

****

Norah's wedding weekend arrives with the promise of warm temperatures and cool breezes. The Clarkes set off to Callwood Bay where her parents have obtained a hotel room for the night and where Norah will get ready for the small ceremony to take place late on Saturday afternoon. Beth outdid herself in the dress department. Norah wanted simple and exquisite—something to serve her through both the wedding and the reception, even though the nights could get cool this time of year.

Her dress is chic and flowing, made of champagne Dacron with a soft lining, providing both breathability and coolness for a warm day. It has spaghetti straps and Beth has hand beaded the top of the bodice with tiny crystals. God alone knows where she managed to get those. Joy's dress is a shade darker and in a lace-covered, more demure design with capped sleeves. Beth has made a wrap for Norah out of the same lace-topped fabric. There's no veil, just a tiny crystal barrette tucked into her somewhat short, straight hair.

As she stands ironing in the hotel room on her wedding day, her dad leans against the wall, watching her with what Norah interprets as deep intensity. There's an auction in the city today, a big one. She wonders if her father misses being there. She looks up at him and smiles, as she thinks what a nice weekend it would be for an auction. He picks up his sunglasses and dashes for the door. On the way out, he tells Paige and Norah he's off to get the car washed, which leaves Norah to question why he bolted so abruptly. He washed it yesterday before they left home.

The ceremony proceeds without a hitch. As weddings go, she's happy with her version of elegant meets simplicity. The chapel is decorated with tiny white and champagne roses. The organist is dramatic without being over the top. The chaplain is funny and serious at all the right times. They adjourn to a small reception hall attached to the chapel, where the bride and groom serve their guests wedding cake and sparkling wine. This unique opportunity to host and circulate allows time for Norah and Sam to visit with their guests, pose for pictures, and personally ensure everyone enjoys the party. Norah, ever alert to the habits of a drinker, worries when she spies Dr. Coderre pass a silver flask to Sam, when they obviously think no one is looking.

The plan is for the reception to conclude and then the immediate families will go out for supper before the bride and groom make their way to a hotel in a nearby town. They'll drive to Montreal the next day. Sam has already given up his apartment and sold any furniture he didn't return to his grandparents' basement.

Dinner will include Norah's parents, Sam's grandparents only—as his parents were unable, for some reason, to make the trip—plus Joy and Guy. Beth was invited but is quite clear in her wish to return to Prestonburg and not stay on. For a wedding gift, Beth gave Norah a sizable cheque, enough to cover the purchase of a quality sewing machine once they get settled in Montreal. Although it doesn't seem like a particularly appropriate wedding gift, Beth makes her choice clear, as she focuses her explanation toward Sam. Norah will be able to craft things like curtains for the apartment, and she feels it's the perfect gift. Sam doesn't seem convinced, but acquiesces on the matter. The cheque is made out to Norah alone.

There is a lot of wine at dinner. Her parents indulge in a glass each. His grandparents and Joy abstain. Guy and Sam make up for everyone. As Norah sits in her beautiful gown, sips her wine, and gazes around the table at her guests, she is alert to a tension building in the room. It rises from Sam and his best man, like steam from a boiling pot. They are, in fact, getting liquored up over filet mignon and rosemary roasted potatoes. She leans over as casually as she can, while all the time aware of the eyes around the table focused on her every move. "Sam, are you watching how much you're drinking?" She knows the minute the whisper leaves her lips that she'll be sorry for the wording.

"I am in total control of how much I'm drinking, my dear. I just got married today and we are celebrating." His response is heard by everyone and he raises his glass in reply to their looks. "A toast, people. Is she not the greatest girl, or what?" He slurps his drink, dribbling a bit on his napkin as Guy claps him on the back and adds his version of congratulations yet again.

They arrive at the hotel in nearby Corkum just after 10:00 PM. Sam opens the door and his first remark is, "If you think I'm going to tote you over this threshold, you're crazy."

She attempts to protect her dignity by pointing out the obvious. This is not their new home and no toting will be necessary, thanks anyway. Sam throws their suitcases on the floor and marches straight for the bathroom, unceremoniously shutting the door without another word. About twenty minutes later, he emerges, dressed in nothing but his underwear. He grabs his coat and scuttles out to the car, returning in a few seconds with a case of beer. He pops a lid. The beer sprays down his hand and on to the carpet. He employs the bedspread as a towel and then stretches out, making himself comfortable. Norah has been sitting at the desk, her wedding dress folded with care on the back of the chair. She is wrapped in a silk dressing gown she purchased especially for tonight. "Are you finished in the bathroom, Sam?" It was all she could muster. "I thought I would take a shower."

"Suit yourself. I'll probably be asleep by the time you come out."

"On our wedding night? What's going on?" Norah shakes like a leaf inside, but be damned if she will expose her feelings to Sam. She's sure he's trying to bait her and she will not get into an argument about his drinking tonight.

"I intend to get drunk out of my skull, period. We did it. We got married. Now I'm going to get plastered. The end."

Norah closes the bathroom door, and locks it behind her. Funny, the things you think about. Norah grew up in a house with no interior door locks. Privacy was automatically respected and a closed door was an unspoken request for that privacy. Somehow, she feels compelled to lock the door in order to guarantee a modicum of separation from the person in the other room. Sadness smothers her. She showers and reappears, naked, pink, and warm under the feathery, cranberry silk. Sam is awake, watching highlights of a baseball game. There are three empty cans on the bedside table and a full one in his hand. He's raided the hotel snack basket and has two big packages of beer nuts open on the bed.

She sits down on the other side, hoisting up her legs and rearranging the dressing gown. She rests her hand, light as a feather, on his arm. She tries to smile and make her voice sound soft and fun. "Are we going to have a wedding night, or what, Mister Sampson?"

He never turns his head as he replies. "For God's sake, Norah, we had a wedding night a long time ago. You get sex. Don't nag."

She slides her hand off his arm and sits up against the veneer and plywood headboard that moves and creaks if any pressure is applied. She stares at the television without stirring until she hears him snoring. She gets off the bed without disturbance, locates the remote to turn off the noise, and once again re-enters the inner sanctum of the fluorescent-filled bathroom. She curls up at the end of the long vanity counter, her back against the side wall and her toes just touching the edge of the sink at the other end.

She thinks about her father as he stood and watched her in the hotel this afternoon. She wonders if she had asked him to run away with her, if he would have. Something in her heart twists just a little as she realizes he was probably thinking the exact same thing.

Norah remains on her perch until she's so cramped she can hardly move. When she returns to the bedroom, dawn is trying to bully its way through a sliver of an opening in the blackout drapes. Without a sound, she dresses in the clothes she'd already laid out for the trip to Montreal, and slips out the door to go for a walk and pick up coffee. She expects Sam will need the caffeine injection when he finally wakes up.

By the time she returns to the room, about an hour later, Sam is up, showered, shaved, and dressed. He looks at her in what appears to be surprise. "Where the hell have you been?" He asks the question but doesn't seem to require any answer. He reaches for the coffee. "We have to get out of here. It's a twelve-hour drive, you know."

Chapter 12

Driving from Corkum to Montreal is an exercise in patience and fortitude for Norah. The Mustang is loaded to the gunnels with their personal effects, kitchen paraphernalia, linens, and a lamp. Soon after arrival, they'll have to buy a bed and a couch. Entertainment will be a clock radio until they can afford a television. They both have two weeks before their jobs start and some wedding money to spend on furniture.

She's excited. He's morose. Norah's valiant attempts at conversation are miserable failures. He drives too fast, does not take breaks, and contributes unduly to the atmosphere of discomfort.

"I imagine you'll have to go to Ecole Notre Dame before the first day of school?" The sentence is said as a question to try, one last time, to elicit some conversation.

"Ya' think?" His curt reply erupts into the car. "Did you get the power turned on in the apartment? Perhaps there's a remote chance the fridge is working and we can find a place to grab some ice on the way in."

Norah misses his point, so enthusiasm bubbles up as she explains the location of a local grocery less than a block away. They're not open twenty-four hours, but are until 11:00 PM, so they'll be able to pick up basics like coffee, milk and bread to have on hand for the morning.

"As long as they have ice."

They travel all day in silence until the sun, blasting through the windshield, succumbs to the hour and disappears. As they approach the city, the sky is purple with dusk and the traffic increases exponentially. It's after ten when, with Norah's researched instructions guiding them, the couple reach the little market within walking distance of Springhill Terrace.

Norah absorbs the culture. This business is owned by a Greek family and she's fascinated with the home-made baklava on the counter and disturbed by the liquor in the refrigerators. Wine and beer can be purchased anywhere in the city. She wheels the cart around and insures she has everything she needs for breakfast, while Sam picks out his favourite beer and finds the chest of ice. After their loot is jammed into the already-loaded car, seeming swollen by its effort to contain their belongings, they drive the short distance to their new home.

Parking was expected to be a challenge, so Norah made arrangements with a resident further down the block to keep a spot open for them on this night. Her plan proves successful. Sam manoeuvres the Mustang as close as possible to the steps at the end of the street, which lead up to the row of converted old homes, one of which houses their apartment.

Unloading the car doesn't take as long as Norah anticipated. As Sam walks around the apartment, he sniffs the corners, frowns into the cupboards, and generally acts like the place will soon be condemned. Norah places a comforter on the bedroom floor with sheets on top. Tomorrow, they'll go and buy a bed. She's wide awake and happy to be busy, so she putters away, putting their meagre groceries and box of supplies into the dreary little kitchen. Her suitcase will remain in a corner until she finds dressers. She suspects Sam won't get a lot of satisfaction out of finally moving into their own place in such an exciting location as Montreal. She doesn't quite know why.

He opens the bottle of Johnny Walker Black Label given to him by Guy just before the wedding, adds the necessary ice, and tips the coffee mug to his lips.

It's well after midnight when they go to bed—or to floor, in this particular instance. Sam falls into a stupor the minute his head hits the pillow. Norah will not think of it as a drunken stupor, but there'll be no intimate time spent tonight. There's no coupling celebration of their new home and new life. She sits on the floor, back propped against the wall with pillows, and begins to question her decisions. She has a promising job. She has secured an apartment within walking distance for her and a short bus ride for Sam. He has a good position. They have enough money to purchase the basics needed for their apartment, and two weeks to put things together.

She knows she would abandon much of this stability for a few moments of affection. Hell, a little unbridled passion wouldn't hurt either. Her back is sore as she stretches out and tries to sleep, as she listens to muffled snoring coming from behind the unapproachable back turned toward her.

****

Excited about her first day of work at Le Blanc and White, Norah's dressed with care and attention for the occasion, not knowing precisely what tasks await her. She's chosen soft linen pants, loose fitting and knotted at the waist. She added a short-sleeved, v-neck T-shirt and an over-blouse—removable if it gets too warm.

Early fall in Montreal can be unpredictable. She carries a small knapsack with her wallet and lunch inside. The walk is interesting and will change every day as the shop windows along the busy thoroughfare are dressed for different occasions.

She arrives almost an hour before she's expected. Since she has no keys, and the main door on Rue Ste. Catherine remains locked unless the public is invited to a showing, her only option is to ring the bell and hope someone is even earlier than she is. Her ring elicits the attention of a man she comes to know as Phil Thibodeau. Phil is barrel-shaped with a reddish complexion and balding hair. He has chosen to shave his head, giving him the aura of a wrestler. He meanders over to the plate glass entrance doors as Norah stands outside and peers into the darkness beyond.

"What can I do for you?" he asks in perfect English, accented only slightly with the romantic flair of French.

How do people automatically know she's English? "I'm Norah Clarke, well Norah Sampson now, but I was Norah Clarke when I got the job," she sputters, wondering if this man is even privy to the hiring habits of Bertrand Le Blanc.

Phil smiles, pulls the door wider, and extends his hand. "You are the new appraiser and designer from Nova Scotia," he booms. "I am Phil, Phil Thibodeau, and Bertrand's man-of-all-things. Come in. Come in. You are early. We will have a tour and then I will make you some coffee. It is a grand start on a first day, to have coffee in the lunchroom with the man-of-all-things." He laughs out loud and the sound echoes across the marble floors. For whatever reason, Norah trusts this man and takes him at his word.

She giggles to herself. It appears job descriptions are a bit inflated in this place, since she's quite convinced Phil is the freight guy and she considers herself to be an assessor. She rationalizes that it's better to be elevated than depreciated when it comes to how people see you in your job, and shakes his hand. Norah follows him into the cool, dark foyer, and deeper into the building soon to become her home away from home.

She looks around at the skeletal remains of the old movie theatre. The once popcorn-scented candy counter is now the reception area where people sign up for auctions and obtain a bidding number. The swinging doors to the theatre area reveal original seats, reupholstered in a rich blue. They sit as sentinels facing a curtained stage. She feels propelled back in time. Phil explains the process whereby auctions are carried out. He tells her about the big screen where pictures of the items on sale are projected. Before the sale, bidders go upstairs to view the items.

They turn toward the stairs which are extra wide, with brass handrails polished to vibrancy. The carpet is a deep blue tapestry reflecting the blue inside the theatre. The top of the stairs opens into a great room the size of the whole bottom floor. The space is lighted by the arched window located above the original marquis and visible from the street. Schoolhouse style white globe lights drop down on long pendants around the room, augmenting the natural light from outside. Furniture pieces sit in disarray, abandoned without rooms—seeking context.

"We're getting ready to photograph," Phil explains. "Bertrand said you would assist with the arrangement of some of the glass displays once you got here. It will, I think, be your first assignment but he'll explain when he arrives. For now, we'll go to the basement, where all the magic happens." He waves both hands like fans for effect.

They take the lumbering freight elevator to the basement. When the big folding doors creak as they finally open, Norah is provided with her first glimpse of a space that doesn't look like a basement at all. There are work rooms and offices. There's a protected area that has double doors and resembles a surgery suite. This is where any painting, lacquering, or staining takes place. The space is ventilated, a model of safety, and located well away from the staff.

Most offices on this level open into the hall as well as into an anteroom or workroom. Phil leads Norah to his office, in the middle of all the others. His desk is cluttered, but in an oddly organized kind of way. He points out a vinyl chair to Norah and turns toward the kitchenette across the hall. Moments later he returns with two cups of coffee, along with cream and sugar on a tray.

"We will give you the guest treatment this morning because you came in before the birds are out of bed." He smiles down at her. "After this, you are on your own, and you must tell no one I made you coffee. I am considered a bit of a tyrant around here." He winks, sits down, and opens the bottom drawer of his desk to stretch out his legs. "Your office is just down the hall. You'll share with Dorothy—Dorothy Chipman. She is Bertrand's assistant. Your office adjoins a workroom where you can research items, spread out books, do whatever it takes. We have a collection of Limoges and a box of antique kitchenware I think will end up in your workroom before the day is over.

Norah sips the coffee as her mind races. Phil has a picture on his desk of himself with his arm around a frail-looking woman with masses of long, thick, black hair. He notices her looking at the photograph. "That is me with my wife, Madeleine. We will have you and your husband—did Bertrand not tell us you are a newlywed?—to our house for dinner soon. Madeleine is a wonderful cook. We will be friends. You'll see."

He explains his role at the auction house. Phil manages all the freight going in and out. He also makes minor repairs, as needed, and keeps track of inventory being stored for future sales. He cleans, polishes, and sets things in place for display and photography. He has two other men who work under him.

Bertrand, all spiffy in a navy-blue suit, golden patterned tie, and very polished shoes, suddenly appears at Phil's door. "I thought I might find you down here." He speaks with familiarity to her, but turns to Phil and asks, "Did you take Norah to her office or were you kind enough to leave some of the Show-and-Tell to me?" He turns back to Norah. "This guy always manages to scoop the new employees and show them around before I get a chance. Have I told you how much you can annoy me, Phil?" He is not the least bit annoyed. Norah can tell.

She thanks Phil for the coffee, and follows Bertrand down the hall. The office assigned to her is small and will be shared. Dorothy's space is obvious—until today she had the whole office. Bertrand looks around with haste, obviously assessing the situation. "The desk in the corner will be yours," he sputters, removing a stack of ledgers and invoices from the top. "I asked Dorothy to make sure your desk was outfitted and ready. She must have gotten swamped last week and didn't get to it," he adds as an apology for the mess. "Take a look through the drawers and make sure you have all the supplies you need. If not, ask Dorothy. On second thought, ask Phil to take you to the office supply room to get what you need." He looks flustered.

Norah helps move a few things off the desk. She tries to exhibit a calmness she doesn't really feel. She's determined things will be fine. Her eyes travel to the closed door and almost at once, Bertrand rushes forward to open it for her. "This will be your workroom." Norah sees the trestle table clear of any lingering work projects of Dorothy's, so she relaxes a little. "You can request a collection, or particular items, be moved in here so you can work on them. I have a couple of things for you, but we want your help upstairs right now. A collection of glass requires set up for pictures, and we then need it displayed for the up-coming auction."

Bertrand turns to see Dorothy standing in the doorway. Not strictly late for work, she is strolling in at precisely 9:00 AM. Norah wonders if she sat in the coffee shop around the corner to watch the time in order to make such a precise entrance.

Wearing jeans and a sweat shirt advertising a rock band from years ago, Dorothy is a big woman with dark, straight hair and rimless glasses, too small for her face. Her voice booms and grates at the same time. "So this is the new girl, eh?"

Bertrand steps forward and introduces them. "Dorothy, this is Norah Clarke. She's our new appraiser and designer from Nova Scotia. Norah, this is Dorothy Chipman, my long-suffering and hard-working assistant. You two will be sharing an office, as you both already know." He casts a sideways glance at Dorothy. *Is he trying to pacify her with the compliment?*

"Suffering is right," responds Dorothy as she turns back to her desk, ignoring Norah's outstretched hand. "Now I get a demotion—no more private office. Great!"

Bertrand appears indignant, or perhaps exasperated. He motions to Norah and they leave at once. Norah thinks about dropping her bag on the floor beside the now clutter-free desk, but follows her boss out the door with it still slung on her shoulder. They climb into the elevator and are hoisted to the display area where Phil has just had a complete collection of Nova Scotia pressed glass delivered. Norah will spend the day assisting with the photography and identification as well as setting all the pieces up for public display.

It feels wonderful to be surrounded by beautiful pieces of glass; to have people ask her opinion and follow her instructions. Time flies by and soon everyone breaks for lunch. Norah grabs her bag. She intends to return to the staff room and hopes to be able to see Phil again. Maybe she will take a stab at befriending Dorothy. She pops her head into her shared office and sees a telephone and set of keys on the desk. No sign of Dorothy.

As she enters the room and picks up the keys, Bertrand's assistant appears like a threatening force out of nowhere and shuts the door behind her. "Down for lunch?" She offers a vacuous smile as Norah is startled and attempts to hide her reaction from this woman who is somehow projecting such negativity.

"Yup. Just saw the keys on the desk and thought I'd grab them first." She tries to sound casual but feels nervous for some reason. Dorothy strides over to the desk and flops into her chair. It struggles under the assault of both weight and pressure. The springs protest with a soft groan. She crosses one generous thigh over the other. Norah catches herself thinking about Beth and the difference between people when they like themselves and when they don't.

"I want to find out some things about you, and tell you my rules. You can go off for your lunch in a minute. Sit down. Don't hover," she commands and Norah, for want of options, sits down. Dorothy proceeds to rattle off her expectations. She speaks as if Norah is disorganized and wanting in most areas of office management and protocol. It seems Dorothy rules the office roost. She does not ask Norah anything at all about herself.

"Dorothy, I like to think I'm pretty organized and responsible. I hope we'll be able to work together. I expect I'll meet your standards." She fails to prevent the sarcasm from creeping out, but manages to keep her voice from vibrating as, and in one motion, she is up and out the door.

Norah, with a deep sigh, sits across the table from Phil and one of his assistants. Her face is flushed and she's still shaking just a tiny bit.

"Don't let Dorothy get under your skin, Norah. She's all bark." Phil nods his shiny dome toward a fresh pot of tea on the counter.

Her first day flies by. Norah's late. She wants to get the glass all set up before she leaves and it's almost 6:00 PM as she steps behind the main-floor counter and says goodnight to Bertrand. The walk back home, on the opposite side of the busy street, provides a change from the morning. Norah window shops her way along. She passes a pet shop and thinks of Bijou. It would be nice to have a dog again. Perhaps she and Sam can get a dog.

The apartment is dark and cold as Norah unlocks the door and enters the tiny vestibule. She expected Sam to be home early and have supper started but maybe he had a long first day, too. She turns the corner and there he is, seated in the new chrome and leather Eames lounger reproduction purchased with the money they had earmarked for a table and chairs. After they bought the hide-a-bed couch and the bed, the money left somehow got used for this modern monstrosity. As a result, Norah's search of vintage outlets for a storage piece and a kitchen set, was to no avail.

In the end, she managed to stretch her sewing machine money far enough to purchase an old walnut sideboard from a second hand store nearby. At least it would serve to hold towels and a television once they could afford one. Sam insisted he have a stylish chair regardless of how it would blow the budget. He's kicked back with Johnny Walker at his elbow, already red-faced, eyes hooded, and muscles relaxed.

She attempts a smile as she looks across the room. "Hard day?" Norah tries to keep the irony out of her voice.

"It's a job. I got through it. God, I hate having to work!" He doesn't inquire as to her experience. It would be so nice to share the ups and downs of her day, but tonight she knows there will be no sharing.

"I'll start supper. You sit still." She makes her way into the bedroom to change her clothes first, and thinks that with this type of home life, she will soon turn into a morose and pathetic newlywed.

Chapter 13

Norah adores her job, despite the ongoing trials of sharing an office with the demanding and rigid Dorothy. Dealing with constant criticism and the undermining nature of such a personality propels Norah to pursue other contacts at work.

She and Phil become fast friends. She is confident Bertrand is impressed by her knowledge and research abilities. She's never at her desk, having adopted an area in an empty workroom down the hall, thanks to Phil and his helpers. All of the items assigned to her for study are collected in this room. The move down the hall happened as a simple means to an end. Dorothy was not coping with the stacks of boxes and organized clutter that is the lot of the researcher and appraiser. She complained constantly to anyone who would listen. Norah started working down the hall and, in the end, this turned out to be the best option to avoid conflict.

Life on the home front has not resolved itself with any similar or obvious solution. Sam continues to drink. He also spends money at an alarming rate. Norah guards every dime. She accepted the role of bill payer but it's challenging to perform this thankless function with no money. Sam lives for his post-work sojourns to the bar with like-minded teachers and the tab for any one night can exceed a hundred dollars. He also often comes home with some ultramodern—most often chrome or silver and probably useless—ornament or utensil for the house.

In the last three months, he's purchased crystal salt and pepper shakers with silver and onyx tops, a crystal decanter set with twelve glasses, chrome salad servers, and a wooden salad bowl set. Everything goes on the credit card and when the bill arrives, he doesn't want to discuss the consequences. The monthly charges to the local liquor store are creeping dangerously close to rent territory, and Norah catches herself obsessing about bills and thinking of her mother.

As she lives with a husband who would rather drink himself to sleep than make love to his wife, Norah is starved for affection and companionship. Sam would rather spend his spare time in a smoky bar than at home and when she peers ahead at her future, it seems bleak indeed.

****

Beaded and mesh handbags from the 1920s are one of the hottest collectibles around these days and Norah has been assigned the enviable task of researching and cataloguing a collection of fifteen such bags to be photographed and prepared for auction just before Christmas.

Her work table supports a large white dressmaker's box filled with individually wrapped bags. She sits in front of the table and carefully unwraps to reveal each work of art snuggled into its tissue paper cradle. There are two made in France, having intricate beading in shades of silver and gold with clasps of twisted gold and tiny chains for carrying. There are three German made pieces, with delicate floral bead-work. One has a beaded fringe and a sterling-silver clasp. There is a small German bag, more the size of a modern change purse, with a butterfly of beads embroidered into the design and silver cherubs on the clasp. There's an English purse, woven with seed pearls and cream-coloured beads. Norah wonders if it was carried by a bride on her wedding day. Each unique creation is catalogued, and a price it might realize at auction is determined, based on the documentation she reviews. She picks up the phone to contact the in-house photographer and an appointment is made for the next afternoon to take pictures for the auction catalogue.

After she painstakingly places each purse back in the box, she calls Phil to let him know the Nippon collection can be delivered to her workroom anytime. She looks forward to handling the assortment of Japanese hand decorated porcelain pieces Bertrand acquired on a recent trip to a home where he went to appraise a desk. The woman had a curio full of the delicious ware produced from the late 1890s to September 1, 1921 and known as Nippon, "Land of the Rising Sun." This grouping contains some exceptional pieces and Norah anticipates tomorrow will be a great day of study.

First thing the next morning, Bertrand appears in her workroom just before Phil shows up with the Nippon. "I'm having my annual Christmas soiree at my home in Westmount in two weeks and I would be tickled pink if you and your husband could come." He's quite formal, in an exaggerated way, and bows slightly, looking at her over reading glasses perched on the end of his very Roman nose.

Norah has heard whispers about this party and is anxious to accept, mindful of the formality of checking with Sam first. He's made no noises about a teachers' party although she can't believe there won't be one. "I'm sure we can come. I just want to double check with Sam." She smiles at her boss. "Can I confirm tomorrow?"

"No problem at all, my dear. It's just a simple get-together. Tell your husband we're suggesting attire be dressed-up casual. Hilary and I take care of everything. All you have to do is come. Starts at 8:00 PM on Saturday, the fourteenth. Let me know tomorrow, if you can." He breezes out of the doorway, turning back just in time to tell her he likes the work she's compiled on the purses and will wait with bated breath for the information she uncovers about the Nippon. "You do excellent work, Norah." She nods her head, feeling a slight flush of warmth from the compliment, just as Phil comes down the hall wheeling a two-tiered cart laden with newsprint-stuffed boxes.

Norah's anxious to get home and share the excitement of the party invitation with Sam. She's already thinking about making something special to wear, having seen a white cardigan in a shop window on the way to work. It was made with a glittery wool and mother of pearl buttons down the front. She could make a long skirt or trousers to go with it. Searching out sales was becoming a hobby, of sorts, considering her ongoing financial dilemma. Perhaps she can make do with what she has. Her mind races as she explores her options and unlocks the apartment door. Although not at all late, she finds Sam sound asleep on the sofa. There's a shot glass and two beer cans on the cloth-covered crate that serves as their coffee table.

She makes supper. She stands in the kitchen while the rice cooks and the vegetables steam; not entering the living room to turn on the news or sit in his lounger to read the mail. She eats alone at the counter and then makes up a plate to cover and leave in the fridge. She goes to bed to read, and hopes she'll be asleep before he wakes up. About 10:00 PM, on her side with the light out, she feels him crawl into bed beside her. Before long, his snores become rhythmic. It's a long time before she drifts off.

The next morning, Norah ignores the evening before and simply tells Sam they're invited to Bertrand's on December fourteenth for a staff Christmas party. She says they'll take a cab. It will be wonderful. She says she's anxious for him to meet her co-workers.

Later on in the day, Norah's surrounded by porcelain when Bertrand pops into the workroom. She accepts his invitation and takes down his address. For the remainder of that week and the next, she immerses herself in all that is Nippon—the shapes, the hand-painted designs, the colours and textures of moriage, the dragonware, the cocoa pots, the children's dishes, the makers' marks, and the valuations. There are more than fifty pieces she catalogues before having them moved to the showroom for photography and display. The last auction of the season is on Thursday evening, just two days before the party.

****

Norah's home life continues as nothing short of miserable. When Sam is home, he's rarely sober. He spends much of his time out and about. He spends money in bars, or on clothes and useless accessories for the apartment. He shows up one evening with a gift—a huge box from Ogilvy's that contains a charcoal suede maxi coat with a white fox-fur collar. She knows he means well, but the charge placed on their credit card almost takes her breath away.

Shortly after Sam gives her the coat, she calls the office to say she'll be a bit late due to a personal appointment, and walks the extra ten blocks to Ogilvy's, intent on returning the unworn coat they so obviously can't afford. It's raining, a cold early December sleet-like mixture that fights to solidify into the first snow of the season. Her feet are wet and her hair sticks to her forehead as she makes her way through the beautiful department store to the return counter. She feels sorry for herself and more than a little humiliated when the clerk looks across and asks the reason for the return. "It just wasn't the right style." She mumbles the lie softly. She attempts to gather her dignity in front of this woman she will most likely never see again. "I guess my husband meant well." Norah's smile is empty. Relieved the charge is reversed, she walks to work, unable to prevent her hot tears from mixing with the cold rain running down her cheeks.

****

The day of the staff party finally arrives. It doesn't start well. She makes the mistake of trying to appeal to the gentleman she still has faith is hidden deep inside her husband. She asks him to refrain from drinking at the party.

"Are you afraid I'll make a bad impression?" he asks with steely calm between sips of black coffee. She wonders how much pleasure he gets out of watching her squirm.

"Not really." She tries to put the best possible spin on the situation. "I just want them to see the real you, Sam. If you drink too much, it's not the real you." She does not want to whine.

He raises his head and looks at her long and hard. "I'll see what I can do, if it'll make you happy."

It starts to snow just as dusk unrolls across the city. Light reflects off the snow back up to the sky and an eerie quiet settles over the neighbourhood. The snow is heavy and accumulating at an amazing rate. The roads will be greasy and dangerous on the way up into the hills of Westmount. The party starts at 8:00 PM, so she calls the cab company an hour earlier, expecting to give it lots of time to get to them. The dispatcher just laughs, and says that if she wanted a cab for 7:30 PM, she should have called when it started snowing. They would be at least an hour, if not more. Norah stands in the window and gazes out at the snow-covered pathway. She has dressed with special attention. Her second-hand white sweater sparkles in the glow of the living room lamp. It suits the grey velveteen trousers she made especially for the evening, perfectly. The reflection back into the apartment reveals Sam at the fridge, popping ice into a glass and reaching for the Johnny Walker. "I thought you weren't going to drink." She makes the statement, not turning around and not looking for an answer.

"I thought we were going to a party, but that doesn't appear to be happening either." He smiles, unfriendly and challenging, into the window and turns on their "rent to own" television.

It's an hour later when the phone jangles Norah. It's the cab company to tell them their ride will be there in about twenty minutes. She had almost lost hope, as she watched Sam mix his third highball. After waiting a few more minutes, they bundle up and begin the slippery trek down the path and then the steps leading to the street below. Norah didn't miss the flash of silver as Sam tucked his flask into the inside pocket of his top coat.

The snow falls without mercy. It's built up on the sidewalk and on the steps as they descend to Springhill. Eventually—and none too soon, as Norah's hands start to go numb inside the leather gloves her mother gave her for Christmas two years ago—a blue Caprice sedan, with its white taxi light, turns the corner and fishtails down to the end. It slides, with a kind of lumbering grace, to a stop about a foot from the stone wall supporting the staircase leading to the terrace.

They pile into the back, and direct the driver to the corner of Chemin Argyle and Avenue Churchill, a posh area in the Anglophone neighbourhood of Westmount.

He heaves a sigh and looks at Norah via the rear view mirror. "You might have to get out and push, to get me up the mountain, you know." He isn't laughing. The big, rear-wheel drive classic Ford manages the trip with occasional skids and periodic curses from the driver. He pulls up in front of an English Manor style stone house, vaguely Tudor but with a French flair. Likely built around 1928, it sits with sedate grandeur on a corner lot. There is a garage underneath, with its entrance on one street. The stone steps that lead up to an imposing leaded- and bevelled-glass entry door with matching sidelights, face the other street. The skeletal remains of creeping Boston ivy cover most of the lower half of the facade. There is an obvious lack of embellishment, except for two conspicuous roof peaks and an overhanging, upstairs bay window.

A front yard of shrubs and flowering bushes are bedded with professional care for winter. As Norah picks her way up the slushy stone steps, with Sam muttering at her heels—reminding her of a misbehaving mongrel dog—she sees twinkling white lights and a curving staircase through refracting glass.

The door is opened with a flourish and Bertrand fills the entry. Dressed in a navy corduroy sports coat paired with a grey, cashmere turtle neck, he is every bit the man about the manor. He looks at Norah and then down at the stairs. "My God, I just cleaned those steps off not ten minutes ago! This party might turn into an all-nighter if it gets much worse!" He leans over and gives

Norah a peck on the cheek as he extends his hand to Sam. "I'm Bertrand Le Blanc." He jumps the gun on the introductions.

Norah turns to her husband. "This is Sam, Bertrand. My husband, Sam Sampson."

Sam stands a couple of steps below Norah and looks up. "Your steps are slippery."

Her boss lowers his hand and looks at Norah. She had not expected her husband to be so surly and hopes Bertrand isn't put off. Ever the gentleman, he moves aside to allow them entry just as his wife, resplendent in a black taffeta skirt and silver shell top trimmed with sequins, breezes into the black and white tiled foyer. She's carrying a glass of red wine in a piece of stemware the size of a brandy snifter. Bertrand makes the introductions, and Hilary shows them into the office, just off the entry, where they can drop their coats onto a pile already established on Bertrand's cleaned-off, massive, antique mahogany partners' desk.

Hilary is tall and thin in a super model kind of way. Her blond hair is pulled to the nape of her neck and held in a casual knot with a tortoise shell clip that permits tendrils to escape in all directions. Her ears are trimmed with exquisite diamond studs. "I have been so anxious to meet you." She leans over and whispers in Norah's ear. "Bertie says you're a whiz with glass and china. Come. May I get you something to drink?" They cross the hall into the living room that encompasses almost the full length of this side of the house, and move seamlessly into a dining room capable of seating twelve. The walnut table is laden with all manner of hors d'oeuvres and the sideboard holds a selection of wine and spirits to rival any public house.

As Norah takes a glass of white wine, Sam spies the scotch and helps himself before Hilary has a chance to extend an invitation. "Well! I like a man who knows what he wants. Bertrand is a scotch drinker, himself, when he bothers to have a drink at all. He prefers the hunt and has a little collection in the bar downstairs." She sets her glass on the table and links arms with both of them. "Now, let's go see who's here." The three of them turn their attention to the living room where most of Norah's colleagues are seated or standing. They called out greetings as she and Sam followed Hilary to the bar. Now they're all ready for introductions.

The living room, anchored by a Carrara marble gas fireplace, is furnished with classic pieces. The couch and English club chairs in pale tapestry fabrics stuffed with down, sit with comfortable elegance on the heavy pile French Aubusson carpet. The room is peppered with tiny side tables of different vintages. They are made of various woods, some with barley-twist legs and others with little removable glass tray tops.

The Christmas tree, in the window, just brushes the ten-foot ceiling, and is decorated with antique ornaments from all over the world. The space is stunning, and Norah hopes she hasn't let her mouth hang open. They make their way from one group to the next. Norah introduces Sam to Phil and in turn, gets to meet his wife, Madeleine, for the first time. Norah's seen her picture on his desk but it does her no justice. Dressed in a simple blue silk shirt and winter white palazzo pants, she's stunning and waif-like with long, dark hair and a pale complexion. The blue seems to make her look all the more pale, but her smile is warm and she greets Norah as if they have known one another forever.

"Phil has told me so much about you. We want to have the two of you over for dinner after the holidays. Will you come?" Like a child, she seems anxious for an answer right away and Norah nods her head.

"We ought to be able to work something out, Madeleine. I look forward to it." While Hilary attends to her guests, Norah manoeuvres Sam around, introducing and explaining who people are, their connections to her work, and a few words about what they do.

A few people look unfamiliar at first. Phil's two helpers, Dan and Jean Pierre, are both there with girlfriends. She's never seen them look so put together and grown up. It's kind of funny. It reminds her of her life-guarding days, when it was sometimes hard to recognize a swimmer with regular clothes on when you met them in the grocery store. Later, she sees Dorothy is there. She appears from the kitchen where she's been helping Hilary replenish plates of tourtiere, mini quiche, and cheese platters. She still wears the now-familiar ensemble of sweat shirt and jeans, but this time the sweat shirt is red with Santa on the front and the jeans look less old, not frayed at the bottom like Dorothy's work attire most often is.

She approaches Norah and whispers in her ear as she eyes Sam sitting in a large Mission recliner by the fireplace. "Going to introduce me to your old man? He doesn't look like your type. Is he drunk already?" She smiles, but Norah can't decide if she's being nice or mean. They turn toward the fireplace and Dorothy pushes ahead. She extends her hand. "I'm Dorothy. I'm sure you've heard all about me. I'm the office bitch."

Sam does not get up but manages to shake Dorothy's hand. "Never heard a word about you." He looks at Norah as he extends his arm. "Nice to meet you." He takes a last gulp of his second drink since arriving, and resets the lounger, with clumsy determination, so he can go back to the bar for a third.

"Great guy." The sarcasm drips from Dorothy's voice. "Lucky you. I always thought married couples talked." Dorothy then turns her attention to Phil and Madeleine, making a snide remark about "Phil's child bride." She passes the veiled insult off as a joke.

Norah's attention is soon redirected when Bertrand announces he'll give people a tour of the house if they're interested and haven't been there before. Sam and Norah accompany a couple of other people through the French country kitchen with its slate floors and double oven, on to the family room, and upstairs to the beautiful bedrooms including the master with the bay window she saw from the street. Each of the four rooms has its own bath and the whole place is a collector's paradise of furniture and *objets d'art*. As they proceed to the lower level, Bertrand reveals what he calls the playroom. There is a bar, a pool table, a television, a large leather sofa, and lots of pillows on the floor. He points out the glassed curio behind the bar. It houses his collection of single malt scotch whiskey, some bottled after fifty years in a cask.

Norah knows next to nothing about whiskey but finds it interesting that Bertrand would collect liquor. He's not much of a drinker. Sam stays behind to play a game of pool with Jean Pierre and the remainder of the entourage returns to the living room, where Phil is regaling everyone with a story about a lady at the last auction who wanted to buy all kinds of stuff but hadn't bothered to take the time to obtain a bidding card.

Little more than an hour later, people start to make anxious noises about leaving before long. The storm is much worse and some have a considerable distance to travel. Although the offer is made for people to stay, there is a general reluctance to remain overnight at the boss's house. Hilary goes to the phone and calls the closest cab company, ordering half a dozen taxis to make their way to the Westmount neighbourhood as soon as possible. Guests will leave as the cars turn up. Norah notices Jean Pierre has been in the living room for quite some time and Sam is nowhere to be seen. Perhaps he's playing pool with someone else, but there appears to be no one missing. She assumes that she leaves the living room unnoticed, and tiptoes downstairs.

Sam is stretched out on the leather sofa, staring at the acoustic ceiling tiles, barely holding on to a half empty bottle of scotch. He looks up as she comes around the corner. "Look what I found." He holds up his prize. "This stuff was distilled back in 1960. It tastes better than any scotch I have ever drunk. Speaking of which, I think I might be." He punctuates all this with a giggle.

Norah feels sick. If the scotch was in the curio, then it's precious to Bertrand. "Sam." She almost spits his name as she whispers, "Did you get it out of the cabinet behind the bar?"

"What if I did? We're at a party. Everybody's drinking. I can have a few." He pouts and whines.

Norah grabs the bottle and places it on the counter. "Hilary has called cabs. The weather is ferocious and we have to get home. Get up." She feels a little panicky. Sam gets to his feet and allows himself to be propelled up the stairs and into the foyer where Norah's friends and colleagues are climbing into boots and wrapping themselves in scarves. Two cabs are already waiting. Norah rummages for Sam's coat, as well as her own. They'll wait for another taxi. She will not leave before talking to her boss.

She finds him in the living room, standing by the tree, his hands folded with precision behind his back. He's looking out the window while watching the snow and the approach of another cab trying to make the corner on the unplowed road. "I need to apologize for my husband." Her voice is fragile and soft.

He turns to her, and with a dignity and grace she knows she will forever appreciate, tells her it's okay. Jean Pierre has already broken the news to him. "He got into my Glenturret 1960, Norah. It's a Highland Single Malt Scotch Whiskey bottled in 1978. I planned to open it for our twenty-fifth wedding anniversary. Your husband is a very heavy and somewhat thoughtless drinker, my dear."

"Bertrand. I am so sorry. Can I buy you another bottle? Can you take the money out of my pay? I can't tell you how embarrassed and sorry I am.

"You take him home, Norah. You have much worse problems than my 1960 Glenturret. See you Monday."

It's a long and treacherous ride back to Springhill Terrace. Scrunched into the corner of the backseat, seemingly swallowed by his overcoat and scarf, Sam continues to pout. "I think Jean Pierre might be gay," is the singular remark he makes.

Chapter 14

Before 7:30 AM. Norah lets herself into the cool dark interior of Le Blanc and White on the Monday following the party. Since it's so close to Christmas, and the last sale's been completed, there'll be few people in the office now until after the holiday. She's embarrassed following Sam's behaviour at Bertrand's, and hopes to hide away in her workroom documenting realized prices from the last sale. She switches on the stairway light and walks down one floor. Her key sounds hollow as she turns it in the lock.

By 9:00 AM, she hears staff making coffee, chatting about the holidays, and scampering up and down the hall tidying up loose ends before the weekend. It isn't long before there's a tap on her door and Bertrand pokes his head in. He looks quite festive in a red plaid waistcoat and matching red tie. His appearance feels soothing for some reason. Norah, a sad smile nudging her lips up at the corners, motions for him to enter and sit.

He pats her on the arm and says he'll just be a minute. He inquires about her records, and if she has all the sales information she needs. "Don't worry about Saturday, Norah. Sam meant no harm. It wasn't your fault."

Her forced smile fades. "He can be such an ass when he drinks. He promised me he wouldn't drink and then he started when the cab was late!" She blurts all this into the open space between them and then wishes she could gather up the words and hide them away. It's one of the few times she's admitted there's an issue.

Bertrand's gaze is intense. "I am your boss, but I would like to think I am also your friend," he begins. "You may ask me for any help you might need. Hilary and I will always support you, no matter what."

Something brittle and clenched seems to relax inside Norah's chest. She returns her boss's stare from misty eyes and an imperceptible nod conveys her thanks. At this moment, Phil chooses to push open the door a tiny bit further and thrust forward a mug of coffee, freshly brewed. "Someone brought short bread. It's in the kitchen." He sets his offering on the corner of the table and turns tail back to his office.

Bertrand gets up to go, changing the subject as he stands. "Plans for Christmas?"

"No. We talked about going to Sam's parents' place in Florida, but there was some sort of change. Just a quiet few days off. I'll be back in between Christmas and New Year."

She avoids mentioning that Sam called his parents. Mr. and Mrs. Sampson suggested they weren't enthusiastic about spending another drunken holiday with their son, despite his recent marriage and the fact they have never met their daughter-in-law. Although she knows her parents would welcome them home to Prestonburg, she's reluctant to ask, given how close they are to the holiday and how much she wants to avoid any scenes Sam could create.

"Hilary and I are going south for a couple of weeks. Today is my last day before we leave, so I guess I'll see you in 1986!" He makes every attempt to laugh, as he edges his way out into the corridor.

Later on, Norah works up enough courage to leave her room and trudge down the hall to thank Phil for the coffee. His desk is unoccupied but Jean Pierre is sitting on a stool alongside, cleaning some piece of equipment unidentifiable to Norah. He's in blue jeans and a green denim work-shirt, open at the neck. His blond hair cascades around his face. It is an attribute of envy among most of the staff, both male and female.

He glances up as she approaches, then drops his head to his work, mumbling hello without meeting her gaze. "How are you this morning, Jean Pierre? Recovered from the weekend?" She's trying to sound cheery. He nods but still doesn't look up. Something's wrong. She can feel it. "Jean Pierre, what's the matter? Have I done something to offend you?"

He looks up at her, shakes his head and puts down the contraption he's holding, heaving a huge sigh in the process. "Phil has gone to get some stuff at the hardware store. Close the door."

Norah does as she's told. An icy sense of foreboding ripples along her spine. She remembers Sam's remark in the cab as they were driven home from the party. It was stupid and said by a drunk. Did he say something to Jean Pierre? Even if he did, she's certain Jean Pierre wouldn't take anything Sam said seriously. Her mind races, but she's still not prepared for his disclosure, blunt and stabbing.

"Your husband made a pass at me." He crosses his arms and tilts his head to one side. "I wouldn't like him even if I was gay," he continues. "He stole the boss's scotch and didn't give a crap what anybody thought."

"There are times I don't like him much either, Jean Pierre." She tries to smile and make a bit of a joke at Sam's expense. "He drinks too much and behaves badly. All I can do is apologize on his behalf."

Jean Pierre sips his coffee and picks up his project again. "He's not a good guy, Norah. It would be smart if you keep him away from here. This is a pretty nice family," he adds, almost as an afterthought.

****

On her way home from work the following Thursday, just as darkness settles down on a city preparing for the biggest holiday of the year, Norah activates the tinkle of bells when she pushes open the door and enters the pet shop. She is instantly assaulted by a smell of shavings, pet food, and something medicinal which she's sure is meant to cover up the ever-present essence of cat pee. At the back of the shop, past harnesses, coats, litter boxes, and stuffies are the kennels of puppies playing, sleeping, and waiting to become "the one."

Norah chooses a tiny female, mixed breed beagle. The clerk describes her as a runt and says she's expected to be no more than ten to twelve pounds when fully grown. The puppy sits in the back of the glassed-in kennel and looks at Norah with expectant eyes. Her oversized ears hang almost to her front paws, framing a perfect brown and white dog face. "You will be my dog tomorrow," Norah whispers to the pup she has already named Ivy in her mind. "Don't go anywhere."

She returns to the front counter, asks the clerk for additional information about the little beagle, and leaves a deposit. Tonight, she'll take food, treats, a dog bed, and a couple of toys—making the trek easier tomorrow. More snow is expected. She'll pick her up after work and since they have no plans for Christmas, she can be at home with Ivy and start to train her. At fourteen weeks old, she's more than ready to learn her manners. Sam will be told tonight. Her dog. Her say. Her Christmas present to herself.

Sam informs Norah they're invited to a party on Saturday, but she's getting a puppy and doesn't want to leave it alone. He's annoyed, whines, opens a fresh bottle of Johnny Walker, and tells her having a dog is one thing, but she has to be able to leave it to go to work or to a party. Okay. She'll come to the party, but no scotch. He's to take some beer instead. The bargain is struck. Sam accepts the addition of the puppy with a measure of disinterest. Norah will leave Ivy at home on Saturday evening. They'll make an obligatory appearance at the house of one of Sam's teacher colleagues and stay only a short while. He'll take beer and not indulge in any of the scotch that turns him into someone she feels neither one of them particularly likes. She never mentions Jean Pierre.

Norah is beside herself all day Friday at work. She decides to leave mid-afternoon. No one is doing much anyway, but to prevent Dorothy from having a field day with her departure, she puts a note in Bertrand's mail slot to inform him about Ivy and her plan to leave early to pick her up. The streets of Montreal swarm with people. It's December twentieth and shopping is in high gear. She gets to the pet store and bursts through the door. Ivy has been moved to a little wire kennel by herself near the cash, as staff wait for Norah to swoop her up and take her home. Norah opens the kennel and reaches inside. Ivy emits a tiny shiver and then nestles into Norah's neck as she holds the little dog close to her. She breathes in the sweet and familiar smell of warm puppy and cannot believe the feelings flooding through her for this tiny being she clutches against her cheek. Ivy is going on her credit card. There's no extra money, but Norah has made up her mind—she doesn't care.

She cooks supper and puts Sam's in the fridge, as she's done many, many times before. Tonight is different. She spends her evening with Ivy. They play, they cuddle and watch TV, and they go out on the terrace sidewalk in front of the converted mansion row houses. People stop to speak, asking about her puppy. All of a sudden, she has neighbours with faces and voices—people she never even noticed before.

She starts to teach the attentive little dog to chase and fetch a ball, and to walk on a leash. She doesn't pay much attention when Sam manages to haul his inebriated self into the apartment well after 11:00 PM. By this time, Norah and Ivy are curled up in bed. Norah hears him enter the bedroom, as Ivy attempts a tiny little dog growl that goes unheeded. She lowers the puppy into her basket on the floor.

By the time Sam drags himself into the kitchen to locate the coffee the next morning, Norah and Ivy have been out a couple of times, breakfast has been served and enjoyed by them both, and Christmas background music is playing on the radio. "I see you managed to pick up the little mutt." He gazes down at Ivy through bloodshot eyes. Ivy wags her tail but makes no move to approach. She lets out one sharp yap and runs in the other direction.

"She wants you to play." Norah attempts to engage the two of them.

"For God's sake, she just ran away! There better not be any more yapping. Nothing worse than a dog barking all the time. Be prepared to get rid of it if that happens." He pours coffee from the pot Norah has just brewed and ignores the dog.

Norah removes herself from the kitchen and Sam's company, picking up her puppy and whispering, "Nothing worse than a husband drinking all the time, either."

****

The party is at the apartment of a single teacher with whom Sam works and, Norah presumes, parties. As they arrive a bit late—getting a cab was as challenging as the week before—she realizes the small third-story walk up is wall-to-wall people. They have to sidle their way between bodies and bottles, so Sam can maneuver his precious beer into the kitchen fridge. Music is blaring. A couple of people lean over and whisper introductions in Norah's ear. Sam just hollers over the din. He tells people she can't speak French and waves his hand as if to indicate it's a lost cause.

Norah finds a stool beside the front window. It looks like it came from the garbage, with its gold-coloured legs and twice-ripped black-and-white vinyl seat. After she sits, all she can see are waists and legs, as so many people are packed into the tiny space.

Much to her surprise, a familiar face approaches about five minutes later. Marcy leans over and says she's going to scare up some white wine and would Norah like a glass. Feeling like a rescued wallflower, Norah nods with enthusiasm and moments later, none the worse for wear, Marcy returns with two vessels holding wine. One is a Mason jar and the other is a Royal Albert coffee mug in Lavender Rose pattern.

Marcy is Dan's girlfriend. Dan is one of Phil's two helpers and they met at Bertrand's the week before. She is quite short and dresses in clothes a little too tight and revealing for Norah's tastes, but she's kind, full of smiles, and ready to have a good old-fashioned chin wag on the fringe. Since Dan's sister dates the guy having the party, Marcy is in the same boat as Norah. She knows no one except the two siblings. They have a lot to talk about, since she turns out to be a collector of jadeite, a passion they have in common, and Marcy's mother has an extensive collection of folk art from all over eastern Canada. Norah opts out of a second coffee mug of wine, expecting she and Sam will leave soon. She's anxious to get home to Ivy, who cried a little when they left, the sound twisting Norah's heart as she locked the door.

As Norah regales Marcy with puppy stories, a thunderous clamour of cursing, breaking glass, and screaming comes from the kitchen with a sudden abruptness that halts any form of one-on-one conversation in the apartment. People are stunned. They look like they're in a stop-action scene in a movie. Marcy stares at Norah, eyes wide and mouth bow-shaped and open in surprise. "Sounds like someone threw something across the kitchen," is her analysis once she regains some of her composure.

Norah looks at her new friend, eyes knowing, as she resolutely sets her cup on the floor and wiggles through the guests to the kitchen, afraid of what she's going to find. She hears before she sees what's going on. "You drank my last fucking beer, you asshole! That beer was mine! You owe me beer!"

Norah shoves her way past the gawkers standing at the kitchen door just in time to see Sam start to move toward the guy holding the beer. The refrigerator is face down in the tiny space, contents splayed in all directions, cord pulled clean out of the wall, and hinges bent. The poor thing looks like it could be the body at a crime scene.

She starts to make her way toward Sam, before he hits the guy, and then she spies Dan. She leans across and whispers in his ear, "Did he do this?" Dan nods without looking at her. "Can you get someone to help you pick the thing up? I'll see if I can manoeuvre him out of here before all hell breaks loose." He nods again. She continues to move toward her husband, who's still cursing, although it appears as if people are trying to look away. He's a mess.

She reaches for Sam's arm and he yanks back from her touch. Undeterred, she grabs his hand, hard. "We are going home now," she says between clenched teeth. "We will call a cab, wait downstairs, and go home." She continues to hold his hand in a death grip, as she drags him through the crowd in the kitchen, her head down until she gets to the hallway. Not letting go, she manages to root out their coats.

Marcy appears from around the corner. "I called you a cab, Norah. It should be here before long." Her smile is sad. "I really enjoyed our visit tonight."

"Thanks. Me, too." Her face is grim. Sam sits on the floor now, like a cranky little boy mid-tantrum.

After the effort of man-handling him down the three flights of stairs, the cab mercifully arrives. She shoves him into the backseat ahead of her, climbs in, closes the door and gives the driver their address. Sam continues to mumble and whine about his stolen beer.

When they get out on Springhill and she leans toward the front window to pay the driver, Sam sits down on the steps leading up to the terrace. "You have lots of trouble," the cabbie says in broken English. "Young girls don't need such trouble." The sympathetic man waits until she has him up the steps and into the building before he turns the ancient diesel-spewing Mercedes around.

When they walk in, Ivy appears, all wiggles and squeals. The paper is wet, but only the paper. Norah grabs her leash, picks up the puppy, and goes back out. She leaves Sam standing in the hall acting like he's in the wrong apartment. It seems he's forgotten about the dog. They walk up and down Springhill Terrace a couple of times while Ivy sniffs, does her thing, and jumps in little piles of snow left after shovelling. Norah catches herself wishing, for the first time, she could just keep on walking, but it appears she has nowhere to go.

She trudges, with reluctance, back to the house and their door. It's locked and her keys are inside on the table where she placed them when they got home. She knocks and hears a slurred "Go away," coming from the bedroom. Thank God it's just 10:30 PM. She goes back outside and over to the brick low-rise building opposite the row houses.

The manager is home and kind enough to come and unlock her door, chastising her in a soft, French accent about learning to take her keys when she walks her new puppy. He coos to Ivy and opens the door, only to hear Sam inside, grumbling to the walls about his stolen beer. He looks at Norah without saying anything for a moment and then he smiles. "Perhaps it is another apartment you need, Madame. Not the keys to this one." He pats her arm and leaves her to her drunken husband and yet more humiliation.

* * * *

Sam spends the entire holiday either drunk or getting drunk. Norah focuses all her attention on her dog. Her parents call on Christmas Eve and are ecstatic she has chosen to have another pet. What did Sam get her for Christmas? Oh, you know—the usual. And thanks for the fabric. She will make trousers with the traditional Campbell wool tartan. It'll be a challenge to match the plaid, but she's looking forward to it. No, no plans for New Year's Eve. Yes, a young couple needs to go out and celebrate but she would rather stay home with Ivy. She tries to sound upbeat. She tells them she loves them.

Chapter 15

Standing in line under high ceilings, on marble floors in her neighbourhood bank, Ivy nestled in the crook of her arm, Norah feels like a traitor to Sam and to her marriage. Some version of a preservation instinct, buried deep inside, has successfully propelled her to this point. She will start depositing half of their household budget requirements into their joint account, and place the remainder into her trust savings account, opened so long ago by her parents. It's remained untouched since she finished her degree. She feels a certain urgency to protect at least some of her hard earned money from Sam and the local bar scene.

Norah's not looking forward to the summer. Sam will be off. It's the busiest time of the year for the auction house. She has no desire to take a vacation with her husband in any event, but the anticipation of hot summer days in the city with a husband at home, either drunk or hung over, causes a miserable mixture of anxiety and depression to roll over her in waves. She isn't sleeping well. She's not eating well. She goes to work at the crack of dawn and comes home late. After almost a year of marriage, her enthusiasm has vaporized, and she often catches herself daydreaming about living alone.

Her mind drifts back to their last social engagement, a dinner at Phil and Madeleine's. Sam manages to stay almost sober, being polite and respectful until well into the evening. Out of the blue, he makes a remark about Madeleine's age and repeats his accusation about Phil robbing the cradle. Despite his rudeness, they take it well, used to people making remarks about their age difference. In actual fact, Madeleine is about ten years younger than Phil, but her Greek heritage has given her youthful looks and a china-doll complexion, fooling many into thinking she's much younger. No big deal, until Sam suggests Phil might be into little girls. The evening degenerates from there, and it isn't long before Norah is making the familiar apologies and calling a cab.

She shifts Ivy to her other arm and moves up in the line. That was the last time they were invited anywhere. She's doing the right thing.

The Monday after their evening at the Thibodeau's, Phil taps on her door following lunch, carrying a cup of mint tea and asking if they could perhaps have a talk. Norah heaves a sigh and motions him in; accepts the tea with gratitude and moves aside the dead-eyed bisque statues cluttering her worktable.

Phil starts off with characteristic gentleness. "Sam is quite the drinker." The statement falls between them, dead words on the floor. Norah doesn't respond. "Is he the same at home, or just when you two are out socializing?"

As much as she likes and admires Phil, Norah is not about to confide in this man, at least not a lot. "He drinks pretty much every day, Phil. Most of the time, I can tell when he goes over the line, but I lost my concentration. I enjoyed your company and the conversation the other night, so I didn't keep track." She smiles, but it's a sad smile, one of both regret and apology. "I'm sorry for his behaviour," she says.

"Not your fault. Is he an alcoholic?"

Norah is aghast! An alcoholic! She has never before given Sam's drinking any kind of label. She has always just assumed he preferred drinking to other things, and he could choose options if he wanted. "God! I don't think so, Phil. He often says he won't drink." She stops and thinks for a second and nods her head. "And then he finds some excuse, or picks a fight, or gets a call. Who knows?" She tries to make it sound irrelevant. "He doesn't hit me or anything, if you're worried." The forced smile feels more like a grimace.

"I have another question and I don't want you to get mad at me." He leans over, holding his mug in both hands, elbows on his knees, and stares directly into her big green eyes. "Jean Pierre has made a few comments. Is Sam gay?"

Norah tries not to react. She holds her emotions in a vice grip as she attempts to take control of the situation. "Sam and I have been together a long time and married for almost a year. His past has nothing to do with our relationship. I have no doubt he's faithful. He is just a very heavy drinker." The repeated words sound hollow, even to her.

Phil sits back in his chair, as if he's studying Norah. "You can call on me anytime, you know." He picks up the empty mugs and leaves her workroom.

Norah leans into the bank wicket as the teller admires Ivy. In completing the transaction, she feels a sense of satisfaction. It mixes with a measure of foreboding as she navigates the granite steps on the way out.

****

Their anniversary passes without so much as a card exchanged between them. Norah goes to work as always. Sam spends most of his summer wandering the streets of Montreal, coming home at odd times, drinking himself into a stupor, and remaining in bed long after Norah and Ivy leave for the auction house. The little dog has fallen into the work routine and become a bit of a mascot at Le Blanc and White. For whatever the reason, Norah is uneasy leaving her at home with Sam. She has no evidence he's been mean to her, but she remains apprehensive, nonetheless.

At work, Ivy stays by Norah's side, padding along down corridors and up stairs. She settles into a small basket in the workroom, a basket that appeared like magic out of nowhere one Monday morning. Norah still has no idea where it came from.

Dorothy is having a fall barbecue to celebrate the end of a busy and successful summer but Norah's not invited. There have been other parties—they are a very social group. Norah's heard whispers in the corridors and lunchroom, but never received any invitations. People are entitled to invite whom they want, she rationalizes, and she refuses to feel snubbed.

Dorothy clomps into the workroom, uninvited, one Tuesday morning in September. She's curt. "I'm having a barbecue at my house on Saturday. You are more than welcome to attend as long as you don't bring your drunk of a husband." She turns on her heel and walks out, leaving Norah feeling sideswiped and numb.

She walks down the hall to Dorothy's office with reluctance, and knocks on the door frame. "Can we talk about this?"

"Nothing to talk about." The reply is typically blunt. Dorothy never turns around from her desk, her broad back representing her. "I'm not like other people. You're on the staff, and I'll invite you and you may come. I don't want your old man there, though, so you can tell him spouses aren't invited or tell him he's an asshole. I don't care."

"I can't come to a party and tell him spouses aren't allowed, Dorothy, but thanks for asking me and having the guts to tell me the truth." She turns on her heel and leaves before Bertrand's assistant has time to spin around in her chair and nod a response. Just as well.

****

As Christmas approaches, the auction house is ramping up for pre-holiday sales. Norah's workroom is never free from cardboard boxes full of newspaper-wrapped items. Her table is covered in research texts and notebooks. She's happy, ensconced in work she loves. She can forget about her non-existent home life when knee deep in Limoges china or Depression-era glassware.

Bertrand's party is coming up in a month. Everyone on staff is anxious and there is a buzz as they wait for invitations. No one makes any holiday plans until they know the date of his party. Everyone attends. Norah makes a most difficult decision, in order to avoid disappointment for herself or embarrassment for Hilary and Bertrand.

She approaches his office after confirming with Dorothy he has no scheduled appointments. "May I talk to you for a minute?" He nods and motions her in, getting out of his chair just like the perfect gentleman he is, and motioning for her to sit in one of the two leather club chairs in front of his desk. "I suppose you're gearing up for another great Christmas party." She tries to keep her voice casual.

He's looking at her over tortoise shell reading glasses. "Indeed we are. Did you need to know the date right away in order to make plans?"

"No, Bertrand. I want to tell you Sam and I will not attend this year." Then, despite her attempt at control, the words cascade out. "Listen. I know people have had parties and I haven't been invited because of Sam. Dorothy made it very clear, in September. I could come to her barbecue but Sam wasn't welcome. At least she was honest. I just want you to know, it's easier to tell you we won't come than to worry you won't invite us at all, or you'll just invite me, or I'll have to bear the burden of taking him to your house again. I just can't do it. This way, we can say we were invited but we had other things to do, and nobody has to feel bad."

"You feel bad," he says, still looking at her over his glasses.

"I have to deal with it, and I'm trying. If it weren't for work, I don't know what I'd do." Her gaze is steady as she looks at her boss.

"I would very much like to talk with your husband. I would like to make a referral to AA for him. I would like to tell him what a lovely wife he has and how he is making her sick and sad and lonely. You are more than welcome to come to the party and bring him, or not. This will be your choice. Hilary and I both appreciate your company." He gets out of his chair and rounds the desk as Norah rises to leave. "Whatever decisions you make, and I'm sure you will be making some, talk to me. I can help. Things may seem bad now, but in the grand scheme of things, this is just a paragraph in the story of your life." He pats her shoulder as she departs the office.

Later, at home, Sam is being very considerate and his behaviour is suspicious, to say the least. He's prepared dinner, even set the table. He has candles and wine, of course. Norah asks what the occasion is and he declares it's time for him to chip in a bit. Over a dinner of steaks and salad, he mentions he's been talking to his parents. All Norah can think about is the long-distance bill being run up. His parents have relented and perhaps they could fly to Tampa for Christmas this year.

Norah looks up from her steak, done in the exact way Sam likes it. She heaves a sigh, feeling like she's forced to be the one who states the obvious. "We can't afford to, Sam. The credit cards are maxed out. I thought we would just stay put. I already wrote my folks and told them we were staying here. They're disappointed but understand."

Sam gets up from his seat and goes to the cupboard holding the scotch. He drops ice into his glass and pours substantially more than two fingers of the amber liquid. "You have a bank account with money in it. We could use some of that. My name should be on it, too. After all, we've been married almost eighteen months."

Norah remains calm. She pushes her dinner aside and picks at the roll on her side plate. "Supper was great, Sam. No, we'll not use my trust savings to go to Florida for Christmas. The money is for me to do a master's degree some day. Besides, making reservations now would cost a small fortune. If you wanted this, we could have been saving all summer. Instead, you drank any extra money. Not my fault." She gets more agitated as she speaks, and tries to calm herself. Escalation is not a good idea.

Sam takes his drink, plods toward the couch and pushes Ivy out of the way with his foot. She skitters across the parquet flooring and lets out a tiny yelp. Norah rushes to pick up her dog. She grabs the leash, her coat, and her keys. She leaves the apartment as quickly as she can manage. She refuses to discuss this any further, and he'll not get his hands on her trust. Her sudden and unbending determination is surprising, even to her.

****

Later in the week, the bank calls her at work. Sam is there trying to get her trust account made joint. Of course, the bank can't do this without her permission, and of course, Norah summarily refuses. After she returns the phone to its cradle, she picks up Ivy and sits there staring at the Royal Worcester china on her worktable. She sips licorice tea that seems to have lost all of its flavour.

She feels frozen in time. It will be humiliating if she has to call her parents to tell them she has failed for the first time in her life. Marriage is a pretty significant first failure. She hates the thought of having to return to the apartment tonight. She has some decisions to make.

Their relationship deteriorates more quickly than Norah could have imagined. Sam never comes near their bed. He sleeps on the couch, most often passed out. They exchange words on an as-needed basis, and no longer eat together. Norah's written all the credit card companies except her personal card, and had her name removed from any correspondence. She's notified them she will not be liable for unpaid balances. She has visited the credit departments of all the big stores in Montreal—Eaton's, Ogilvy's, Birks, Mappins, and Hudson's Bay—discovering charge accounts at every store with her name as a co-owner. No more.

****

By the spring of 1987, she is, at least mentally and emotionally, separating herself from her husband.

While busy working on a display for the photographer, Dan approaches her and asks if she would be able to help him. "I have to take my cat to the vet and I have no carrier. Since you have one for Ivy, I thought I might borrow yours."

Norah continues to arrange antique dishes into a display for the photographer. "I can't give you my dog carrier, as it's just for Ivy, but I think we have an old duffel bag at home. I'll look for it tonight and bring it in tomorrow, if you like. What's wrong with your kitty, Dan?"

"Marcy says she has to have shots. I've never had a pet before, so this is all new."

"Pets need shots." Norah is matter-of-fact. "I'll let you know tomorrow if I can find the duffel. The apartment isn't very big." She smiles as he turns toward the elevator to go get another load for display.

As usual, Norah arrives home to a cold and empty apartment. She has no idea when, or if, Sam will be home although he's never managed to remain out all night, regardless of his condition. She puts Ivy down and pads into the bathroom in her stocking feet, to rifle through the extra blankets on the floor of the built-in cupboard in search of the duffel for Dan. No luck.

She returns to the hall closet, knowing all the while, it's not there. Perhaps it's in the storage locker in the basement. If so, she'll have to wait until Sam is able to give her some assistance. As a last ditch effort, she gets down on one knee, lifts the bed skirt, and peeks under the bed. *There it is!* She reaches for the handles to pull it out and realizes it's not empty. She opens the zipper and stares at the contents in utter disbelief.

Inside, on top of a stack of magazines, is one with a picture of two men having sex. She removes it from the bag and another emerges from underneath. The duffel has at least a dozen magazines with different titles but similar images. She flips through the first and then slams it back into the bag. After replacing things as she found them, Norah returns to the kitchen and feeds Ivy. She has trouble organizing her thoughts.

She tells herself Sam's sexual orientation has not been their issue. His drinking has been the issue. They're fine if he isn't drinking. When was the last time they had sex? She can't remember. Someone said people have sex almost every day for the first couple of years they're married. She always just blamed his drinking for their lousy sex-life.

Does Sam want to appear heterosexual to better fit in at work, just like Jim Brooks said back in Prestonburg the year before she and Sam got married? Her mind races, remembering what Beth said, remembering remarks Sam has made. Episodes and incidents are flying through her mind, confusing the image she thought she had of her marriage and of Sam.

"Dan." At work the next day, she looks at the young man who has been so nice to her. "Can't find the duffel bag. Maybe you need to just break down and buy a cat carrier. They have them at the pet store I pass everyday on my way in. They aren't expensive."

He nods, although Norah can tell by the look on his face, that she has probably been too abrupt. "No problem. I told Marcy if you couldn't find the bag, I'd pick one up today. Thanks anyway." He continues down the hall, not even breaking stride.

Norah marvels, silently, at how something as insignificant to this young man as the duffel bag, may well be the final factor that changes her life forever.

Chapter 16

She trudges upstairs to Bertrand's office with Ivy tucked under her arm, and sounds a soft tap on his door. "Come in. Entrez." She hears the characteristic response. As she eases the door open, he motions for her to sit, even though he's still on the phone.

Ivy wiggles. She loves coming to Bertrand's office. There'll be treats.

No longer engaged, he opens the drawer and Ivy trots over to his side. She exhibits her bilingual obedience skills when he states the command to sit, in French. He obviously loves dogs, but he and Hilary manage to live without. "What brings you two up here today, Norah? Trouble with the Limoges pieces? I thought they looked quite good."

"They're fine, Bertrand. I'm almost through. I wonder if it would be okay for me to take a couple of days off." Her tone is resigned and she's unable to prevent the sadness from creeping out.

Her boss looks at her with questioning eyes. "Of course. You could just give the paperwork to Dorothy. No problem. Is everything okay?"

Instead of responding with a simple "yes" and continuing to maintain the privacy she so carefully guards, she surprises herself when she leans back in the chair and sighs. "I need to find an apartment, Bertrand. It looks like Ivy and I are going to leave Sam." She has to tell someone and her head aches with the tension of holding the words inside. Now it's out there.

"Norah, you may have whatever time you need." He comes around the desk, sits on the corner, and looks down at her with what appears to be a fatherly expression, although it seems odd coming from her boss. "I have a friend who is just about finished renovating the third floor of an old English-style brownstone just a couple of blocks away on Rue de la Montagne. You must know the spot. Salon de Mademoiselle Faubert is at street level with an apartment upstairs. The third floor area would be perfect for you. Shall I call him and ask if you can go see it?"

Norah is a bit taken aback. She expected to visit the rental office of her current building manager in order to get a sense of what else might be out there within her price range. She knows she'll only be able to afford a studio, one that will permit her to have a dog. She's progressed no further in the process. "Of course! I would love to see it, but I imagine it'll be too expensive, Bertrand. Even for a third-floor studio, it'll be a lot."

"Nonsense," he replies at once. "Josef is looking for a long-term, reliable tenant and doesn't want students who, he thinks, will trash the place in next to no time. The tenant just above the dress shop is a professor at McGill. She writes and researches and keeps to herself. We talked about all of this just last week."

Arrangements are made and she meets Josef at the brownstone. It's a beautiful old building housing a designer on the main floor. A bay window sits at eye level, just above the black wrought-iron fence across the front. A tiny gate opens off the sidewalk, inviting customers up the sandstone front steps. Just beside the glass entry to the business, is a shiny black door with two push bells. It's locked and Josef opens it to let them in.

It reminds Norah of the entrance to Beth's apartment above the antique shop in Prestonburg. They go up the first flight of stairs, past the apartment door of the tenant in Number One, around a small corner, and up a second set of stairs to the third floor studio. Their footsteps echo off the high ceiling. A shiny number two has obviously just been secured to the door, which is ajar to reveal the painters inside. Josef, a tiny, round, anxious little man opens his arms and introduces her to the space, proud of the work being done.

Norah gazes about the big room, for this is precisely what it is, one very big room about thirty by thirty. Although the building, itself, is bigger, stairs and utilities have gobbled up a portion of the third floor living space. The studio runs from the front to the back of the building. The ceilings are slanted and the back is where the bathroom has been situated. The window was removed to make room for a shower. It's fresh, white, and almost spa-like. The studio's one window is a large gable overlooking the busy street and a seat has been tucked into the box-like area under it. There's an alcove housing a new kitchen—limited but adequate—with a small stove, under-counter refrigerator and a couple of upper cabinets. The hardwood floors have been sanded and stained a warm golden oak. The original baseboards and mouldings, huge by 1980s' standards, remain and are painted white. The cabinets are crisp natural, flat panel birch with porcelain pulls. The wall paint colour is ivory drifting toward a buttery cream. Everything smells like lacquer. There's a good-sized closet in the back corner of the main living area. Norah struggles not to fall in love before she knows the facts. She's sure it'll be more than she can afford.

She knows Josef is watching for her reaction. She can't prevent her eyes from smiling as she looks around. "Cute dog," he says as he pats Ivy on the head. She has not put her down. The men are painting. "It is okay for dog. No barking?"

Norah shakes her head. "No barking. Ivy comes to work with me. I don't go out much, so she's almost never alone. No barking, Josef."

"Okay, okay. Ready in one week. Two hundred and I pay your heat and hot water. You pay electricity. Good deal?"

She looks down at him and narrows her eyes. "I work for Bertrand but do not make a big salary, Josef. How about you pay the power, too, and we have a deal?"

He nods with enthusiasm and pats Ivy. "Okay, okay. I drop keys off next Tuesday. You move in after."

Norah returns to the apartment on Springhill Terrace to wait for Sam to get home from work. It's going to be a long night and she prepares to stay up for the duration, if she has to, or go to the office if she needs to get away. Her purse and Ivy's leash are on the counter near the door. Her coat is on a hook nearby and her key ring is in her pocket. She gears up for the worst.

She makes a pizza and cooks it so they can eat—or not—whatever happens. She has decided to keep it simple, to be forthright and pragmatic.

He comes in, gives her an odd look like he can smell something's amiss, and pours a stiff drink. She has to do this quickly. He'll be drunk in no time. "Sam. I found an apartment today and I will be moving at the end of next week. All I want is the couch and my oak side board, as well as some kitchen stuff. We don't have much to split."

He looks at her from his position in his fancy lounger, as if she's some alien species communicating in a language he doesn't quite comprehend.

Before he has a chance to respond, she continues. "This isn't working and we both know it." No accusing. "Your drinking is a problem for me. I don't like having to worry about money. I know you aren't happy and I can't help." Her voice becomes quiet, as she looks down at the floor

"You're mad because I went to the bank and tried to break in to your little nest egg." There's the slight indication of a snarl in his voice that Norah chooses to ignore.

"Yeah, I was cross, but we have worse problems than money. I offered to loan Dan the duffel bag to take his cat to the vet last week." She pauses to watch his face blanch. "This marriage is not working. I don't want to be roommates. I want a relationship with someone who cares about me, Sam." Her voice softens again.

"I care about you, Norah. Always have. You are the only woman I have ever cared about. Why do you think I thought this would work? Do you have to leave?" As has become predictable, he starts to whine a bit, now. "There's a studio, in the house next door, coming up for rent. Could you just live there?"

He's kidding, right? Hard to tell. The whole conversation feels like the script for a bad movie. "No, Sam. I will not move next door. I've found a place over on Rue de la Montagne; a brownstone owned by a friend of Bertrand's. It's nice."

"Right." The tone is snide, now. "Bertrand wants to get you set up in a little nest somewhere, right? I always wondered about you and Frenchie."

Norah laughs out loud. "So, you want to think I'm stepping out with my boss? Will it make this whole thing easier? Come on, Sam. Just call it a day. You tried your best to live the straight life, but it isn't working. Be who you are. I'm moving the end of next week. Do you want pizza, or not?"

"I'm going out." He gets up, grabs his jacket, and slams the door. It's the first time he doesn't come home at all. Later the next day, she wonders if he even made it to work in the morning.

Norah reports to Bertrand about her meeting with Josef. She likes the funny little Polish man and is confident they'll have a good tenant and landlord relationship. Bertrand offers her a truck plus Dan and Jean Pierre on her moving day. She's overwhelmed by his generosity. "I don't have much. There's a hide-a-bed and an old oak sideboard I bought at a second hand shop when we first moved here, a few boxes of dishes, and a couple of suitcases, maybe a lamp."

"Good. The boys can use the small truck and it shouldn't take long. Perhaps we need to have a little house warming for you, to get you some things you need." He's rubbing his hands together and his smile is indulgent.

Norah is unsettled. "I don't think I want a party, Bertrand." Her eyes fill with tears. He hurries to pat her on the shoulder. "No problem. What day do you want the truck? I'll speak to the boys."

****

Austin answers the phone. Norah knows he'll be worried, receiving a long distance call in the middle of the week from his only child.

"Dad, it's me."

"Are you okay, honey? What's the matter?"

"I'm okay, Dad, just sad. I'm leaving Sam. I just can't manage the drinking and the stress about money all the time. I should have known he wouldn't stop just because we were married."

The sound of the extension being engaged tells Norah her mother's on the other phone.

"Hi, Mom. I'm fine. I have a new studio apartment and I'm leaving Sam in a few days. A couple of guys from work will bring a truck and help me."

"Are you okay?" her mother asks. "Do you need money or anything?" Norah has never accepted offers of help before. With the exception of the trust, which actually was earned money, she's always struggled with accepting help. They even offered to pay for the young couple to come home last Christmas, but Norah flatly refused.

"No, Mom, but I want to come home for a little vacation, maybe next week after the move? I thought I would bring Ivy and come to Halifax on the train. Dad, can you come in to the city to get me?"

"Just name the day and time, sweetheart. How about I call CN and have an open ticket waiting for you at the station. My treat. Okay?" He sounds anxious on the phone. "We want to see you so much. Your mother and I even thought of coming to Montreal later in the fall if you didn't get home this year."

"Sounds good, Dad. I'll pick up the ticket before I get moved."

"Tell us about your place," her mother chimes in, obviously trying to sound supportive and enthusiastic, qualities not often exhibited by Paige.

They talk for almost twenty minutes, a lifetime with long distance charges the way they are, but Norah doesn't care. This would be a bill Sam could worry about long after she moves out.

****

The week at Springhill Terrace with Sam is challenging. He vacillates between anger and sadness. He pleads, and then turns around and tells her he'll be glad when she's gone. He removes items from her boxes. He says they're his things or he wants to keep them—like an egg whisk and a spatula. He's obnoxious beyond description, but she survives.

Dan and Jean Pierre show up just after Sam leaves for work. Norah is thankful for this small mercy. She'll be gone before he gets home. The boys load everything in the truck. Norah and Ivy squeeze into the cab with them and they navigate the few city blocks to her new studio. The men are in good humour despite the prospect of manhandling the hide-a-bed up two flights of stairs.

After her things are unloaded and placed inside Number Two, she offers both young men a cold drink. They look at one another, tell her they aren't quite finished, and trot back down the stairs. A few minutes later they return. One carries a table and the other holds the matching two chairs.

Dan looks up after he places the chairs down on the hardwood floor. "Bertrand says to tell you this is not very valuable now, but might be worth something someday. He thought you might need it." It's a chrome dinette set from the 1960s. The round table is three-and-a-half-feet across with a bright white laminate top and four-inch chrome skirting mounted on a centre pedestal with four support legs. The two chairs are soft green vinyl with a white stripe down the middle of both the back and the seat. They are, indeed, funky and fun.

As she admires them and tries to decide the perfect place for a table and chairs, which she has not had the pleasure of owning before, the boys take off again, clattering down the stairs. In a matter of moments, they return with two stunning end tables, different but the same. Each is dark walnut with a removable glass tray top. One is square with four separate legs. The other is rectangular with a centre leg. They are exquisite. Norah is speechless.

Dan pipes up again. "Bertrand said to tell you these are a house-warming gift from both him and Hilary. I guess they musta' noticed how much you liked all the little tables at his house a couple of Christmases ago." He grins exposing his perfect white teeth.

Norah gets them each a can of pop and sits down on a vinyl chair. She'll write a note to the Le Blancs. A thank-you at the office just won't do. She won't be returning to her post for two weeks, as she's taking the train home to Prestonburg in a couple of days. A note is the best option. Dan and Jean Pierre finish their drinks, admire her new place, and then tell Norah it's time they return to work. They've been very kind.

Her telephone will be installed before the day is over, then she'll do some shopping on the weekend, before embarking on her train trip to Halifax the first of the week. It will be wonderful. She hasn't been home in almost two years.

The apartment comes together for Norah with no real effort at all. She has a flair for such things. She arranges the sparse pieces of furniture into a cozy grouping that takes advantage of the architectural details of the space. She gets her phone installed with a nice long cord so she can move it from the sideboard to be near the couch when she goes to bed. She buys a coffee pot and a tea kettle as Sam refused to let her have either one of these wedding gifts, because both came from friends and family of his. She needs an area rug, but will save for a couple of months before trolling the second hand shops. She makes simple curtains for the gable window. One of her favourite pastimes is to sit in the window seat with Ivy and read. It's a very active street below and she can watch the comings and goings without being observed.

Her first phone call in her new apartment is from Sam. He's been drinking. He wants to come over and visit—with Ivy. She lies. It comes easily. She tells him they're going out. She emphasizes her preference for him to not start to drink if he intends to visit. She remembers when they used to talk long into the night. She swallows down the urge to acquiesce and accept his company, regardless of his condition. She steels herself.

He hangs up the phone.

She sits in the window seat and cries until Ivy lies down on the floor beside her and sighs a pathetic little whimper in response.

Chapter 17

The train trip from Montreal to Halifax, at the end of May, provides Norah much needed solace on many levels. Her father paid for a private compartment. With this arrangement, Norah is able to have Ivy with her. The little room contains a blue leather reclining chair and a small side table, a bed suspended from the ceiling—to be pulled down when needed—and a dollhouse-sized bathroom.

She's able to disembark at various stops. While other passengers run for snacks or stand outside to smoke, she takes Ivy for a little walk. She likes the luxury this privacy provides. She likes being able to curl up with her dog and read without having to make conversation or acknowledge the existence of others. The trip feels rejuvenating and she's grateful to her father for being so generous.

As much as she wants and needs to go back to her hometown for a few days—away from Montreal, work, polite questions, and the newness of her apartment—she's anxious about what awaits her on Tyler Street. Will she have to endure the "I told you so" remarks? Will they feel sorry for her? Will they be mad, disgusted, and aghast? What about Beth? Dear God, what will Beth have to say?

She gives herself a lecture. She decides her response will be a simple explanation about Sam's drinking and the issues about money that propelled her forward to the ultimate decision. To her knowledge, Sam was never unfaithful, so that part has nothing to do with anything. Beth can say whatever she likes. Norah has a plan. She will get a divorce as soon as possible. She will meet with a lawyer at the local Women's Centre when she returns to Montreal. She is in control.

After a night of clacking wheels, and disturbing dreams, about Sam and a vague and mysterious secret life, she settles into the last couple of hours of the trip through Nova Scotia on her way to Halifax. One of the best things about train travel is the scenery. Norah watches as bracelets of houses drift into view and out again while the train clatters along. She loves this landscape. In her mind, as she nears the coast, she feels and smells the rolling ocean. She tastes the salt on her tongue and senses the spray on her cheeks. This is where she needs to be to recharge, to heal, and to begin to feel like herself again.

As the station comes into view, she tucks Ivy safely into the pet carrier and organizes her tote bag. Once they stop, she climbs down the steps with the assistance of an attentive porter. Her suitcase will be along in moments, so she proceeds to the baggage area. She musters the courage to look up and she sees her father, standing on the platform scanning the passengers, bouncing from one foot to the other as he tries to locate his daughter. She expects she looks different to him after two years. He might not even know her. She smiles to herself. She's much thinner. Her hair is longer and not well cut. She just hasn't wanted to spend the money on an expensive Montreal haircut.

She begins moving toward Austin and the closer she gets, the more she feels her composure slipping away. She wraps an arm tightly around Ivy's carrier and straightens her back just a little. She will not go to pieces. This is her life. Her parents can no longer be expected to make things right.

He starts to walk toward her, although walk is the wrong word. He stretches his long legs out one after the other in a gait better described as a slow-motion run. He reaches her and without a word wraps both arms around her body, holding her tight. He smells of old wool and musty newspapers. He probably wore this particular sweater jacket to the last auction he attended.

He has difficulty holding himself together, too. They are a mess.

"Dad. Hi. Let go, now. You're scaring Ivy." She forces a laugh out with the words as she tries to mask the emotion by focusing on her dog.

"You're so thin! Your mother is going to have a fit when she sees you. I thought we taught you how to cook, young lady!" He moves away, but keeps his arms on her shoulders. "We'll get your suitcase and go home. When was the last time you ate, anyway? I brought lunch. Have it in the car. Thought, with the dog, you wouldn't want to go to a restaurant." He stops to take a breath.

Norah looks at him and smiles, but she knows in her heart that her eyes tell a different story. "A picnic in the car sounds wonderful. Let's take Ivy for a little walk and you can meet her while we wait for my suitcase."

After their lunch, which reminds Norah of lunches they took with them to auctions years ago, they make the hour-long trek to Prestonburg. Her father seems to be at a loss for words, and Norah's in no hurry to fill the empty air with polite and useless conversation. She drifts in her own world, stroking her dog and gazing out the window as the familiar scenery rolls by. Most of the time, over the last year, Norah has felt inside her face, peeking out at the world like there's a barrier between her thoughts and any interaction on the other side. She protects herself at all cost.

The fear of revealing how she feels, or of breaking down altogether, is ever present. In a surprising reversal, she finds herself yearning for her window seat in the little apartment on Rue de la Montagne. As much as she wanted to come home, she anticipates this is going to be a very emotionally challenging week.

As they drive past the shop, Norah realizes her mother has closed early—a rare occurrence at Clarkes Antiques and Collectibles. The neighbours will think there's been a death in the family. Paige probably wanted to start supper and have lots of time to visit. When the aging Oldsmobile pulls into the back parking spot, she's at the door waiting. Norah's first glimpse of her mother is of her smoothing her hair back toward that ever-present crooked bun at the nape of her neck, and planting a smile of determination on her face.

When Norah unfolds her waif-like body out of the front seat, Ivy, content in the crook of her arm, just looks up at Norah with questioning eyes. Her mother holds the door so they can come in while her father gets her bags. Once inside, the silence is broken. "I'm so glad you could come home, Norah. We were worried. You're so thin. The dog—Ivy, is it? She's cute. You can put her down. Come in. Come in. Make room for your father." Her words are jumbled, repetitive, and anxious, like she's barely grasping the threads of composure.

Norah smiles down at her mother and gives her a little hug. "I'm fine. A little tired. It was a long ride but the compartment was fabulous. I'm so grateful." She glances over at her father, just as he places her luggage in the hallway leading to her old room. "I don't know how I would have managed with Ivy in the baggage car." She snuggles the dog then sets her down on the floor. "I guess I would have stayed with her all night propped on a pile of suitcases." Ivy sits down beside Norah and plants one small paw firmly on her owner's foot. "If there's time, I'd like to take Ivy for a little walk around the neighbourhood before supper."

Norah and Ivy roam the streets of Prestonburg. Somehow, it surprises her nothing has changed very much. The shops are ramping up for the summer tourist season. Some buildings are being painted; others could use a coat they will never see. Out there, beyond the wall she has built to protect herself from the world, everything seems a curious composite of normal, wrapping around the turmoil in her life.

She is reluctant, but later in the evening, after supper and a lot of prodding, Norah explains to her anxious parents about her plan to visit the Women's Centre and how she'll be seeking a divorce within the next few months. She tells them about her new apartment, and the basics of her work. Then she makes the trek upstairs to visit with her old friend.

Norah feels things cannot be the same anymore. She and Beth will likely never recapture the pleasure in each other's company that they had when Norah was a child. Her long-time suspicion of Beth having an affair with Austin, and now her own wrecked marriage—predicted by Beth herself— will likely cause everlasting scars on the face of their relationship.

Beth is waiting at the apartment door, as she always does. She makes a fuss over Ivy, just like Norah knew she would. Tea is made and brewing in the pot on the tray in the living room, just like all the times before. Norah gets a hug, surrounding her in all that is Beth, just like all the times when she came home from university.

The apartment looks the same, stuffed to the gunnels with yellow bric-a-brac and more angel collectibles than Norah has ever seen. She notes some things *do* change—Beth has more stuff.

They sit. They fuss over Ivy. Beth pours tea, an herbal concoction called Sleepytime. Norah thinks it's an interesting choice, wondering which one of them might be more in need of this relaxing variety, but makes no comment. Back in the old days, she would have asked Beth why she chose this tea, but Norah doesn't have a lot of energy to ask questions when she doesn't care about the answers.

She waits for the "I told you so" conversation, and has steeled herself with prepared answers. Instead, Beth asks about her job and about the new apartment. She wants to know every last detail and follows up with the suggestion that maybe she could come to Montreal for a visit at the end of the summer break, after her course is finished. She still manages to try and upgrade her credentials every summer. Beth chats away like Norah's marriage never happened.

Finally, she says how she feels. "Norah, you made a good decision. Anything I can do to help, you can count on me." Her eyes are a tiny bit wet and she holds her mug of tea a tiny bit tighter, but the tremor of nervousness creeping out does not escape Norah's notice.

Norah lets her shoulders relax. "Thanks, Beth. I was worried you were going to point out the painfully obvious. I'm so happy to be home, with people who care about me no matter what. My colleagues at work have been super supportive, but it's not the same. I'm glad to be home for a while, just to get some rest."

"And to eat, I hope! My God, girl, you are like a matchstick! No need to let the idiot make you sick!" She smiles. "I couldn't resist just one little dig at the asshole. Oops! That was two!" She bobs her head back and forth for emphasis. Her blond curls, dyed to perfection, wiggle with the effort. "I'll stop now. No more snide remarks, I promise." She giggles as she repositions herself in her chair and Norah forces a smile. Beth is Beth and there is a measure of comfort in the familiarity. It's good some things never change.

What turns out to be a wonderful week is topped off by a Saturday auction that reminds Norah of happier days, from what seems like a hundred years ago. With her mother managing the shop and dog-sitting Ivy, Norah and her dad spend the sunny spring day at an outdoor event where furniture and box lots are lined up for viewing; where people bring their own lawn chairs and a lunch; where the grass is damp and the breezes are cool off the water.

Austin buys glass, china, and two parlour tables. One has brass lion-paw feet. Each paw is grasping a glass ball. There are no carpets to speak of— nothing big enough to suit her new place. She tells her father it'll be easier to buy one in Montreal than to try and manhandle something home on the train. He agrees.

****

Upon returning to Montreal, Norah is rejuvenated and feels both a sense of contentment and a security that she really is loved. Her parents didn't pry. They allowed her to say what she wanted to say, without offering judgment.

They permitted her to be her newfound self. She took long walks, sat by the ocean, spent quiet time reading, and mended without pressure.

As Norah looks up at her apartment, while getting out of the cab on Rue de la Montagne, she finds herself happy to be home and looking forward to her return to work. She's also anxious about starting the divorce process. She hopes Sam will cooperate.

A few days after getting back, Norah makes an appointment to see a lawyer at the Women's Centre on Cote de Neige, near her home. This is a support agency for women needing assistance to navigate through the myriad of both federal and provincial laws governing a variety of issues. Norah knows it'll take patience, but she expects things will be easier for her now as a new Canadian Divorce Act came into being just this past year. The biggest change is in the shorter wait time for no-fault divorce, reduced to twelve months. Her goal is to have her divorce by the end of the next summer.

****

Sam says he'll cooperate. After months of taking his drunken calls, listening to ice tinkling in his glass at the other end of the phone, and responding to his complaints and issues, he has agreed to sign the papers—when needed. He succeeds in complicating Norah's best-laid plans when he moves to Toronto quite unexpectedly. He swears he'll be in court on the appointed day. She hopes, once the divorce is final, and with Sam off in Toronto, the threads of their marriage will be forever severed, and he will stop trying to weave some unlikely relationship out of the tattered remains. She wants to apply to graduate school and create new fabric, fabric devoid of all that is Sam.

Norah's little studio on Rue de la Montagne has become her sanctuary. After scouring the antique malls and second hand stores throughout the West End, she located what she thinks is the perfect oriental tapestry carpet to suit her aesthetic and her eclectic grouping of possessions. The search was assisted by a very helpful cheque from her father that she found tucked in her bag when she returned from her trip to Prestonburg.

The neighbourhood provides comfort in its familiarity. It reminds her of her childhood on Tyler Street, with shops and restaurants downstairs and interesting characters living above. She now thinks of herself as one of

158

those interesting and somewhat mysterious characters, although everyone recognizes the tall girl from the auction house who is always in the company of the little beagle-mix named Ivy. Norah has met many local residents with dogs. Everyone knows the names of the animals and rarely the names of the people. There's a dog park just a couple of blocks away and, other than at work, this is where she meets almost everyone she knows.

****

After six months of being on her own and continuing at Le Blanc and White, Norah decides, with much soul searching, to apply to graduate school and give up her job, if she's accepted. It'll be very difficult to part company with those who supported her through her ill-fated marriage and separation, but she feels it's time to make a move.

She's not sure how she'll manage without the kind advice of Bertrand, or the insight she's often received from Phil. She wants to try for a graduate position at McGill University in Anthropology and Sociology beginning in the winter of 1988. She thinks about Bertrand and Hilary's wonderful party, and how this next Christmas gathering may be her last.

The first week of November, on a miserable and gloom-wrapped rainy day, when her mood parallels the weather, Norah leaves her workroom filled with boxes of Japanese Lustreware and piles of Newfoundland hooked rugs. She walks up the stairs to Bertrand's office. The time has come to let him know her plans. Ivy pads along behind her, ever the watchdog, alert for anyone who might bend down for a pat and a hello.

She enters his office at the prearranged time and he's waiting for her. She doesn't immediately sense her boss's anxiety. He jumps up from his chair and runs around the desk, indicating for her to sit while he gives Ivy the requisite biscuit. His expression, framed in a chiselled look of aging handsome, is unsettled. Norah wonders why.

"Sit. Sit." He flutters. He doesn't look at her. He focuses on Ivy. "What can I do for you today? I've been very curious. You made an appointment. So formal." He's running on.

Now Norah senses his distress. *Let's get this over with.* "Bertrand, I've been accepted to graduate school at McGill, starting in the winter semester. I'll be doing a master's degree in Sociology and Anthropology and plan to write a thesis about collecting." She looks at him and grins. "Think I can manage writing about collecting?"

He obviously tries to sound supportive and casual, but Norah can hear the underlying anxiety in his voice. "What are your plans? Do you want to work here part time to help with your expenses?"

"Would it be possible?" Norah's surprised at Bertrand's offer. She intended to use her education trust to pay for school as well as living expenses. The thought never crossed her mind the business would put up with a student working part time. "My classes will be two days a week and I'll have to do research as well."

Bertrand leans over. "Norah, you can work whenever you can. We'll arrange work around your classes. You may interview collectors and buyers through the auction house. Hilary and I both want you to stay with the company. You are an asset, you know."

The Le Blancs must have suspected her aspirations all along. Norah, as is always the case, continues to be surprised when people notice or care. She tends to feel invisible and gives herself no credit for friendships made or lives touched. She'll stay with her job, working two or three days a week including, perhaps, auction days on the weekends. It'll be the perfect fit.

$$\mathcal{Chapter}\ 18$$

Life settles into a comfortable rhythm, starting in January. Norah, who has always loved learning, quickly embraces graduate school life. She eagerly anticipates spending time researching.

Her classes are minimal. There's one, Advanced Anthropological Studies and another, Research Techniques. Each chews up an afternoon of seminar-style class time. There are a mere half-dozen students in each group. Her thesis research involves extensive interviewing of avid collectors, as Norah attempts to discover the personality characteristics of individuals propelled into extreme collecting.

Her first major interview is with a husband and wife, introduced to her by Bertrand. They are regulars at the auction house and collect Fiesta pottery. Part of the thrill of collecting this particular pottery is because many pieces, like covered onion soup bowls, were made over a very limited period and examples are scarce. Monsieur and Madame Cloutier have a complete set of onion soups. They took it upon themselves to learn to speak English, so they could travel to the United States without language issues. Since Quebec's importing habits in the 1930s were significantly different than other areas of the continent, they often go to Ohio and search out rare specimens not likely to ever be found in Canada at all, let alone nearby.

Bertrand introduced Norah to the Cloutiers during an auction. He told them Norah was doing her master's degree, and wished to interview serious collectors. The couple invited her to their home to see their accumulations.

At the appointed time, Norah arrives on the doorstep of the Cloutiers, in a suburb of Montreal, called Longueuil, just off the Island. They live in a traditional split entry bungalow built in the late 1960s.

Norah rings the doorbell, which is answered with such haste, she wonders if the woman was standing at the window awaiting her arrival. She removes her jacket as her gaze roves from one area to another.

There are examples of Fiesta pottery everywhere. Bowls line the stairs. The light is on in the family room below. Norah can see only a portion of a Hoosier cabinet, but can tell it is burdened to overflowing with product. She inclines her head to better view a shelf installed about a foot below the ceiling, all the way around the living room. Every available inch of the space holds Fiesta.

Madame Cloutier, a little woman with pin curls in a tight, cap-like arrangement around her head, and bottle thick spectacles, ushers her in and begins the tour. Her husband, also small and significantly shyer when it comes to speaking English, sits in a rocker by the fireplace, under a mantle covered in Fiesta coffee pots of every hue. Norah doesn't know where to look. Pottery obscures every available surface, fills every cabinet and cupboard, and sits in disarray on the floor. There are many rare, one-of-a-kind pieces sold to Fiesta diehards right from the original factory collections. She asks if she can take a few pictures, and some notes. The little woman tells her that as a friend of Bertrand's, Norah can do whatever she likes. They will have tea and Norah will get to see everything.

After two hours of touring and being regaled with stories about every rare find and every decision, Norah concludes that the couple has built their whole married life around collecting this brightly coloured, heavy pottery. Their vacations before retirement were planned to take advantage of sales. Now, their social life is comprised of attending fairs and meetings all over North America—trading, but most often buying.

They have no children and no extended family even remotely interested in an inheritance of such unmitigated vastness or peculiarity. "One day our collection will hit the market in a big sale at Le Blanc and White just like the many sales we have attended in the past. I think we have more than six thousand pieces, but I don't know for sure." Madame Cloutier claps her hands together for emphasis as she looks up at Norah. "I guess we just want to own it all!"

People like the Cloutiers are the bread and butter of auction houses as well as antique and collectible businesses. Norah knows full well the best customers are the ones who show up, see an item they collect, and cannot bear the thought of anyone owning it but them. Norah saw a woman come into Clarkes Antiques and Collectibles one afternoon and buy every cream and sugar set in the shop. She bought fourteen sets, including china, glass, and silver. She had over a thousand at home but she felt compelled to own every other set she saw. Human beings collecting. It's a fascinating affliction.

****

There are men in Norah's life as well. Her first encounter, after her separation, is with Conner Elliot, a draft dodger from the Mid-western United States. He enlisted in the US military and said he was fine until they asked him to carry a gun. He reacted by jumping on a train and making his way to Winnipeg. Because he had friends in Montreal, he continued on to Quebec. He rotates around to various apartments. Norah meets him at the dog park where he spends a great deal of time taking care of the pets of friends and friends of friends. The problem with the Whippet currently in his charge is that the dog doesn't seem to like men much and wanders over to Norah, determined to keep company with her. As Norah introduces herself and Ivy to the nervous dog, Conner appears, sits, and gets comfortable on the park bench.

He's about Norah's age, tall and lanky, with naturally curly blond hair down to his shoulders. His ears are pierced and he most often wears a turtle neck sweater under a pair of red and green paisley overalls. He looks like the quintessential idea of a hippy propelled from the mid-1960s to the 1980s. He's friendly, polite, and curious. He asks Norah out to dinner and she accepts. He suggests they meet at a bistro, in Old Montreal, for supper the next night.

The restaurant is down a creepy little alley off a cobblestone pathway. Norah has never been there before. She had to call the establishment and get directions to the place, so she could make her way after getting off the bus at the nearest stop. The darkness makes her nervous. She doesn't like the area.

Dinner is fine. Conner is funny, and they enjoy each other's company.

"You know, I could stay at your place for a while. Take care of Ivy. Help out." His indigo eyes twinkle at her.

"Ivy comes to work with me, Conner. She doesn't need a babysitter. And besides, my apartment isn't big enough for long-term guests." *Thank God!* He continues to stare at her, head tilted, putting on buckets of charm. She decides not to linger at the restaurant. This decision will enable her to catch an earlier bus home.

"I've a busy day scheduled tomorrow, Conner. Think I'll just leave now. Thanks for the company." She sounds formal, even to herself, as she makes her goodbyes after placing crumpled bills, to cover a significant portion of the tab, on the table. There is no move to escort her to the bus. This is probably because she made it clear he could not come back to Rue de la Montagne with her.

He calls often over the next month or so. They exchange greetings in the park whenever he turns up, but Norah starts to sit with other people so she's never on a bench alone, and eventually the calls stop.

****

After almost nine months in her studio, walking by apartment Number One numerous times a day with Ivy, Norah has only exchanged simple pleasantries with Alina Van Essen. She is a Professor of European Cultural Studies at McGill, and specializes in changes effected by World War II. She's about sixty years old and has lived in the building for more than ten years.

It appears she only ventures out to work or to get groceries and wine. Norah's observed nothing else. No one seems to visit and there are never any sounds of television, radio, or music coming from her apartment. They have never run into one another on campus.

Just as Norah reaches the landing in front of Number One, the door snaps open and out pops Alina. "Do you like tea?" With Ivy under her arm and lost in thought, Norah almost tips backward down the stairs. "Careful. Don't fall."

Norah gathers herself and replies. "I love tea. Do you like dogs?"

"Never had pets growing up. Just another mouth to feed, but you can bring it in, sure." She glances toward Ivy without interest. "You never seem to be without your dog."

Norah is unsure if this is a statement of fact or a criticism of some sort. Alina's manner is abrupt, if nothing else. They enter the apartment behind the professor and Norah pulls the door closed with care. She looks around. Alina's design aesthetic appears to be library meets cafeteria. There are books everywhere. Norah's neighbour is not a good housekeeper and any surface not holding a book is supporting an empty cup, a plate, or a few utensils. Her place smells like the garbage needs attending. The table, covered in papers, holds a typewriter barely visible through the debris.

"Don't mind the mess. I think more clearly when I'm surrounded by clutter. It makes my mind feel liberated." She turns to Norah and shrugs. "I don't know why I am like this."

Norah makes no judgment. She has learned, over the years, to make assessments of people on their treatment of her rather than on the state of their carpets. Despite being a bit of a neat freak herself, she no longer expects others to share her passion for order. "No problem, Alina. Ivy and I will just sit over here." She's spied an armchair in the corner with only a couple of reference books on the seat. She places them on the floor by the chair and sits down.

Alina disappears into the kitchen to retrieve the tea. Norah looks around. The apartment is a considerable size, bigger than her studio, with a separate kitchen, a living room with a dining alcove, and two bedrooms. The guest room has pocket doors opening to the living area so the space looks bigger than it is. Alina, taking full advantage of this, uses the added open space as her office and she's spread her work out significantly. The furniture is old and tattered. It looks like it's all from jumble sales and second hand shops—which can be a good thing—but it's obvious Alina hasn't had someone with Norah's experience to guide her.

The floor is partially covered by a spotty rug and department-store curtains try their best to hang on the windows. Norah knows the woman has lived here for many years and is sure Josef would paint and do upgrades if she asked. *Curious.*

Alina is tall, taller than Norah which says something, and she's thin. She is not thin in a good, healthy way. She is thin in a neglected way. She walks with an osteoporosis bend. Her hair is of medium length, mousy brown, and crying for attention both in the cutting and conditioning departments. Her skin is marked. Her features are mannish with heavy eyelids and wide lips. She wears clothes too big for her, and today she sports a long flannel skirt and a man's sweater with pockets, reminiscent of Norah's father's preference.

She returns to the living room with two mugs, both sport tea bag strings and small squares of identifying paper hanging over the side. There's no offer of cream or sugar, no spoon to remove the bag. The cup is pottery and chipped. Norah rearranges Ivy beside her in the chair, accepting the mug with a smile. Alina sits down on a footstool just across from her and settles. "So, tell me about yourself. I decided if we are going to be neighbours for a while, I should get to know you better than just saying hello." She smiles at her guest and Norah notes her teeth require attention.

"I agree." Norah nods and returns the smile. She tells her neighbour about her work at the auction house. She tells her about her work at McGill. Alina mentions her teaching and her research. They pet the dog. An hour is spent immersed in the benign pleasantries of sharing surface information with someone you have just met.

Norah never mentions Sam. Alina avoids any reference to her personal life. They are both relaxed—happy the ice has been broken.

****

True to his word, something Norah finds difficult to believe, Forrest Sampson does, in fact, appear in divorce court at the Palais du Justice in Montreal on a perfect June day in 1988, ready to say he wants an uncontested divorce after a year of separation. He arrives alone, nervous, and shaking. Norah imagines he would like a drink. Their nods to one another would be imperceptible to anyone interested enough to look.

The courtroom is crowded. There are twenty-five divorce cases scheduled today in this room alone. Norah's lawyer, Miss No-Nonsense Shirley Cohen, has her papers well prepared and assembled in front of her when the clerk announces, in French, for the case of Clarke versus Sampson. Sam climbs into the box when called and swears he will accept the divorce as uncontested. Since there are no children and no assets, things go ahead at lightning speed. The judge looks down from his lofty perch at Miss Cohen. "And why is this young woman receiving no support?"

The lawyer, taken aback by the question, responds. "No need and not requested, My Lord."

The judge disagrees. "I will add a caveat so Mademoiselle Clarke will have the right to ask for support, if the need arises, for the next five years." He looks at Norah. "Is this acceptable to you?"

"Yes, My Lord," comes her response as she rushes to her feet, impressed with herself since she actually believes she understood the entire exchange, although it all took place in French.

"A decree nisi is hereby granted and final papers will be issued in ninety days. Merci.

Norah turns to cast a quick glance at Sam behind her. He nods acknowledgment, as Shirley sweeps her papers back into an already-stuffed briefcase. She leans over to Norah. "That's it. We're out of here!" She pushes back her chair, straightens her powder-blue suit jacket down over a very tight pencil skirt, and leaves the courtroom.

Norah mumbles her thanks to the woman's back, feeling somehow like she's been hit by a bus and not sure why. It's only 11:00 AM but seems like the end of a long day. Sam approaches her with arms outstretched for a hug. "See? Told you I would show up. Can I take you to lunch?"

Although not intending to spend time with him, she had taken the day off from work and school, so nods her consent. Words are having trouble making their way from her brain to her mouth. *Can you be in shock after getting divorced? Should she just leave and go home? What might the proper protocol be?*

They lunch in Old Montreal, near the courthouse, at a sidewalk cafe with umbrellas to protect patrons from the sun. The area is a favourite haunt for artists who sketch and peddle their wares nearby. It strikes Norah as odd how everything seems to be fine around them. No one senses how weird this all is. Sam orders two sangria, but Norah sticks to water and, in the end, he manages to drink hers as well. Then he orders two more. She eats a salad with no flavour. They talk about his new job at a private school in Toronto, about graduate school, about the auction house, and about Ivy.

Although Norah is the one who instigated divorce proceedings, Sam seems to be the one discovering the thrill of new-found freedom. Without reservation, and obviously choosing to treat her like an old friend, he regales Norah with stories of one-night stands with men he has met in a bar or through other friends. Norah thinks he's playing fast and loose with his health, considering the AIDS and HIV scares dominating the news. It appears Sam is flaunting his disregard for his personal well being.

By the time Norah finishes with the cardboard and sawdust salad she has tried to consume, Sam has drunk six sangria and eaten virtually nothing. He is to catch his bus to the airport in an hour and return to Toronto. Norah drops some money on the table and organizes herself to leave. She looks across at the blotchy face and hooded eyes, as Sam begins to disappear behind his alcoholic shroud. She's anxious to get home to Ivy. He tosses her money back at her, saying he is quite capable of taking his "wife" to lunch.

She thanks him, tells him to take care of himself, picks up the bills she has just put down, and leaves without looking back. She walks for a dozen blocks before she catches her bus, although she could have waited in front of the cafe.

****

Bertrand and Hilary set up a date between Chandler Le Sage and Norah. Chandler is the indulged son of some very wealthy friends. They arrange to meet at a posh restaurant in Montreal's West End, a few blocks from Norah's apartment. She protects her privacy with a vengeance and has developed a reluctance to share the exact location of her home with anyone she's just meeting. A single woman living alone in the city can't be too careful.

She dresses with care. She hates blind dates, but trusts the judgment of her friends, especially Hilary, who is so thoughtful and gracious. She wishes the Le Blancs had just invited them both there for dinner. She wears a mid-calf length suede skirt in a soft biscuit shade, bought during Mademoiselle Faubert's rock-bottom, one-day-only discount sale just after Christmas.

In the spring of 1990, the news is full of stories about the Cold War, and Nelson Mandela has just been released from prison. The designer located on the main floor of Norah's building is ahead of her time showing a sixties' influence. Norah's skirt is paired to perfection with a black tank top and a frayed jean jacket, providing a silent nod to grunge, an element of pop culture to which Norah merely has a passing acquaintance. It's simple. She loves the jacket and the way it looks on her.

She walks up the stone steps and into Barton's entry at precisely 7:00 PM, scanning the patrons for someone who looks like he might be her dinner companion. She expects a thirty-something blond man who, according to Bertrand, tries to look like a Wall Street executive. She has been told he'll inherit his father's wealth management business, but is having trouble organizing himself to settle down and practice the financial strategies he learned while studying business at Laval University.

No one looks appropriate, so she asks the maître d' and is led to a small table in an alcove where Monsieur Le Sage is seated. He gets up when he sees her approach and she extends her hand.

In the half glow of the candlelit table, she assesses a young man who looks about twenty years old—her height—but pudgy with baby fat-like qualities that make him appear shorter. He's dressed in blue jeans and an ill-fitting sports jacket. There's nothing remotely Wall Street about him, so Norah determines she'll come to her own conclusions. He bows in an exaggeratedly formal and sarcastic way as he takes her hand in his. "Finally, I get to meet the mysterious Norah Clarke." His tone is mocking.

"And I finally get to meet the Chandler everyone has been telling me about." She smiles and sits down opposite him, noticing the high ball of whiskey at his right hand.

"I just got another drink." He waves down the waiter. "What will you have, Norah?"

The word "another" does not escape her attention. "Herbal tea." She looks up at the waiter. "A chamomile, if you have it?"

He nods his assent and turns to leave, as Chandler makes a remark about what he perceives as her obvious disapproval.

"No disapproval intended." Her response is blunt and pragmatic. "I don't drink much and would prefer tea. It has nothing to do with you. I couldn't disapprove of you. I don't know you." All this is said with quiet resolution. A smile plays at the corners of her mouth and her deep green eyes try to burn a hole into his brain. She can feel him squirm and doesn't care much.

He tries a new tack. "The Le Blancs tell me you just finished a master's. Care to tell me what it's about?"

She could take the chance and relax, but prefers to stay aloof. She isn't sure why, but instinct tells her not to enjoy herself too much. "Cultural Anthropology. I study collectors and the human nature of collecting. It's a good fit with what I do for Le Blanc and White. What do you do?"

"Pretend I work for Daddy. He likes to think I'm his right hand man, and he pays me so he can think so." His grin is smug, like he's smarter than his father and has just shared this fact with Norah.

They order dinner. Chandler insists on chateaubriand for two, a huge and expensive meal for which Barton's is renowned. It would take two sumo wrestlers to eat it. Chandler digs in, enjoying another couple of whiskeys along the way. The conversation is idle and about nothing. Norah wants to go home. She finds herself wondering if Alina's lights will be on; if perhaps she'll have a visit with her neighbour later. Finally, they're finished. No dessert, thank God.

Chandler offers to drive Norah home, but she's having none of it. As they leave the restaurant, he points out his 1989 silver Audi 100 diesel, turbo charged, fast-back parked across the street. "Now, wouldn't you like a drive home in my baby?" He puts his arm around her shoulder and sways into her.

"Sorry, my friend." She attempts to sound gracious. "I just don't drive with someone who's been drinking. I'll walk."

She starts to pull away from his arm, and he holds on just a little tighter while he fights with his pocket to retrieve a set of keys. He grabs her hand and drops the keys into her palm. "So you drive, Miss Chamomile Tea."

"I couldn't possibly drive your car." She steps back as he sways against the handrail and loses his balance. She steadies him.

"Sure you can. Be a good girl and drive me home. Then Dad's driver can bring you back to your place. No problem. I can't leave my baby here on the street all night." He gazes with drunken lust at the car. "You can help. Come on." He's snivelling now, and starting to make a scene as they block the steps.

He collapses into the leather bucket seat on the passenger side. She opens the door and eases herself down into the very low slung driver's side. The car is beautiful, smells new, and wraps around her just like the ads on television say an Audi can do. After getting her bearings, as well as Chandler's address and directions, she eases the car out into the street. Before long, they're in six lanes of traffic on a very busy Rue Sherbrooke.

Chandler, belted loosely in beside her, is all hands. He tries, without much success, to get one of them up under her skirt which, much to his annoyance, extends down well below her knees. She moves his meaty mitt more than once. He leans further over to her side of the car and she's having trouble concentrating on driving. "Stop it. I'll wind up hitting something with your beautiful car." This might sink in.

For a minute, he retreats to his side. Without any warning, he lunges toward her and the car swerves, just enough to scare her. She says nothing. She engages the hazard lights and stops the car. Horns honk all around her. She checks her mirrors with care, gets out, closes the door and makes her way through snarled traffic to the opposite side of the street. She is a mere three blocks from home and disappears down a side street. She can hear sirens.

Chapter 19

Bertrand is taking a back seat role, and enjoys being less hands on. Norah basks in the glow of her present situation. She's completed her graduate degree with resounding success, and is again working full time at Le Blanc and White. Her position has expanded. She now does many of the initial visits with sellers and determines the projects accepted by the auction house.

Beth is coming to visit. She's talked about travelling to Montreal ever since Norah left Sam, but despite her considerable time off as a teacher, has never managed to fulfil the commitment. Norah is beside herself with excitement. She wishes Beth could stay with her, but her studio won't support the addition of guests, and Beth, to her credit, wants Norah to arrange a place for her at a small boutique hotel not far north, on Rue de la Montaigne.

In a state of flurried excitement, she prepares for the coming get-together with her old friend and mentor. She plans a cocktail soiree of sorts, so Beth can meet her colleagues from work, as well as Alina, and Luc Tondreau, her latest flame.

Luc is an interesting character. He's significantly older than Norah, in his mid-forties. He owns four restaurants on the island. They met quite by accident when she decided to treat herself to dinner out a few months ago. She went to a small bistro about two blocks away. While sitting and reading Margaret Atwood's latest contribution to the world of Canadian fiction, *Cat's Eye,* Luc approached the table, introduced himself as the proprietor, and commented that a beautiful lady should not be dining alone on a Friday evening. "Perhaps I could join you for dessert after your meal?"

Luc is very tall and in good shape. He is fashionable and put together, always dressed in slacks and a sports jacket. He is never without a tie when in one of his establishments. His hair is short, sandy, and greying at the temples. His features are chiselled, and his skin has seen far too much sun. He is a gentleman to the fourth power, and Norah is smitten the moment he approaches her.

They have seen a lot of one another since that first night. He is the one man, besides Sam, whom Norah has taken to her bed. She's still discovering the joy of intimacy with an experienced French lover, whose primary concern is her welfare.

One night, he arrived in his bottle-green 1967 Jaguar XKE convertible roadster, and whisked her off to a restaurant in an east-end neighbourhood of Montreal unfamiliar to her. They walked into a dining room bereft of patrons. A number of waiters in very formal black and white attire stood in a line along the perimeter. One table was dressed. They were ushered to this table and service swiftly began. Luc just smiled, reached across the expanse of white linen to hold her hand, and nodded wordless instructions to anxious staff.

When Norah tried to speak, he put a finger to his lips, never taking his eyes from hers. She started to get nervous. They had not known one another long enough for him to propose; although, despite her misgivings about marriage in general, she could be talked into thinking Luc was the one.

After what seemed like forever, he broke his silence. "I hired the whole restaurant tonight so we could have some privacy and the place to ourselves. Do you like this?" He glanced about at the exquisite surroundings. "This is my favourite spot. I don't own it yet, but want to buy it. First, I want your opinion. Do you like it? This will be a business I buy for us."

* * * *

Getting Beth comfortable at Hotel de la Petite Montagne is no small feat. Although she doesn't complain or criticize in so many words, she wants to ensure all the amenities are equal to a big chain motel, whereas small, boutique hotels like this are geared toward the tourist spending more time outside than in. She needs ice. She wants extra towels. She wants an alarm clock. She wants to find out if the window opens, but perhaps it will be too noisy. The air conditioner must be whisper quiet. It's an ordeal. Norah exercises patience, waits, and assists as required. Once Beth feels suitably settled, they walk the three blocks down the street and up the two flights to Norah's apartment.

Beth is not impressed. The weather is oppressively hot and muggy, lying like plastic wrap on warm skin. Weight loss has never been one of her priorities, so her feet are heavy on the sidewalk as they make their way. She huffs up the stairs, and Norah is a bit taken aback considering Beth needs to climb stairs every day to get to her own apartment in Prestonburg.

"I guess I need more exercise." Her statement is sheepish and uttered through a face too pink for comfort.

Her childhood friend compliments Norah's efforts with the apartment, although she manages to note the minimalist nature of possession accumulation. "How do you manage with so little stuff?"

The answer is simple. Norah wants little and doesn't buy for the sake of buying, unlike Beth who was compelled to shop on the way to the apartment, buying two T-shirts with pictures of Montreal on the front.

Norah's excited to tell Beth about the details of the party tomorrow. Luc has insisted on having his nearby bistro cater the affair, and she has no idea what will arrive the next afternoon. He has declared, with authority, he will handle the decisions. All she had to do was invite her guests.

Bertrand and Hilary are coming. To Norah's surprise, they were very pleased to get an invitation. She thought they would decline, but there was no hesitation whatsoever.

Phil and Madeleine will be there. Madeleine, of course, wants to come ahead of other guests and help, but Norah assured her all was taken care of.

The additional personnel at work, those with whom Norah interacts on a daily basis, are all invited and have accepted. Jean Pierre is coming with his latest girlfriend. Dan is now married to Marcy, and they will both be there. Norah and Marcy have enjoyed the company of one another over the years. Norah has never forgotten how kind Marcy was the night Sam killed the refrigerator. Much to Norah's surprise, Dorothy accepted Norah's invite as well.

Just on a chance, Norah called the parents of her old college friend, Joy Scott. Joy happens to be in town, and says she wouldn't miss this party for the world. At least there will be another person Beth has met before.

Alina will be there, and any minute she'll join them for supper at a terrace restaurant nearby. Nothing like Montreal on a sultry August night. Everyone will be on the streets, and it will be the perfect venue to give Beth a little taste of life in downtown Montreal.

Beth and Alina are not a good fit. They spend most of the evening sizing one another up like two old cats in the barnyard.

"You wear very fancy clothes." Alina is her usual abrupt self, directing her remarks at Beth who is resplendent in a pink sleeveless sequined shell top and a long tie-dyed skirt.

"If you think this is fancy, you ain't seen nothin' yet." Beth's reply is in her best down-home vernacular. Norah is a little worried about what she will choose for tomorrow's party. "Do you want some tips?" Beth smiles across at Alina.

Alina glances down at her navy blue slacks, slightly short and a bit pilled from many washes, and at her flowered blouse that doesn't button well. She gives Beth a look of disdain. "Perhaps I think there are more important things in the world than clothes. Perhaps I am not trying to hide anything."

Norah's thankful the evening isn't reduced to fisticuffs and heaves a sigh of relief, matched with a measure of disappointment, when the ordeal is over.

The following morning, she leaves Beth to her own devices and cleans her apartment until the very hardwood shines. She expects Luc and his staff to turn up about 2:00 PM, although she hasn't a clue what to expect. Her guests will be arriving around 4:00 PM to have cocktails and hors d'oeuvres. She has tried to plan, but it's a challenge when she doesn't know exactly what will be coming in the door.

As expected, Luc's caterers arrive. There are two waiters and a wine steward. They even bring a collapsible buffet table and portable mini bar. They move furniture. They unpack crystal glasses in about ten different shapes and sizes. They have white china plates and silver cutlery. They have trays of food. She has to ask what things are and they tell her not to worry, each chafing dish and platter comes with its own identification card handwritten by a professional calligrapher.

She roams around examining the water chestnuts wrapped in bacon, the Santa Fe chicken spring rolls with sauce, the filo asparagus and Asiago cheese, the filo raspberry almond and Brie, the petit crab tarts with cranberry, and the requisite platters of vegetables, fruit and cheese, just as Luc enters the studio in all his glory. He's helping the bartender with a case of wine. Deservedly or not, and even though she originally felt fabulous in a new, halter-top dress she just made, Norah is entrenched in the feeling of country bumpkin. She's overwhelmed by her perceived inadequacies. She feels her little party may be getting away from her.

"So what do you think? Have I succeeded in pleasing you? Do you think your friends will be impressed?"

"Everything is fabulous, Luc." She doesn't want to sound ungrateful. This is his business. He's in his element, and knows what he's doing, but her intent was to have a nice little get-together so Beth could meet her Montreal friends and her lover. Her intent was not for Luc to try and win points with everybody else in the room. When the four men are busy at the table, she snatches up the plastic cutlery and paper plates she purchased for the occasion and jams the evidence into the nearest kitchen drawer. She pulls the boxes of wine from the refrigerator and wedges them into the back of the pots and pans cupboard.

Luc turns around, takes two broad steps across the expanse of her main room, encircles her with his arms, and kisses her temple. "Don't be nervous. I will make sure all your friends have a wonderful time." He looks around the apartment. "We have got to get you out of this hole in the wall." His comment is said almost to himself as he gazes toward her coveted window seat and adds, "I think we need something in Outremont, about three thousand square feet." He looks at her. "We will talk about this later but think about what you would like. We can move before Christmas, I am sure."

He turns to the waiters and barks some last minute instructions Norah can't quite translate.

People start to arrive. Beth is first. Dressed in honour of the occasion, true to her word, she is decked out in a floor-length golden chiffon sun dress, with hair coiffed this morning at a nearby salon, and eyelashes firmly glued in place. Her expression indicates she's bowled over by the catering experience, and by the panache of Luc. He introduces himself, before Norah can grab Ivy to prevent her from getting tangled up in Beth's yardage of shimmer. He pours her a glass of wine, and only then acknowledges Norah who continues holding her dog in her arms, watching the operation take place before her.

Beth rolls her eyes at Norah. "Quite the guy," she stage whispers. "Do you even know what this food is? I don't care, mind you. I intend to try everything."

Bertrand and Hilary arrive right behind Beth. *Thank God.* They're more like Luc, and in his league when it comes to entertaining. Norah feels out of her depth. Ivy trudges over to see Bertrand, who somehow managed to remember to put a dog cookie into his dapper and expensive sports jacket, in honour of his meeting with Ivy here at home. Norah is touched by his thoughtfulness. Hilary and Bertrand are also introduced to Luc by Luc, despite Norah's attempts to perform this function herself.

Hilary refuses the initial offer of a drink, and makes her way over to Norah. She gives her a huge hug, places a long, narrow parcel wrapped in silver foil and red ribbon on the counter, and turns to Beth. Norah wonders if it's salad servers. For once, she's able to take the initiative with introductions.

Although Beth doesn't make the effort to rise out of her chair, Hilary shakes her hand, and they exchange pleasantries about Beth's visit and her plans for the next few days. At one point, Hilary takes a moment and whispers instructions for Norah to tuck the present away for later.

"It's for you. Open it when you are alone." Then she adds with a little smile, "If you happen to be alone."

The boys all seem to arrive at once. The noise on the stairs is deafening. All the clatter should inspire Alina to come up as well. Luc is a great host by any measure. He meets people. He remembers who they are, and introduces those who don't know one another. He even manages to worm a smile out of Dorothy Chipman, who walks in the door and declares she doesn't intend to stay, but has done her duty and shown up.

Norah does not feel like such a great hostess. She senses herself fading into the background, as if she's sliding down into a hole of her own making. She has to focus and deal with her guests. People are eating. They're enjoying the food, and talking to one another. Everyone has met Beth and Alina. She has a great visit with Marcy, who's expecting a baby and over the moon about the experience.

A little tinkle of glasses. Norah looks up from her conversation with Alina, and sees Luc as he tries to get everyone's attention. "Thank you all for coming. Norah, where are you? Oh, there you are. Come and stand here by me while we thank our guests and make our announcement."

Norah heaves yet another sigh and goes over to stand by Luc, who puts a possessive arm around her waist. *What's he talking about and why is he thanking her guests?* "This will be the last time this little spot will hold a party for Norah. I have decided we will buy a place in Outremont together. She is going to help me run my restaurants. We are going to have a wonderful time." He raises his free arm high in the air, saluting the room with his wine.

Norah cannot prevent the look of total surprise crossing her face for all to see. There's a hushed silence in the room. She recovers, pats Luc's arm, and smiles with feigned indulgence, she hopes looks authentic. "Speculation, I'm afraid. All speculation. It appears my friend and I need to talk things over.

Who knows what the future holds? Now, can I get anyone another glass of wine, and who would like me to put the kettle on?"

She moves across the floor to the kitchen alcove. She occupies herself with the kettle and the teapot as conversations in the room resume. Bertrand is beside her in an instant. "Are you leaving?" The words are soft by her ear.

"No," she sighs with quiet resignation. "It appears I may have a pushy boyfriend who thinks he can make unilateral decisions about my life. It'll take more than crab tarts with cranberry to persuade me to leave my job." She looks him in the eye. "I hope that's okay with you."

Bertrand's smile lights up his whole face and he squeezes her shoulder. "I am so glad to hear you say that, Norah. Hilary and I want you to have a bit more responsibility, and we would be lost without your help. I think, in the fall, you will need to hire yourself an assistant."

A few minutes later, Norah leans down to whisper in Beth's ear. "Don't go. I would like you and Alina to stay after the catering is cleared away, and Luc leaves. Can you remain?"

"Just try and get me out of this chair," Beth replies without moving her head to look at Norah. She wiggles her chiffoned bum further down into the seat for emphasis, just as Joy approaches to say goodbye.

Norah wanders over to where Alina is sitting on the window seat visiting with Marcy, who gets up to try and convince Dan it's time to go. "Stay put, if you can, Alina. I want Luc to have to leave because you and Beth won't go."

"No problem, Norah. More tea." She holds up her empty cup. Norah smiles to herself, as she plugs in the kettle, yet again.

After everybody makes their way out, the caterers start to clean up the mess by piling everything in boxes for transport back to the bistro. Luc hints, subtlety aside, about staying, but Beth and Alina make no move to leave. After a couple of futile attempts, Norah suggests Luc call her tomorrow. She will entertain her friends and they will walk Beth back to her hotel later in the evening. He has no choice but to make his departure, although his annoyance begins to seep through his impeccable French manners.

By 8:30 PM, the three women sit together with a fresh pot of chamomile tea, and Norah points out the elephant in the room. "It appears Luc thinks I'm going to leave my life and jump into his without as much as a discussion."

"He's very well off." Beth's remark is blunt. "It seems he would like to have you for a partner in life and business." She wiggles around in the chair to settle herself. Ivy has managed to crawl onto her lap. Norah is on the floor while Alina perches on the edge of the couch. She has said nothing, so far.

Norah opens her mouth to reply but Alina, with unanticipated force, butts in. "He is a male chauvinist pig! He wants you to do whatever he says. He thinks, just because he is a successful businessman, you will fall at his feet and be grateful for his crumbs. You are better than this."

Norah looks over and smiles. Her eyes twinkle as she admonishes her friend. "So tell us what you really think, girl!"

Beth throws her head back and laughs until tears cut a trail through her expertly applied make-up. "I love a woman who says it like it is! Bravo." Perhaps the two old barnyard cats will get along after all. "As for you, my girl, I think you have a problem. I bet this guy will be hard to dump." There's a certain element of caution in her tone.

Alina and Norah walk Beth back to her hotel later in the evening. It's a gorgeous night, and it feels like everyone in the city is out wandering about. Although the offer is there, neither woman needs more tea as they leave Beth, and Ivy leads them home at the end of her leash. As they enter the building, Alina turns to lock the outside door. "Do you expect him back?" She pauses before turning the bolt.

"No, no. Let's lock up." Norah sighs as they walk up the wide stairs together.

Much later, after the bistro has closed, Luc turns the knob on the outside door of Norah's building only to discover it locked. He knocks. Nothing. He rings the little black bell just below the N. Clarke, hand written by Josef. Nothing. He backs out on to the sidewalk, looks up at her alcove window, and calls her name. The apartment is dark with no sign of life. After a full five minutes of knocking and calling, he turns to leave while looking over his shoulder and up at her window one last time.

Upstairs, Norah sits tucked in behind the curtain, looking down on the street below. She sees him try the door. She lets the bell ring. She hears him shout out her name, in the accent she has come to love. She doesn't move, except for rhythmically sliding her hand down the warm little body of Ivy snuggled beside her.

He'll call tomorrow and she will deal with him then. Tears creep, unattended, from the corners of her deep green eyes.

Chapter 20

The paper feels smooth and rich in her hands. She hates to destroy the mystery and anticipation by opening the pretty silver package given to her by Hilary the other night. She peels away the layers, and discovers a name plaque ready to be installed on the door of her small office just next to Bertrand, on the main floor of the auction house. Underneath, it says "Manager" in white relief against a brown wood grain background.

The Le Blancs are making their intentions clear to Norah. She is part of the family and they want her to stay. She's grateful. It would be tougher to turn her back on someone like Luc if she wasn't happy in her current situation.

Luc is difficult. He is mad about Norah, unable to understand why she doesn't want to live with him and pursue his business interests by his side. He offers to drive her home to Prestonburg, in the Jaguar, so he can meet her parents. He offers marriage before living together. He gets nowhere.

Norah stands her ground. She's done. It takes months before he stops calling altogether. She hears a rumour that the neighbourhood bistro has been sold, but she never goes back to the quaint little restaurant.

* * * *

Sam, as has been his habit since they first separated, still calls and sends cards. The cards show up for her birthday, and at Christmas. He always calls on their wedding anniversary though he didn't acknowledge any of this when they were married. The phone will ring very late on some Friday or Saturday night.

If it's after 11:00 PM, Norah can be almost certain it's Sam. His voice will be slurred, and he'll complain about his life and how he wishes they were still married, inviting her to Toronto for a visit so she can meet his friends. She

179

listens. She declines. She shares very little of her personal life—struggles, or successes. She knows he only calls when he's drinking and she never considers the contact more than a mild irritation.

Norah's world consists of work and friendships. Although able to afford substantially more than the studio apartment on Rue de la Montagne, she stays put following Alina's example. Josef is a kind and considerate landlord. The location is ideal and the rent reasonable. Both women feel safe and secure—no small feat in the middle of Montreal during this time.

Both her role and her responsibilities have expanded since she first started with Le Blanc and White. Bertrand, although still involved at a macro level, has turned over most of the management duties to Norah. Phil, along with Dan and Jean Pierre, remain on staff, but the cranky Dorothy has long gone. Norah was thankful when Dorothy made it clear to everyone she was taking a government position in order to get more benefits. Norah hired a young man straight out of community college to replace her. He shows enormous promise.

Frederick Zuckerman, born and brought up in Montreal, is twenty-two years old and prefers to be called Freddie. As Bertrand and Norah's Administrative Assistant, he brings a fresh new dynamic to the auction house. He's funny, easy going, and efficient in the extreme—the polar opposite of Dorothy. He has an uncanny way of anticipating next moves of those around him, and always seems on top of everything. His olive skin, his skinny build, and his flirty attitude have made him a hit with all the staff from the time of his interview.

No one, including Bertrand, misses Dorothy Chipman.

Norah, with calculated and measured steps, lets go of her role as appraiser and assessor. She turns over much of this work to various staff members who have expressed an interest in picking up the slack. Just like Bertrand used to do, she keeps her hand in by double-checking at every level of the process. The reputation of the business is uppermost in her mind. To this end, Norah has managed to improve her French. More than half of their clients, both sellers and buyers, are Francophone. Norah's biggest challenge has been to develop competent communication skills in French.

As she picks up the reins from Bertrand, she decides she's reached a point where she has the nerve to ask her boss and mentor about the elusive "White" on the masthead. It would not look good if a client asked for Mr. White and she had no idea what to say. "I've never learned anything about your partner, Bertrand. Did something happen to him a long time ago?"

Bertrand leans back in his office chair, sips coffee, and gives his very capable manager an indulgent smile. "You have not figured it out? I am surprised no one has spilled the beans. I expect Phil knows the answer to your question." He is evasive, but in a teasing kind of way. "There is no Mr. White or Mrs. White at all, unless you want to count Hilary and me. Never was. I chose the name to match my own so the public would think we were a company with both English and French owners."

He's laughing now. "We have never been labeled a French auction house or an English auction house. We have always been a Montreal auction house. My deception has worked all these years. It's been pretty good for business, don't you think?" He looks at her over his reading glasses.

Norah is taken aback. She always thought White was dead, or in a nursing home or something, and that the Le Blancs just kept the name for continuity. She smiles at her old friend and boss. "You are a scoundrel. Fooling the public all these years! Has no one ever asked to work with White? What do you tell them?"

"It has never been a problem." He takes another sip of coffee. "The name gives the business balance. It is everything the public wants."

****

Norah expands her horizons as she continues in the auction business. Often asked to lecture in the Sociology Department at McGill, she's become a regular guest for course topics about modern cultural anthropology, and has been seriously bitten by the teaching bug. She loves preparing and researching for a lecture. She likes meeting with the students. Those who come to her classes are not bound by any criteria. They attend out of interest, and it has become a very rewarding experience for her.

As time goes by, she starts to explore the possibility of going back to school to obtain a PhD, and start a teaching career. By 1997, she's examining programs with a genuine desire to move forward. At thirty-four, she wants to make a change to a more academic setting, to return to her roots, to take a chance on herself.

It is both painful and complicated to even contemplate leaving the comfort and security of Le Blanc and White for an undetermined and unpredictable future. Could it be almost twelve years since she looked through the plate glass entry doors into the dimly lit art deco theatre foyer she would come to think of as her second home?

After being accepted into the PhD program at her old alma mater, Callwood College, and managing to land a teaching assistant role with an Anthropology professor, she prepares to tell Bertrand and the rest of the auction house staff, of her plans to leave her position and return to Callwood Bay.

It is June, 1998, and Norah waits in her office for Bertrand to arrive. He most often appears mid-morning. The letter is composed. The formality of the situation has been addressed. The difficulty will be telling this man, who has become like another father to her, of her intentions to leave in two months and move back to the east coast. She's nervous.

Ivy, the fur around her muzzle white with age, is curled up in her basket just under Norah's desk. Ivy doesn't bother pattering about after her person now. She is content to sleep in her tiny bed, or stretch out on the cool tile if temperatures warrant. She's an old dog and Norah dreads the day a decision will have to be made. She hears Bertrand enter his office. She heaves a sigh and lifts herself out of the office chair, rolling it backwards as she leans down to speak to Ivy in a soft voice before leaving the room. "I'll be right back. You stay put." The little dog opens her eyes just enough to see Norah, and responds to the pat by closing them again.

Norah taps on the doorframe of her boss' office. He looks up and she's greeted as always, with a smile of welcome. They have had a connection from the beginning, based on respect and a mutual love of the business. This makes her task that much harder.

"Come in. Come in. Everything okay?" His voice sounds anxious. She knows the envelope in her hand will not go unnoticed as she steps into the inner sanctum and takes a seat. "What are we up to today?" His attempt to sound cheerful has a hollow echo, despite his obvious efforts. The jig is up. He's figured it out already.

Norah leans over and smiles, although her eyes are sad as she places the envelope in front of him. "No need to mince words, Bertrand. This is my resignation." She rushes on as she sees the look of pain on her dear friend's face. "I've been accepted to do my PhD at Callwood College. I'm going to teach, I hope." She adds the last bit, despite her ultimate confidence everything will, in fact, happen exactly as she wants. "You and Hilary have been so good to me, Bertrand. Do you know it's been twelve years since I started with you? I don't think I could ever have gotten through my divorce, if it hadn't been for you. As a matter of fact, I'm not sure I could have gotten through my master's, if it hadn't been for you. I'll never be able to express my gratitude."

The rush comes to an abrupt halt. Her eyes are soft and moist. "You know I could never thank-you enough for all you've done for me." She remains leaning forward, looking her boss in the eye; waiting for a response she fears isn't going to come.

Ever stoic, and ever the gentleman, Bertrand smiles although his face is drawn when he looks at Norah. "Congratulations, my dear. I suspected as much. Hilary and I have often thought you could run this place without me now, but we haven't been eager to retire just yet. We know you want more." He shakes his head as he continues. "I just don't know what it will be like without you. You have left your mark on Le Blanc and White. Have you told any of the staff?"

"Of course not!" Norah is a bit shocked he would think of her jumping the gun in such a fashion. "I haven't even told my parents yet, or given notice to Josef! I wanted us to be okay, first." Her voice is quieter as she utters this last part.

"When do you want to leave?" She knows he wants to hear the details from her.

"Two months. Early August. It will give me time to get settled in Callwood Bay before the fall term. I have to find a place to live where dogs are allowed." On cue, Ivy wanders out of Norah's office and into Bertrand's. She trudges over to the cookie drawer for her obligatory treat, coupled with a pat.

Bertrand looks up. "Hilary and I will have a little send-off for you. We'll decide on the details later. Have Freddie send a memo to all the staff and we will go from there." He gives her a moist-eyed smile that clearly says he knows her well enough not to even try and talk her out of this decision.

It's a big change for everyone. The staff flutter around. They wish her luck and wonder why she would ever leave such a great job to go back to school. Alina supports Norah's goal of entering the world of academia, but states with all too familiar bluntness that Norah should go back to McGill and stay put in her familiar surroundings.

Norah knows her father is happy to think of her near home. He wants to assist with the move. Her mother can't help but express her nervousness. What if she can't get a teaching position after investing in a PhD? What then? Norah responds with a laugh. She could always move home and run Clarkes Antiques and Collectibles. Beth is suspicious. Is Norah running from something? Is she involved with someone else like Luc, and has to move in order to get away? Sam is aghast. She will be so far away, making it hard for him to visit. *Visit?* He's never visited—yet another Forrest Sampson pipe dream.

Austin becomes Mr. Mover and Mr. Real Estate agent all rolled into one. He makes plans to rent a truck and come to Montreal. He spends days in Callwood Bay until he secures the perfect rental for his daughter. He pays an extra month's rent to secure the property, and calls her to tell her all about it.

"Dad. Slow down. I'm having trouble understanding you. Tell me again. All I got was how this place is two blocks from campus, and I can run home for lunch. What else?"

Austin inhales in what is a familiar, albeit fruitless, attempt to curb his excitement. "Norah, this is one of four apartments in a converted turn-of-the-century mansion just off the main drag. It's owned by a local contractor who fixes houses and sells them, but he rents this one out. Yours is on the main floor. You go in the front entrance and the door is on the right. The living room is where the old front parlour would have been. The kitchen is just behind and there's an alcove for a table. There's a bedroom with an attached bath and another little room you could use as a spare, storage, or as an office. The ceilings are high. The windows are new, and the floors are wood. You can have Ivy." He pauses to take a breath.

"The other three apartments are rented, all to professors and graduate students. There's one married couple and two singles. Since we have it a month early, I thought I would go ahead and paint. He said he'd buy the paint if we do it. Do you want off white walls, or something else?"

Norah is not sure whether to laugh or cry. It's been a very long time since she needed to play parent to her father, trying to curb his unbridled enthusiasm about one thing or another, but she gets back in the swing of things without much trouble. "Dad. Let's wait on the paint until I get there." Her eyes travel over the soft biscuit walls of her studio apartment. There's much she will miss. "I'll have almost a month before school starts, so we'll have lots of time.

I'll let you pick me out an apartment, sight unseen, but I just can't pick paint colours over the phone." Her voice is indulgent and her father responds by recognizing that it's obviously time to stand down.

"Okay, okay, but I want to help you."

"And Mom's reaction to you spending all your time in Callwood Bay?"

A short silence ensues. "She's excited you're moving closer to home, too, Norah. She just worries."

Chapter 21

Norah, the newly minted PhD candidate, and her father arrive in Callwood Bay on a beautiful summer afternoon the second week of August. The leaves on the maple trees are as big as saucers, and drape over the tiny side streets, caressing the truck as it creeps toward their destination. Ivy is curled up on the bench seat between Austin and Norah. As they approach the house, a familiar form rises up, with a mixture of heavy reluctance and anxious anticipation, from the old granite stone called a front step. As if she's waited to be sure, she starts to wave a fleshy arm at the approaching rental truck. There seems to be an unusually large number of cars parked on the street. The small front-yard parking lot—asphalt where grass once thrived—has been rendered empty by one Miss Beth Hanley, who must have approached the residents and convinced them to move their vehicles. Known for her organizational skills in Prestonburg, she was obviously determined to unleash them on an unsuspecting Callwood Bay.

Between the three of them, they get the truck unloaded. There isn't much. Norah has her art deco chrome kitchen set, her hide-a-bed, and Beth's version of the most comfortable chair in the world, her kitchen stuff, the end tables given to her by Bertrand, and the gift given to her by everyone at work when she left—an original piece of art done by Hilary Le Blanc. She created the acrylic painting of the landscape of Rue de la Montagne, she said, so Norah would never forget them. Norah could look at it for hours, getting lost in the buildings and dissolving into the neighbourhood. All that remains are her clothes and books. Although Norah has a reputation as an expert when it comes to collecting, she, herself, remains a minimalist.

Of course, Beth has brought supper, including all the dishes and silverware, so Norah doesn't have to start unpacking right away. The apartment has been cleaned until it sparkles. The phone is scheduled to be installed the next day,

187

and the landlord will be by later on. The truck will be returned tomorrow, and Austin will be back in a couple of days. They need to shop for paint, a real bed, and for the first time in her life, Norah wants to buy a car, or maybe a truck. Living with easy access to public transit all these years, she now finds herself excited about the idea of owning a vehicle.

So after they leave, and her new landlord, a rather gruff and untidy man named Leo, has come and gone, Norah searches out the box of linens, makes up her couch bed and falls asleep exhausted but happy, with Ivy tucked in beside her. Her new life has started.

****

August flashes by in a blur of painting, Prestonburg, parents, and preparation. With early September coming into focus, Norah must meet several professors, her adviser, and her students. She must outline her plan of expanding her master's thesis into a doctoral dissertation. Life is now diametrically opposed to the reliable routine that was work at the auction house. She misses the structure.

The Victorian four-plex houses an eclectic mix of inhabitants. Eva and Bennett Whitelaw occupy the unit across the hall from Norah, on the main floor. They're English professors and appear, at first meeting, to be quite proper and reserved. They've exchanged pleasantries in the foyer, but nothing further. Above Norah resides the black sheep of the building—as Norah has come to think of her. Audrey Pippins is a Fine Arts graduate student, doing her master's in printmaking. She is in a perpetual state of messy, paint-covered, and complete disarray from her untidy and knotted hair to her jeans with no knees. Audrey is noisy—both in her heavy tread on the stairs, and in her musical taste. Irwin Fairbanks lives above the Whitelaw's and they lucked out in the upstairs neighbour department. He appears older than the average graduate student. He's doing a master's in Commerce and Norah has never seen him without a jacket of some description, and a tie.

Much to her surprise, just before the fall semester gets into full swing, she gets invited to a small open house gathering at the Whitelaw's. Eva suggests Norah and her neighbours will be able to get to know each other a bit better than the simple cordiality of saying hello in the hall. In addition, some of their English Department cohorts will pop by, as is the tradition every September.

Norah, with a bottle of German white wine in hand, crosses the hall after she hears welcoming noises coming from Eva. Not wanting to hover at her peephole for fear they'll sense her breathing, she can't determine if this is Irwin from upstairs or someone else. In any event, she won't be the first arrival, so, after insuring Ivy is settled, off she goes.

The Whitelaw apartment is almost the mirror image of Norah's, but looks much smaller. It's designed á la Sherlock Holmes, with floor to ceiling bookshelves and faded tapestry furniture, befitting the architectural setting. The curtains are heavy green brocade with floppy gold tassels holding them back, exposing aged and discoloured sheers instead of the front yard outside. This choice in window treatment subdues the whole room into a vague imitation of a Gothic movie set. Eva leads Norah into the centre of the space, acknowledges her husband and introduces her guest to the other occupant, the man Norah heard arrive earlier.

"This," she exudes with a flourish of her seasonally tinted caftan draped arm, "is our new neighbour, Norah Clarke. Norah, this is our colleague, Parker Dewhurst. Dr. Parker Dewhurst to be precise."

Parker, seated in a decrepit-looking, turn-of-the-century rosewood slipper chair, rises with an outstretched hand. "It's always nice to meet a new neighbour of the Whitelaws. People seem to come and go in here, don't they?" He glances back at Eva.

He's tall, much taller than Norah, and appears to unfold as he gets up from the very low piece of furniture. He's dressed in the uniform of professors—blue jeans, a corduroy blazer, and a cotton plaid shirt. His greying brown hair is thinning on top, but hangs down to his shoulders nonetheless. His face is thoughtful and he tilts his head a tiny bit while giving Norah a quizzical look.

She responds without a question. "Here to do my PhD in Cultural Anthropology. I study collecting. I'm an alumnus. Did my undergraduate degree here. Graduated in 1985. Been in Montreal ever since. Did my master's at McGill." *What is the matter with me?* She's rambling, and it's as if she's forgotten how to construct a complete sentence. She feels compelled to fill the air with words.

Parker continues to look at her in the same way. Thank God, the doorbell sounds and Eva welcomes Audrey and Irwin who seem to arrive together. Bennett hasn't moved from the makeshift bar in the corner, laid out with an assortment of bottles, glasses, and mix. Norah takes advantage of Eva's current preoccupation, to slide over toward Bennett, submit her offering, and accept a glass of white wine in exchange.

Audrey is a character, and Norah likes her the moment they meet. She's dressed as if ready to dash off to her studio—torn jeans, T-shirt stained with paint plus yesterday's lunch, and a sweater too big that has seen much better days. Her hair is long and a burnt-brown shade with steaks of silver giving it a unique and sandy hue. Norah has never seen her when it wasn't tied back into a loose ponytail with bits escaping at the sides. Tonight is no different.

The young artist seems to live to embarrass Irwin, taking every opportunity to incorporate a sexual innuendo into the conversation. This makes him blush and causes her to dissolve into peals of laughter. They are quite the comedy team. Irwin doesn't drink anything but soda, while Audrey consumes whatever is passed in her direction. She manages to get quite tipsy, but it becomes obvious to Norah that Irwin has her back. He never takes his deep-set and brooding eyes off her.

Other members of the English faculty arrive for a glass of wine, introductions, and conversations about the upcoming year. People come and go. After much wine, Audrey stumbles upstairs with Irwin at her elbow. Norah's keen sense of observation notices only one door close. Parker whispers in Norah's ear. "May I walk you home?"

Startled, she tries not to show it, and laughs. "I can tell you're a man of big commitments. I think I can find my way." She stops for a second and thinks of Ivy. She would love to get to know Parker a bit better. "On second thought, my dog will need a little walk. You're welcome to join us." They make their goodbyes.

Parker stands on the Whitelaw's threshold and chats while Norah unlocks her door and steps inside to retrieve Ivy, asleep on the couch without a care in the world. Dog under her arm and leash in hand, she returns to the hall where she finds Parker thanking Eva one more time. Off they go, down the front steps and onto the sidewalk, into a velvety aubergine evening. There's not a breath of wind and the maples create an eerie canopy over their heads.

Ivy takes her time. They meander. Parker asks Norah about her work and her time in Montreal. She asks him about his classes and his specialty— *Chaucer, for God's sake!* The walk goes on longer than Ivy is used to, as they are obviously enjoying each other's company. They touch shoulders a little bit, picking their way over uneven sidewalks under dim streetlights. Norah senses him close to her. As her building comes back into sight, Parker heaves a great sigh.

"Must go home. My wife wasn't feeling great tonight, so she stayed behind. Don't want to be too tardy now, do I?" He looks at Norah. His eyes search for hers in the dark. "I've had a wonderful evening. It was tremendous to meet you." He reaches out to touch her shoulder. She takes a short but purposeful step back, steadying imperceptibly with her heel, so as not to unbalance herself.

"Thanks for the company. Ivy, especially, appreciated the long walk tonight." She picks up her dog and steps into the foyer, turning around for just a moment. "It was nice meeting you, Parker. I hope your wife is better soon."

* * * *

As a PhD candidate in Cultural Anthropology, Norah is responsible to Dr. Leslie Forsythe, who was kind enough to take Norah on as her student. There are no classes in this program. Norah is expected to write and defend a thesis, which is somewhat akin to writing a book. The thesis will be an extension of the work she did for her master's degree, which is the norm in most cases. In addition, she'll provide Dr. Forsythe with teaching assistance. This could mean almost anything. Their initial meeting will set the stage for the upcoming three-plus years.

Norah is aware of first impressions. She dressed with care in soft brown chinos, belted at the waist. Her top is a matching patterned shirt, and she threw on her short leather jacket to ward off the fall's early morning chill. She has already sent Dr. Forsythe her master's thesis and research proposal. Her knock is crisp and no nonsense on the paint-chipped, paneled door. After hearing the command to enter, she turns the loose tortoise shell doorknob

Norah finds herself standing in a very austere space indeed, facing her new mentor straight on. It's a stark and cold room illuminated by harsh fluorescent lights overhead. The old hardwood is bare and dusty, as are the floor-to-ceiling bookshelves that cover one wall. Dr. Forsythe sits, protected, behind an over-sized table serving as a desk and a barrier between her and anyone who dares enter. The table is covered with books and papers. A huge and somewhat out-dated computer sits on the desk, dusty and looking like it's seldom used.

Leslie Forsythe is a diminutive woman. She looks miniaturized, sitting behind the big table, in a chair much too low for her petite stature. Her hair is streaked with silver and black, cut in a style looking like a bowl was used to create the effect. She wears what seems to Norah to be a house dress from the 1960s, and an orange cable-knit cardigan—too big and fraying at the cuffs.

Approaching the desk, Norah stretches out her arm. The professor does not rise, but returns the favour and shakes Norah hand. "I'm Norah Clarke, Dr. Forsythe. We finally get to meet in person." Norah attempts to sound enthusiastic, although her intuition is telling her she should feel otherwise. She has met a lot of people in her time. This is one very cold fish.

"Sit down. No need to give me more stuff. I already have what you sent to me here, someplace." She looks at the portfolio still in the crook of Norah's arm while riffling through the disorganized mounds on the desk. Norah drops into the red plastic stacking chair opposite. It feels like a waiting room chair at the dentist's.

Dr. Forsythe remains focused on rustling as she continues. "I want to get a few things straight. Number One. We don't need to spend a lot of time visiting and chatting. I hate that. I'll read your work when you can provide me with a substantial amount, say twenty-five percent. Number Two. I have two introductory courses for you to teach. You said you had done some teaching, so they're yours. The first is Introduction to Cultural Anthropology, and there are fifty-two students. The second is a seminar on Anthropological Theory. There are twenty students. About half drop out by Christmas. The course material is over there." She points to a small table by the door. "One other thing—likely the most important. There's grant money available for your teaching. You can go visit HR after we're through here, and they can give you all the details. Is there anything else?"

Her tone is dismissive. Norah very much wants to visit and chat, but has gotten the message loud and clear. She makes the appropriate responses, saying she'll get the undergraduate schedule and looks forward to the opportunity; it has been nice to meet after corresponding for so long. This takes place while she reaches for the texts and papers waiting for her on the way out.

Norah navigates through the dim and dusty halls of the Sarah McCall Sociology Building. She then crosses the picture-book campus dotted with red brick buildings of various vintages, to Human Resources. She reflects on her first meeting with Dr. Leslie Forsythe who presents herself as a challenging person if Norah expects any kind of relationship. On the bright side, there will be independence and a couple of classes to teach. She's smiling all the way up to her laughing eyes as she approaches HR. The pay won't be much, but who cares? She would work for nothing, in order to be in this place at this time.

As it turns out, her payment for teaching the two courses will be exchanged for all of her fees in the doctoral program. She was right. It isn't much when broken down to an hourly wage, especially when you consider office hours and assignment marking, but Norah is still thrilled. She's given a small office, around the corner from her supervisor. She gets down to business, becoming familiar with course content and determining what will be needed to make her office a cozy home away from home.

Later in the evening, just as she's settled in following her walk with Ivy, Norah takes two phone calls. The first is from Sam. He'll be in Halifax just before Thanksgiving for a teachers' conference. He will stay an extra day if she'll do him the honour of having dinner with him. The second is from Parker. He's been working late and wonders if she's completed her evening walk with Ivy. If not, he would like to come over and go with her, before calling it a day.

Norah's better judgment tells her to refuse the invitations without any remorse, but much to her own surprise, she accepts them both. She will do course prep in her new office tomorrow.

Parker turns up at the front door within minutes. She has just enough time to apply a little eyeliner and roust Ivy, who has already settled in for the night, when the buzzer rings. Always up for a walk, the little dog responds with enthusiastic wiggles and doggy murmurs to the sound of the leash coming out of the coat closet.

Norah can't believe how her heart is racing. This is ridiculous. The man is married, and he just wants to go for a walk before going home. There are no sidewalks where he lives, and darkness drops in with sudden precision this time of year, so it would be dangerous for him to trudge along the side of the road at home. A little voice in the back of her mind responds: *Yeah, right*.

Off they go. It's colder than earlier in the evening and Norah is thankful for her heavy sweater. Parker hasn't said much, just how nice it is to see her again. He gave Ivy a casual, non-committal, not-an-actual-dog-person, kind of pat and held the old front door for her as they left. She tries to make conversation and starts by asking him if he knows Leslie Forsythe. He does, but shares nothing beyond the fact he thinks she's capable.

They walk in silence for a couple of minutes and, without a whole lot of warning, his leather-clad arm is around her shoulder. She looks up at him. His face, difficult to read through the inky shadows created by the soft streetlights, seems poised for her reaction.

She doesn't move away. She likes this man a lot and is comfortable in his company. Without too much guilty deliberation, she could invite him home for the night, but getting wrapped up with a married man would be more than a little complicated. "Parker, it's not that cold and you're married." His arm stays where it is.

"Being married is just a legal entanglement for me, Norah. Don't you feel we have something? I can almost taste it when we're together. I could tell from the minute we met at the Whitelaw party. I couldn't wait to see you again." Now he's dribbling words all over the place, just like she did when they first met. "You've been divorced. You know how these things go."

Now, how would he know that? "You're not divorced, Parker. You're not even separated. You have a home with your wife." She takes a sideways step closer to the edge of the sidewalk, and he moves his arm. "I wish circumstances were different, my friend, but I just can't do this. Life has enough complications." She hates herself, as she hears her voice float on the crisp evening air.

They stop. Parker turns to her and holds her face in his hands. He bends down and kisses her more deeply than she has been kissed in a very long time. "We could be good together. Just think about it." Walking back to the house in silence, Norah wonders if having boundaries is all it's cracked up to be.

＊＊＊＊

Eva dog-sits Ivy. It's a rare occurrence, but driving into the city for supper and returning late in the evening requires arrangements for the little dog, which is now at the ripe old age of thirteen. Eva has made it abundantly clear she likes to go back and forth between the two apartments, sitting with Ivy while doing paperwork, or taking her for walks and returning to Norah's.

Ivy has always managed to make her own friends and seems content to be watched by their pet-loving neighbour.

She's meeting Sam at Embers, a beautiful restaurant near the waterfront, located in a converted fire station from the 1950s. As she takes the hour-long drive to the city in her 1995 Jeep Wrangler, a purchase her parents found both disturbing and confusing, Norah wonders if she's doing the right thing. She hasn't seen Sam in eleven years. Other than the slurred phone calls for her birthday, their anniversary and near Christmas, she never hears from him. Her contribution to the relationship is cards—one at Christmas and one for his birthday. She tries to get very funny cards. There is no other contact on her part other than ensuring he knows her address and phone number when they change.

Keeping casual track of one another has been important to both of them over the years. She isn't sure why.

Norah enters the subdued atmosphere of the restaurant, wishing for a mirror to check and see if she looks as good as she possibly can. It's been awhile, after all, and she continues to want Sam to think she's happy and on top of everything, regardless of what the truth might be. She sees him sitting up on the second level, in the back, looking out through the palladium windows toward the harbour. He's holding the mandatory whiskey straight up over ice. He looks tired and morose, but Norah feels a teachers' conference might inspire such a look. She nods to the maître d', and casts her gaze toward Sam. He leads her up to the table. The server appears at her elbow and offers her a drink. It will be herbal tea tonight, as she anticipates a long and dark drive back to Callwood Bay after supper.

Sam stands. He looks thin and his smile reminds Norah of watery broth. His skin is pale, and he has a lot less hair than when they were married. She leans over and air kisses the side of his face, removing her leather jacket as she prepares to sit. He remains silent.

"Great to see you, Sam. Isn't this a beautiful spot? I thought you'd like it here."

"The restaurant is perfect, Norah. You look fabulous." He sounds wistful.

Wearing black silk pants and a grey-and-white, stripped sweater, the red leather jacket she just removed draws attention to her cranberry crystal drop earrings. Her hair is shorter than before, and stuck behind one ear. For whatever the reason, and it shouldn't matter, she's pleased he has said this, and is pretty confident she does look good.

Conversation is stilted. Norah is determined not to try and pepper the air with words just to keep the space between them occupied. She came to supper because he asked. If he has a motive, he'll have to spit it out soon. She's already anxious to get back on the road, and their meal of crab cakes coupled with a divine salad smothered in Dijon mustard dressing, is just arriving. As she digs in, the awaited shoe drops.

"Kevin died a month ago. I wanted to tell you in person." He has not touched the food and is on his third drink. The muscles in his face have started their familiar sag, but twitch a little as he tries to control his emotions.

Norah is stunned. "Sam, I am so sorry! Why didn't you call me? What happened?" She puts down her fork, leans across the table and pats a shaking hand. Kevin and Sam had been an item for a couple of years. She was under the distinct impression they were going to buy a house together. During one of their phone calls, Sam mentioned meeting Kevin's family and how happy the two of them were. He indicated he wasn't drinking as much. Kevin was having a positive influence.

"It was so damned fast. He had cancer. He hid it from me for a long time, I guess. Once he went into hospital, he went downhill in no time. He was only hospitalized for a week." By this time, the tears are running down his cheeks. "I wanted to tell you in person. I wanted you to know."

The remainder of their time together is spent discussing Kevin, the plans the two men had made, and the problems Sam is having with Kevin's family as, apparently, they want items Sam feels should be his. Death can be complicated.

They hug goodbye. Sam will remain at Embers for one last drink. Norah is anxious to be gone. He'll soon be over the edge, and the conversation is getting garbled, driven by the booze. The trip home is uneventful on this clear and cool fall night. As the Thanksgiving long weekend looms ahead of her, and she navigates her little truck back down the shore, Norah thinks about everything she feels Sam did not say.

She wonders about Kevin's diagnosis, and Sam's vagueness. She wonders about AIDS and her ex-husband's health. She thinks there's a good chance she will not see him again.

Chapter 22

Ivy doesn't travel to the office with Norah as she once did in Montreal. In the winter of 1999, she reaches the ripe old age of fourteen. As current gerontological theory purports, the sphere of her influence has become significantly reduced as she's gotten older.

Norah believes that Ivy's happiest times are when Norah works at home. She settles into the crook of her person's arm, nose snuggled into the elbow of a favourite sweater Norah may be wearing. She relaxes into deep sleep like only a cradled and well-loved dog can do.

It is one of these occasions, as the sound of Leonard Cohen drifts like wisps of smoky velvet through the apartment, and Norah reads a paper about chat rooms on the Internet and how this type of introduction has changed the sociology of dating, that Ivy chooses to take her very last breath. It's a few moments, as Norah continues to read, before she's distracted by the lack of rhythmic breathing against her chest. She gets up with great care, holding Ivy as she retrieves her blanket from the dog bed in the corner.

Without a sound and with tears streaming, Norah wraps the little dog in her blanket of soft white velour sprinkled with a pattern of black paw prints, and positions her on the couch, in the corner beside her. Tomorrow, she will take Ivy to the vet for cremation. Tomorrow, she will tell Ivy's friends—Austin and Paige, Beth, the Whitelaws, the Le Blancs. Ivy has been her companion through thick and thin. Tomorrow.

* * * *

After Ivy's death, Norah throws herself into her work with increased vigour, if that's possible. She hates to go home to an empty apartment.

This proves fortuitous, as Dr. Forsythe is becoming a problem and perhaps even a liability for Norah as a doctoral candidate. She oftentimes leaves Norah phone messages, instructing her to conduct seminars with the graduate class because she isn't coming in. She appears to have little or no interest in her own work, Norah and her work, her students and their work, or anything else. Her office is bereft of accoutrements meant to support productivity. The desk is mounded with papers that seem locked in position for days. Her computer remains a dead body, laid out, and dust covered. Her answering machine is always at capacity.

Norah, as focused and driven academically as she happens to be, can get along just fine with minimal input from this potentially troubled or terribly irresponsible woman. Nonetheless, she feels ignored and worries about defending a thesis to other professors in the Anthropology and Sociology Departments when her advisor's feedback has been, for the most part, nonexistent. Norah finds it challenging to determine the exact rules of engagement, or even if she's on an acceptable academic track.

Past experience proves advantageous here as Norah is almost certain Dr. Forsythe is drinking and that her affliction is getting out of hand. On the rare occasion when she actually turns up in her office, she's unkempt and puffy looking. Her skin has a Sam-like cast about it. She is snarly as a bear and nothing interests her. She moves a few papers around, listens to some voice messages, and then leaves without a word.

Norah chugs along with her undergraduates and her thesis work. She loves her two classes with the first- and second-year students. Stimulating interest in cultural anthropology is her primary goal, and she regales them with stories of extreme collectors she's met over the years. She tells them about Roland and Myrna Beauchemin who live in one of Montreal's less prestigious suburbs.

Norah tells how she approached their home after getting a referral from an employee at Le Blanc and White. The employee told her they spoke as if they were going to buy every piece offered at the auction house but then complained to all and sundry about the prices. They told everyone they had hundreds of pieces at home. That boasting resulted in the referral to Norah while she worked on her master's.

The couple are avid Carnival Glass collectors. They reported their collecting started in the late 1970s, and they bought every piece they could find, searching flea markets and garage sales. They accumulated hundreds of pieces and couldn't get enough. The one problem was that almost everything they found to buy had been reproduced, and was available at most department stores.

This very entertaining couple chose to collect in an education vacuum, never reading about their passion, and never learning how to identify the original pieces from the new. Norah shares her collecting wisdom: "Just because someone's grandmother owned it doesn't mean it's an antique. It could have been bought last Christmas brand new!" Her students love the stories, as she brings sociological theory to life.

Through engaging and funny tales like this, coupled with her obvious interest in her students, Norah becomes a popular doctoral candidate and official member of the teaching staff by the time the new millennium rolls around. With Dr. Forsythe's ongoing problems, Norah is asked to join the Anthropology/Sociology Department as a contracted lecturer in 2001, about a year before she defends her thesis.

Professor Forsythe abruptly departs, presumably to facilitate her attendance at a rehab. facility somewhere. Norah is advised she may move her office into the larger space around the corner, previously occupied by her adviser. During this time, Norah is busy preparing for her dissertation. The person who ends up coming to her rescue is Peter Swift. Likely due to the compelling scent of blackberry tea wafting down the hall, Peter starts taking a special interest in Norah and her predicament—the one where she has found herself writing and preparing to defend a thesis with no adviser to organize the process, and no one to hold her hand.

Peter takes on the job with little or no fanfare. He makes it clear that he likes her and thinks someone needs to step in or she'll find another position and it will almost certainly be the Department's loss.

He has little work to do in the way of mentorship. Norah is a leader in her discipline, but responds to his support and encouragement. His job is to navigate the minefield of presentations and readings, provide professorial input at different levels, and to host the big reveal. Norah will present and defend her work to a group of three Callwood College representatives and a fourth professor from an outside university, plus Peter, as her advisor. They must all have copies of her thesis in lots of time to read, ruminate and create questions. Peter will take care of everything related to her presentation, so she can continue to concentrate on compiling her work and teaching her classes. He becomes a friend in the process.

****

The date has been set and everything is in place. Each of the five figures who will sit around her dissertation table has been provided with the finished product in good time. Norah can do nothing, now, but count down the days and review her notes. At the crack of dawn on Tuesday, November 12, 2002, T. G. Norah Clarke turns the key and enters her office, she hopes for the next to last time, as a doctoral candidate.

Norah's dressed in more formal attire than usual for the occasion. She wears a black suit jacket and her mid-calf length biscuit suede skirt known for serving her so well in the years since living over Mademoiselle Flaubert's salon. She will be comfortable, at least. Peter almost bangs into her as he races up her left flank, rattling cups on a tray. He's on his way into the small meeting room and reports, with what breath he has remaining, tea and coffee are being made, the out-of-town reader has arrived, and he's got everything under control.

She smiles at him with genuine fondness, her eyes lighting up in the process. "Peter, you look more nervous than me. Can I help you with anything?

"Not a chance. You just compose yourself and come down when you're ready. I'll ply them with hot drinks and cookies." His smile is conspiratorial.

"Peter, I cannot believe you made cookies for my presentation!" Norah feigns being horrified. "You didn't have to pull out every stop."

Since his hands are full, he's prevented from flailing them about. Instead he rolls his head from side to side and laughs, obviously missing her sarcasm. "Are you kidding? I bought them, but the thought is there. Must keep them comfy. Now you know my strategy." He turns on his heel and struts down the hall, continuing to torture the poor cups that are probably chipped by now.

Norah enters the room a full ten minutes before she's scheduled to begin. Her notes are placed in order on the head table. She sets up the LCD projector and ensures her computer is ready to go. It's not long before the three local professors appear and Peter, still somewhat flustered, rises to make introductions. He acknowledges Dr. Brenda Strang, a professor in Indonesian Cultural Development from St. Augustine's in the city, first.

Dr. Strang's a mousy-looking woman, middle-aged, and preoccupied with her leather-bound agenda most of the time. Although requiring no formal introductions, he also presents Norah to Dr. Michael Burke, a professor in the Sociology Department, Dr. Mary Biggs, a Callwood Research Fellow in the Anthropology Department, and Dr. Sophia Bonnheim, a visiting professor from Germany who specializes in European Culture.

As Norah nods and speaks to each of her examiners, her thoughts drift momentarily to Alina. It would be nice to have her old friend at the table. She thinks Alina would be proud of her today.

Dr. Burke, in his mid-sixties and very formal, spends most of his time looking at the table. He's tall and elegant in Clark Gable fashion. Norah wonders if he's reviewing what he plans to ask her, or if he's just too shy to make eye contact.

Dr. Biggs is in her thirties. She's bird-like, with hawkish features and a piercing voice. Being a Research Fellow means she has a grant to work in the Department but does little in the way of teaching. She guest lectures on occasion. Few people know any details about her research.

Reminding Norah of Alina in many ways, Dr. Bonnheim is a large, deep-voiced woman with an abruptness that can be off-putting. She's managed to rub a lot of people the wrong way during her short tenure as a visiting professor, and Norah is more nervous of her than anyone else at the table. After they exchange nods and hellos, Peter explains how Norah will complete her presentation, they will have a ten-minute break, and then the floor will be open for questions.

With that, the endurance test called a dissertation defense begins.

Norah enjoys presenting and teaching. It shows. She's animated and relaxed. She doesn't read from prepared notes although they remain on the table as a guide—should she need them. She looks her examiners in the eye, leaving no one out. She talks to them about the culture of collecting in general, and the idea of extreme collecting in particular. There are the hoarders. There are those who focus on the mundane and those who must own every one of whatever they collect.

She shows them museum collections that have lost focus. She shares pictures of famous collections and amusing excuses for collections. She speaks about how it all starts and the consequences when it ends. Norah's research is not laboratory or literature based. It rises from a deep knowledge, extensive field experience, and a life surrounded by all things collectible in the eyes of particular personalities. Her work is considered qualitative, as opposed to quantitative. Her stories are funny, sad, and even bizarre. She opens up doors to a world few have explored. She captures her audience by creating word pictures and bringing her work to life. At the end, someone claps. This is significant in the dissertation world. She isn't sure who it is except it is not Peter, thankfully.

During the short break, the atmosphere in the room is electric. Her examiners are smiling, munching cookies and buzzing about her presentation. The questions begin before mouths are empty and bottoms are back into chairs.

"Tell us about your work in Montreal."

"Tell us about your family antique business."

"Do you think every collector, even the guarded, has the potential to become extreme?"

"Did you meet many hoarders during your research, and how did you deal with them?"

The questions are fun and easy for Norah. This has been her life for all of her thirty-nine years. As a mature student, these accomplished academics are treating her as an equal. She is thrilled at how the event is progressing.

After the questions are exhausted, Peter asks with polite formality, if she would mind leaving the room for a short time while they discuss her presentation. He requests that she sit in the chair provided in the hall. They will not be long. She may leave her equipment and paperwork on the table. They will call her in due course.

Norah is taken aback by this. She expected they would notify her of success or failure before day's end, but she thought she could at least go back to her office and relax. Sitting on a plastic chair in the hall for half an hour is not her idea of a good time.

It's a mere fifteen-minute wait, but to Norah it feels like forever. Peter opens the door and, for a split second, lets another conspiratorial smile brush his lips. "Come in. Come in, Norah." Once she's positioned back in front of the presentation table, he very formally steps forward and extends his hand. "On behalf of your Dissertation Examination Committee, we would like to congratulate you, Dr. Norah Clarke." His eyes are a tiny bit misty.

She takes Peter's clammy hand in hers and smiles at the professors as they stand and clap. There is a tiny lump in her throat. Michael Burke, to her surprise, is the one to tell her on behalf of the group, how much they all enjoyed hearing about her work. He said he was thrilled to be a part of the Committee and he read her thesis twice because he liked her style. Brenda Strang adds she hopes Norah might come to St. Augustine's and be a guest lecturer at some point. They each shake her hand and much to Norah's ultimate relief, they finally disperse.

Outside Norah's office, the handyman for the building puts tools back into his pouch. He looks up as Norah and Peter approach. "Hey, Dr. Clarke. Congratulations." She admires the nameplate he has just this minute installed on her door: Dr. T. G. Norah Clarke. She smiles as her mind skips to Hilary and Bertrand and the nameplate she was given by them.

She admonishes Peter, as the handyman lumbers down the hall. "This is your doing, I suppose." She tries to sound cross, but it isn't working.

"Not at all, my dear. Names can't go on doors without Departmental approval. I think you need to stop by HR tomorrow and see what they have to say."

Things proceed at breakneck speed. Convocation is in May, but the university is anxious for her to accept a permanent position as a professor as soon as possible. She sees no reason to decline, wishing to be in no other place than Callwood Bay, which has now become her home.

She spends Christmas in Prestonburg. Life is going to change a bit with her increase in income. Norah wants her own house. She's never lived in a house. Images of the Le Blanc home in Westmount float around in her head. She wants another dog. She's convinced there will not be a second marriage in her future, so her plans are to carve out a life and some semblance of permanence for herself.

There remains one piece of unfinished business. Norah has not heard from Sam since their supper together in the fall of 1998, when she was just starting her PhD. There have been no birthday or Christmas cards; no slurred phone calls in the middle of the night.

She could just forget about it, but for whatever the reason, she wants Sam to know she has succeeded, reached her goal, gotten her doctorate. She hopes he'll be happy for her, but a nagging anxiety prevails. The cards she's sent him over the last four years have not been returned to sender, but his lack of contact is troubling. Sam has always, since they separated, been the one to call. Maybe he's just decided to let go, and she's now the one with ongoing issues about hanging on. Maybe the tables have turned.

Chapter 23

Norah knows the house she wants to buy, but convincing her father she can manage a relic from the 1930s is a tougher ordeal than she imagined. He tears through the place, pointing out everything wrong—and there's a lot. The roof and the floorboards on the front porch are just the beginning. The tired hardwood needs refinishing, the original windows need replacing, not to mention the kitchen. "How is Norah supposed to cook in a kitchen like this?"

She'll work away at it. She'll clean everything, paint, and settle in for a while before getting any work done. It'll be fine. Her father finally sees her vision, whereas her mother just sighs and shakes her head.

In the spring of 2003, Norah moves into her beloved Craftsman bungalow that hasn't seen an upgrade since its 1938 birth date. She makes do with the furniture from her apartment, the carpet she bought in Montreal, the side tables given to her by Bertrand and Hilary, and her funky chrome set that manages to look for all the world like it was put in the old kitchen when the house was built. She cleans, cleans, and cleans some more.

She puts orange tape around the broken floorboards on the front porch. She eyes the light above the front door with disdain. The so-called improvement the former owner completed was to replace what would have been an art deco pendant fixture, with a 1980s' ceiling model from the lumber store. It's cornered the market for ugly meets common.

Norah considers it fortuitous that the other light fixtures are original to the period. To add to her perceived good fortune, she finds doors in the basement, saved after being removed from the two kitchen entries. Both fireplaces, one in the living room and one in the master bedroom, appear intact but have been boarded over—she presumes due to drafts.

The poor old house has potential, but patience and deep pockets will have to be Norah's long suits. She sews curtains. She commandeers her father to help her replace the taps in the kitchen, which were dripping like water torture. He also helps her when she wants to buy a new bathroom vanity top and sink as the old ones were past a restoration option. In the not so distant future, she'll get quotes for the roof and the front steps.

The new Professor Norah Clarke loves her neighbourhood. An avid walker, she spends at least an hour navigating the uneven sidewalks of the area every day. She still misses Ivy. There's a hole in her heart that she knows can only be filled by a dog.

Before college starts in the fall, Norah sees an ad for puppies on the bulletin board at the supermarket. When she calls, the puppies are all spoken for, but they have another dog needing a home. She is house-trained, her name is Violet, and maybe Norah would like to meet her?

Norah travels on a dirt road out of town, following vague directions, until she comes upon a shack-like residence set in the middle of a barren field with the ocean as a backdrop. There are two big huskies chained to a tree near the barn, and she can hear barks escaping from inside the house. She knocks on what appears to be a handmade wooden door, and is greeted by a frail woman dressed in coveralls and wearing a man's dirty beige cardigan. The elbows have holes.

After Norah identifies herself, the woman turns around, her eyes scuttling across the old linoleum kitchen floor. They settle on Violet, under the knife-scarred Arborite table. She's rolling around with another little brown wire-haired dog. The two of them are oblivious to the intruder.

The woman reaches down, and in a split second has Violet by the scruff of the neck. The dog screeches in protest and wiggles to get away. Norah bites her tongue and extends her hands to take the pup.

Norah falls in love with Violet. She's the colour of charcoal cinders with two white front feet and a white patch under her chin—a poodle and terrier cross. Her fur is a mass of soft curls. She's six months old.

Violet settles in welcoming arms without ceremony. The woman obviously reads her visitor like a cheap paperback—perceives her desperate need, her leather jacket, and her almost new vehicle. She charges Norah much more than the original suggested sum.

Before Norah manages to get the crooked wooden door closed on her way out, she overhears the old woman calling for her rusty oil tank to be filled.

Violet is quite a bit different from Bijou or Ivy. She's not the kind of dog who'll just trudge along behind you and stick close by. Violet is more terrier than not. Wild and crazy might well describe her. Norah is a little overwhelmed with this demanding twelve pounds of attitude she's taken on. It appears what Violet wants, Violet expects to get, and she has a way of tormenting Norah into acquiescing in all departments—be it treats, walks, or sleeping on the bed. There seems to be a bit of herding collie in her, and Norah is destined to be her lamb. Despite this, Norah's smitten.

✻✻✻✻

By the time winter rolls around, Norah is ensconced in her old Craftsman, known in the neighbourhood as the professor who is always walking her dog despite the weather. She is successfully progressing through her first full year as Dr. Norah Clarke, Professor of Cultural Anthropology at Callwood College. She is content.

Norah decides to look for Sam. If she searches the Internet for herself, she finds bits of information relating to the university and her research. When she looks for Sam, she finds a newspaper picture of him, with a number of other people, cutting the ribbon in an opening ceremony for a hospice in Toronto. He must have been part of the fundraising operation. The picture is not flattering and again, her suspicions are raised. Something is wrong. The hospice opened eighteen months ago. Their sparse website says nothing else about him.

✻✻✻✻

"Daniel House. How can I help you?" The voice at the other end is male, brisk, and polite in an exaggerated manner.

Norah finds herself feeling nervous and isn't sure why. "I'm trying to locate Sam, ah, Forrest Sampson. He was part of your ribbon cutting when you opened. I came across his picture. We're old friends." She tries to smile when she's talking. Be patient. Be casual.

"There is no one here named Sampson. Who is calling please?"

"My name is Norah Clarke. Sam and I were old friends in university and later in Montreal. I've lost touch with him and when I came across a picture

207

of him and your facility, I thought I would call. Perhaps you would know how I can contact him?"

"Could you give me your phone number—Ms. Clarke, is it? I will get our administrator to call you back. There is no one here by that name." The voice becomes increasing abrupt and more than a little formal. The call is over.

Norah provides her home number and hangs up. For whatever the reason, this is a dead end. Sam must have been part of the fundraising committee but now has nothing more to do with the place. Perhaps he's moved back to Florida. She never managed to meet Sam's parents, but is quite confident that moving to Florida and being closer to family would not be his first option.

Two days later, on a rainy Friday morning, Norah is sitting at her kitchen table, drinking coffee and checking email on her laptop. She has the beginnings of a head cold and has chosen to forego office hours today so she won't spread her germs around. She's busy sending emails to colleagues and students she's scheduled to see throughout the course of the day.

Just as she reaches for the phone, to leave an absent message on her line at work, it rings unexpectedly. She jumps despite herself. "Hello?"

"Hello. May I speak to Norah Clarke, please?"

"Speaking."

"Good Morning. I hope I'm not calling too early."

"Not at all. Who's calling, please?"

"Oh, sorry." The voice sounds nervous. "My name is Anthony Gibbons. I'm the administrator at Daniel House, here in Toronto. I'm given to understand you called on Wednesday, inquiring after Forrest Sampson. Correct?"

Norah is more than a little curious at this point. "Yes. We are old friends. I saw his picture—"

Mr. Gibbons' gentle voice interrupts her. "I know who you are, Dr. Clarke. Sam spoke of you often, and all the cards you ever sent him are with his effects. Forrest died six months ago."

Norah is processing, but not fast enough to keep up with the information. "Effects?" Her voice is soft. She can't hear herself.

"Yes. There was no funeral. All of his effects, although there are few, were boxed up and remain here at Daniel House. His parents said they would retrieve them, but they haven't appeared, as yet. I am terribly sorry you had to find out this way, Dr. Clarke, but the instructions were clear. There were to be no notifications except to his parents and no funeral of any kind. We do things precisely the way our residents request. Sam was one of the first people to enter Daniel House. I'm very sorry for your loss."

"Why are you calling me Dr. Clarke? How would you know that?"

A soft laugh ripples down the phone line. "Forrest kept very close track of you. He often told stories about his "wife." If people didn't believe him, he hauled out your wedding picture. Although very sick at the end, he had our staff watching the Callwood College website. He knew when you received your PhD. He died about two weeks later, as a matter of fact."

Norah is starting to pull herself together. It's obvious Anthony Gibbons is very patient and kind. "He died of AIDS?" She has to ask.

"I am unable to share medical information with you, Dr. Clarke, as I'm sure you can understand, but we are an AIDS hospice. It's what we do. If you have no other questions, I will let you go. Again, I'm very sorry for your loss. Please feel free to come and visit us any time you are in Toronto."

She gets up from the table, picks up her dog, and scuffs on slippered feet to the sofa. Her soft, candy-cane-stripped flannel pyjama bottoms drag on the old hardwood.

Curled up in the corner, patting a snuggling Violet, she stares into space, not quite knowing what to think. Sam is dead. He's been dead for six months. The only conclusion she comes to is that their dinner in the city was to be their last contact, and he knew it. He must have known how sick he was then. He didn't tell her. He didn't want her involved. It sounds like he wanted no one involved. It feels strange to think of him dead. He had a momentous effect on her; changed her life in many ways.

She calls her mother. Maybe talking about it to someone else will make it more real. Paige is sympathetic, but her manner is vague. Is Norah upset? They were divorced for years. Should she be taking time off work because Sam died? People die. Did he have cancer? He wasn't very old.

Norah explains to her mother she's home sick with a cold, and promises to call later. Once her cold is better, she'll come to Prestonburg for the weekend. She wants her parents to meet Violet. She wants Beth to meet Violet.

Perhaps her father would be more understanding, sympathetic, but Austin is out doing errands. She hangs up the phone and wanders into the kitchen looking for more coffee. It feels weird. Her ex-husband is dead.

****

By the time the school year approaches completion, Norah feels she's going to have an emergency on her hands if she doesn't have something done about her roof and her front porch. She can live without a new kitchen. She can manage with the old hardwood floors and the ratty landscaping, but the roof and the porch are a problem.

Her father continues to nag her about it, and says if she can't afford to get it done, he'll chip in. He'll do the porch himself, if she would prefer. *Absolutely not!* He'll loan her money, but she's not to tell her mother. Her mother already seems to think Norah can't afford to maintain a house.

Beth comes to visit. Beth continues to live in the apartment above Clarkes Antiques. "I don't know what you're thinking, plowing every cent you own into an old rattletrap like this. Look at the money you make. You could be travelling all over the world every summer rather than sticking around here, doing research with students, and walking a dog—albeit a cute dog."

Violet is sitting on Beth's knee in the most comfortable chair in the world. They're having tea and Beth has so far managed to get the tea to her lips without Violet deciding this is an opportune time to jump from one side of her ample lap to the other.

They've finished the obligatory tour. Beth is not unkind, but she seems compelled to point out the painfully obvious—the floor boards on the porch, the worn hardwood floors, the missing doors, the old windows.

Norah defends her home as best she can. "Beth, I love the Craftsman architecture. Everything I like—furniture, dishes, and carpets—they're all from this era. It's me. A little time and money and it'll be the perfect place."

"If I tell you I won't come back until it's all done, it's possible I'll never visit again." She sniffs.

"Well, we wouldn't want that," she responds with an indulgent smile. "I'm interviewing contractors next week, since I have more time now. You wait. It'll be beautiful some day."

"You're not getting any younger, Norah."

She interviews and obtains quotes from three contractors. Her father insisted there be three. One man shows up a day late, and his quote is beyond reach. A second man seems too old, and Norah doesn't have a lot of faith in his ability. He must have missed something as his quote is so low. He says he works alone, inspiring even less confidence. The third, Matthew Channing doesn't seem to fit the bill in the beginning, either.

May, 2013

Chapter 24

Joe Waskiewicz enters the Sarah McCall Sociology Building with a determined spring in his step. It's Thursday, May 16, 2013. He defended his thesis in record time, with the help of his mentor, Dr. Clarke, and he's ramped up to graduate on Sunday. This is her last day of office hours as the term has wound down to spring convocation. As he checks his watch—one is never late for a meeting with Norah (he calls her by her given name, now)—he allows himself to be transported, for just a moment, to the miraculous day, a month ago, when he stood before three professors and his adviser to defend his work about Tulipmania.

He was introduced by Norah and when he launched into his presentation, all he could think of was her advice, telling him to: "present his work from the inside out; tell them about what he believes, and how his discoveries and observations have impacted his study; make it his life; and not to present it as a history lesson of research; give them a piece of himself."

He stood in front of his thesis committee and regaled them with stories about tulips in the 1600s. He spoke to them about extreme collecting; about the rise and fall of fortunes; about what we could learn; and what we haven't remembered. He had them enthralled and in the palm of his hand. It was a fabulous experience.

Now, walking down this dreary hall with the worn tapestry runner, just days before graduation, he wants to present another proposal to Norah. Joe wants to do his PhD, and he wants to do it with her. He knows the standard response will be that he needs to spread his wings, and look for other institutions and other advisers—how work can become stale and repetitive if things aren't changed up a bit.

However, his roommates keep urging him to stay, and he could never afford to go on otherwise. If she will agree, he will be accepted. He reaches in his pocket and turns off his cell phone as he knocks on the door. It stands ajar and permits a beam of dust-filled light to sprinkle out over the old floorboards. He would never, on pain of death, allow his cell phone to ring and interrupt a meeting with this woman.

"Come on in, Joe. Right on time, as usual." She has not taken her eyes away from the computer screen. "Tea is made. I thought some Summer Berry was in order, all things considered." She turns in her chair and smiles. He watches it drift, without hesitation, up to her eyes. Joe starts to relax.

He pours tea for them both and places the cups, with practiced precision, on the coffee table set within comfortable reach of all four upholstered chairs.

"You were great last month. I was so proud of you, Joe. Any family making the trip in for graduation?" She moves over to the wing-back just opposite, and sits, crossing long, linen-clad legs.

Joe shifts in his seat almost imperceptibly. His family won't be coming. It's a bad time of year, and money is tight. All he says is that it's a long haul from northern Alberta, but he talks to them a lot on the phone. Changing gears, he jumps straight in. He's learned the lessons of directness quite well from this woman who still presents as more mystery than not to him. "I want to do my PhD with you. Will you be my thesis adviser?"

She looks over the top of her glasses, as she brings the cup to her lips and inhales the essence of strawberry lingering just above the rim. "Are you sure you want to stick with me? The general rule of thumb is familiarity breeds contempt, Joe. The Department will ask questions of you, like: 'Why are you not seeking a doctoral position someplace else? Why do you want to stick with the same thesis supervisor?' Are you prepared for them?"

He's prepared. "I've already been accepted, so that part's out of the way. You're more of a muse than a supervisor, and I think I can do great things with your mentorship. I am home here. I can afford the program if I stay here, and I want to learn how to teach the way you do. I want to show students how much I love this stuff. Is my pitch working for you?"

She's smiling. She leans back in the chair and sips her tea, reflective but teasing at the same time. "Well, Joe. I think we have some work to do over the summer if you're going to teach Introduction to Cultural Anthropology. Give me until the end of the month to get the paperwork over to HR, but you can tell Admissions you have an adviser." She takes another sip of her tea, still smiling.

Joe leaves her office with feet barely touching the floor. He's going to do his doctorate with Dr. Norah Clarke. He'll send her flowers after graduation is over. Perhaps he'll be able to scrounge some tulips. It's a little late in the season for the florists. He might have to raid a garden or two, or pay a small fortune like he did in January.

****

Krista Wainwright has been sitting in the Student Centre since 8:00 AM, although her appointment with Dr. Clarke is not until 9:30 AM. This is her last activity on campus before going back home for the summer. She'll be working at the local library, teaching seniors how to use computers. She hopes it'll be more fun than it sounds. She dressed with care this morning. Her hair is tied back, away from her face. She's wearing white capris and a baggy pink top over a dark pink camisole. Her bare feet are clad in red sandals and her broad shoulder supports a bright red over-sized Lug bag. After her meeting, she'll be catching a ride home with a couple of her friends. She's all packed and has turned in her room key.

She's nervous. Her goal is to convince Dr. Clarke she's worthy of majoring in Cultural Anthropology, and working on her undergraduate project with the professor. She thinks they hit it off from the very beginning, when she and Ashley did the paper about Freud, but Dr. Clarke is a hard woman to read. She doesn't show favouritism and Krista is afraid that maybe she's taken on other students and there won't be room for her. She just can't wait until the fall semester and chance missing out.

As she navigates the corridor toward Dr. Clarke's office, she can hear the familiar sound of Anna Maria Tremonte's voice drifting down the hall. Her professor's radio is tuned to CBC, as usual, and Krista permits the familiar sounds to circle her as she approaches the door. Her tap is light. Dr. Clarke bids her to enter. Her back is to the door as she rises to turn off the radio. She always does this, Krista assumes, out of deference to her student and the meeting they are about to have.

Her instructor's dressed in classic simplicity today. To Krista, it must be in honour of her last office day of the term—that she wears baggy, sea-mist green linen pants cinched up at the ankles, and a soft silk blouse tucked in and highlighting her narrow hips. Her earrings are huge green hoops that shimmer as she moves, even in the subdued office light. "I made fresh tea, Krista. Have a seat. When are you taking off for home?"

"This afternoon. I wanted to talk to you about a request, or maybe it's a proposal, I'm not sure." The tea smells good, like strawberries. She's starting to get used to the tea. She even bought some a month ago, but has made it only once.

Her stomach flips around. *Just spit it out.* She hesitates.

"I was hoping you were here wondering if, in the event you were to major in Sociology, I might be your project adviser." Dr. Clarke looks at her and smiles. It isn't a full smile up to her eyes, but she is most definitely smiling and Krista relaxes.

"How did you know? I'm dying to major in Cultural Anthropology and I want you to be my mentor! How did you know?" she gushes, repeating herself.

"I didn't know, Krista. To be honest, I just hoped you would want to. I'd be happy to work with you." She smiles in the way only Dr. Clarke can.

Krista is over the moon. She takes a gulp of the tea. It's good. She has a plan.

****

Peter Swift turns up a few minutes after Krista's departure. If he were honest, he would say he has been lurking around, waiting for his friend to be free. He has some news for her and he wants to congratulate her. He pads down the hall after she returns with her tea tray and a full kettle of water. He pokes his head around the door casing, not wanting to startle her. "Happy Birthday, my friend."

Obviously touched, she turns around. "You know it's my birthday? Thank you! How did you uncover that little tidbit of information?"

Peter launches into a tale about how Matthew called him last year on her birthday, to find out when she was coming home, and he had come down to her office to ask some strategic questions and report back to her husband. He wrote down the date so he would remember this year.

"Well, you sly old fox. Come in and have tea with me. I have some paperwork to tidy up, one more student to see right after lunch, and then home I go. I'm pretty sure Matthew's at home today making me supper. We bought new wicker furniture for the front porch, and I said it could be my birthday present, so I hope we'll have supper on the porch. Now, what about you? What's new and funny?"

Peter is very anxious to contribute to the conversation. He takes the offered tea, a simple Earl Grey this time. Norah must've had enough of the berries, even though her office is still submerged in the scent of the incense-like brew. "I'm going to spend the whole summer in New York with my new friend. I first went to meet him at Christmas, remember? What I didn't tell you is that I met him on the Internet!"

"Peter, I didn't know you met somebody!"

"I thought people would judge—not you, of course—but I just didn't want anyone to know. Didn't want to jinx the whole thing before I was sure. I've been down twice since, and now I'm going for the whole summer!" He slaps his crossed knee for emphasis. "And, by the way, you look smashing today, birthday girl."

Leaning into the space between them, and somehow creating an intimacy only she seems able to do, Norah shares his enthusiasm. "Tell me all about him, Peter. I'm so happy for you."

Peter spends the better part of thirty minutes sharing information about Harold, a teacher from Brooklyn, New York, who works at a private school and has a small apartment nearby. Peter is serious. They want to be together, and they are both searching job opportunities—meaning there will eventually be a move for one of them. Right now, Peter feels the chances are better for him to find a position than Harold, so he hopes to relocate within another year. It's a big step, to contemplate giving up a tenured university position, but it'll be for love. He's told no one but Norah.

****

At 12:30 PM, on the dot, in comes Damien George. He loves to visit Dr. Clarke and is looking forward to a summer assisting her with information gathering for her latest paper. She will be examining the difference between modern day entomologists and their insect collections, as compared to avid collectors from the late 1800s. He'll do research for her from July second until August thirtieth. He might even get to interview some collectors and see some bugs.

Damien invested a lot of effort in cleaning up his act so he could compete for a chance to get this position. His sneakers are tied. His jeans fit, and his T-shirt is plain white with no slogan. His haircut is reasonable, if not perfect. The rucksack remains his calling card. He tries hard to make eye contact with his professor, as he knows this is important to her. He likes the tea, and he doesn't give a damn what kind she pulls out.

They talk about the work, what she expects, where his space will be in the Department, hours, money, and all the other details.

His parents are thrilled he'll be working with one of his teachers for the summer. Money isn't a serious issue, so six weeks of research is better to them than four months of work at a fast food outlet. He'll go home for a break now, and spend time with his folks.

When he leaves Norah's office at 2:00 PM, Damien feels like an adult; like a man with goals and aspirations; like he doesn't have to apologize any more for never having been to a real school.

****

Paige is ready to go to Callwood Bay by 10:00 AM. She's anxious to get there so Norah will be surprised when she arrives home from work. At seventy-five years old, she's frail but in good health, having managed her husband's sudden death, a year ago, with more dignity and grace than many would have given her credit.

With the burden of business ownership behind her, she has taken to popular culture with a vengeance. She records television programs so as not to miss anything, and oftentimes attends movies with Beth, just like her daughter once did. She dresses in soft cotton pants with drawstring waists and matching blouses with little flowers appliquéd on the collars.

Her current ensemble is pale blue, and the sales clerk told her the fabric is crinkle cotton, whatever that means. It washes like an old rag and was on sale. Paige's biggest excitement today involves her collaboration with Matthew to find the best birthday present they could for Norah. Paige used her contacts from the antique business, and Matthew will employ his handyman skills. It will be perfect.

Beth's appearance at the door is no surprise. Paige is ready, as there's no mistaking her coming down those stairs. The older woman has learned, over the years and especially since Austin's death, how to temper her criticisms.

She always knew Beth had eyes for her husband. Austin was too much of a gentleman to ever say anything, but they both knew. A woman in love can't totally hide the look in her eyes. Beth hasn't been as adept at concealing her feelings as she thinks.

****

Today, Beth is wound as tight as a drum. She's so excited. Norah's fiftieth and a surprise to boot.

Beth's contribution is the cake and she's anxious the three-layered masterpiece will make it to Callwood Bay without collapsing. She's placed it, with ultimate care and caution, in a Styrofoam cooler and wrapped it in blankets to keep any warm air out. She's told Paige she'll be driving with the Malibu's air conditioning going full throttle, "so to bring a sweater and no complaining about the cold."

Despite frequent walks and fewer desserts, she still managed to put on a few pounds over the winter, so black capris are Beth's default fashion option. They should have some slimming effect. Since black is so dreary, she's topped them off with a melon chiffon blouse and a multi-coloured scarf from India, given to her by one of her sewing class students.

Beth is growing comfortable in Paige's company. With Austin gone, and Beth now owning the building, their relationship has become more equal in many ways. Beth makes a conscious effort to include Paige in her little events in the craft shop, and her attempts appear appreciated.

Their common denominator is Norah. Beth refuses to believe Paige ever knew about her ongoing mental love affair with Austin. That thought is followed by a sudden flood of emotion. She's stunned as the familiar feelings of loss rush over her for the umpteenth time.

****

Matthew is just a little panicky. Beth and Paige will be arriving any minute. Dinner is organized. He expects Norah at about three, and worries there'll be a call to say she'll be home early. He also hopes she doesn't wonder, as she walks up the street, why every remaining tulip in the yard is missing.

The house is filled with Norah's favourite flower for her fiftieth birthday. He has six vases scattered throughout the downstairs and a special one of all whites in their bedroom.

Paige and Beth will want a tour because the kitchen is done, and the pocket doors are installed. He hopes they'll be impressed with the hardwood. It was a bitch to get those floors refinished. Norah would have nothing to do with the idea of replacement.

The phone rings. He jumps to catch it, almost tripping over Violet in the process. It's Beth. "We're fifteen minutes away. I have the cake. Do you need anything I can pick up on my way into town?"

"Everything is fine, but I'm running out of time to do the installation. The sooner you get here the better."

Matthew does a last-minute check, for maybe the third time. Shrimp is in the marinade. The barbecue has adequate propane. Baked potatoes are ready for the oven. Salad greens are washed and chilling. Violet has been out. Wine is in the fridge. The tea things are assembled on the veranda table. He hears the car pull in.

He rushes out to get the cake, and instructs Beth to move the Malibu up the street to the driveway of the first house on the extension. They're away this week, and it'll serve to hide the familiar amber bronze vehicle to maintain the surprise. Violet, pawing on the top of the porch gate, peers over at her visitors. These are people she knows and her tail begins its salute.

Matthew grabs the cake and Paige eases herself out of the passenger seat and opens the rear door to retrieve the box in the back. As Beth parks the car and makes her way with deliberate effort back down the street, Matthew helps Paige into the house.

"Let's leave the tour for Norah when she gets home." He sees Paige looking around but wants to get to work. He figures he might have thirty minutes before she gets here. He opens the box. The antique pendant porch fixture is nestled among mounds of tissue in the middle of the space. It's a caramel glass diamond-shaped drop fixture, with tiny bits of coloured glass around the collar where the glass meets the neck. It's breathtaking. His mother-in-law must have called in a lot of favours.

Matthew looks down at Paige. Her eyes are wet as she watches her son-in-law's reaction. "Man, Paige, this is extraordinary! It must have cost a fortune! Are you going to let me help you pay for this?"

"Not a chance!" Her voice is emphatic in its finality. "Your contribution is to put it up." She takes a breath for emphasis. "Now!"

The old light is already down, the breaker off, and the ladder tucked into a corner behind the front door. Matthew moves to hang the fixture, authentic to the Craftsman period, and the job is done in no time flat. The two women admire his work, giving him a little clap as he descends the ladder.

After the tools of the trade are stowed away, after the cake is relegated to the fridge, after the tea things get reorganized on the table yet again, Matthew ensures one of his wife's favourite singers, Adele, is floating through the air, courtesy of the CD player inside.

Violet is alerted to Norah's steady step approaching. It's a quiet spring afternoon with just the bare essence of a breeze rippling in the new-born maple leaves beginning to create their annual canopy of green. Violet barks, and they see Norah look up. Matthew turns on the porch light, hands Violet to Beth, and opens the gate.

Down the steps he flies. His long legs propel him across their patch of lawn. He reaches his wife's side, just as she looks up to wave at Paige and Beth standing on the front porch. He watches her expression, as the most beautiful art deco pendant porch light he feels sure she has ever seen, registers in her smiling eyes. She extends out her hand to him.

"Are you surprised?" He puts his arm around her waist as they finish the short jaunt back to the yard. She says she is, but somehow, he knows better.

About the Author

L. P. Suzanne Atkinson was born in New Brunswick, Canada and lived in both Alberta and Quebec before settling in Nova Scotia in 1991. She has a BA in Psychology from Mount Allison University, a Bachelor of Social Work from McGill University, and an MA in Sociology from Acadia University. Suzanne spent her professional career in the fields of mental health and home care as both a therapist and trainer. She also owned and operated, with her husband, both an antique business and a construction business for more than twenty-five years.

Her philosophy of life is based on two qualities for which she continually strives. They are her benchmarks. First: there is no better descriptor than to be called a kind person and good friend. Second: a lesson learned and not shared is information squandered.

Suzanne writes about the challenges inherent in aging and about the unavoidable consequences of relationships. She uses her life and work experiences to weave timeless stories that cross many boundaries. She and her husband, David Weintraub, continue to make Nova Scotia their home.

Email – lpsa.books@eastlink.ca
Website – http://lpsabooks.wix.com/lpsabooks#
Facebook – L.P.Suzanne Atkinson – Author